THE SOCIETY
OF TIME

The Original Trilogy and Other Stories

THE SOCIETY OF TIME

The Original Trilogy and Other Stories

The Original Trilogy and Other Stories

JOHN BRUNNER

edited by

MIKE ASHLEY

This collection first published in 2020 by
The British Library
96 Euston Road
London NW1 2DB

Cataloguing in Publication Data
A catalogue record for this publication is available from the British Library

ISBN 978 0 7123 5382 3
e-ISBN 978 0 7123 6772 1

Frontispiece illustration shows a gathering of Spanish and Native American men
during the conquest of Mexico, from Antonio de Solis y Ribadeneyra's *Historia de la
conquista de Mexico...*, Brussels, 1704. Image copyright © The British Library Board

Cover design by Jason Anscomb.

Cover image shows a detail of a diagram depicting René Descartes' Vortex Theory,
from *Principia Philosophiae*, 1644. Image copyright © The British Library Board

Text design and typesetting by Tetragon, London
Printed and bound by CPI Group (UK) Ltd, Croydon CR0 4YY

CONTENTS

INTRODUCTION   7

The Society of Time Trilogy   13
  Spoil of Yesterday   15
  The Word Not Written   65
  The Fullness of Time   115

Father of Lies   167

The Analysts   239

INTRODUCTION

Caring for Worlds

The stories collected here take you to three very different worlds—the world of the Society of Time where the Spanish Armada was victorious, the world of a psychotic imagination in "Father of Lies", and a future world reached by complicated topology in "The Analysts". John Brunner was a genius at creating worlds, whether almost the same as ours or utterly alien, but all ones we need to understand and explore. That's what Brunner encouraged us to do in over one hundred books and more than two hundred stories. He wanted us to consider these strange worlds of his imagination and compare them to our world and see what thoughts they provoked. Because deep down in most of his stories are warnings, about ourselves and how we treat the planet.

John Brunner established himself as a premier writer of science fiction with *Stand on Zanzibar* (1968) which went on to win the Hugo Award as that year's best novel. This dystopian work, which included attempts at population control in a world where population growth was rising exponentially, revealed to the wider world that Brunner could deliver a sophisticated multi-layered work of fiction with significant impact.

He went on to cement that reputation with *The Jagged Orbit* (1969), portraying a future with interracial tension, a new wave of psychedelic drugs and an increase in readily available weapons, *The Sheep Look Up* (1972) where pollution sees many species on the brink of extinction, and *The Shockwave Rider* (1975) showing a world of social chaos and over reliance on computer networks—Brunner coined the word "worm" for computer malware. All three worlds now seem disturbingly familiar.

Those who knew Brunner's work, though, knew that he had always been experimental and provocative. Though he was one of the more prolific British writers of science fiction and fantasy in the late 1950s and 1960s, his work was seldom formulaic as he found bold ways to explore familiar themes. Before *Stand on Zanzibar* caused the world to sit up and take notice, and before the so-called New Wave sought to shake out the tired and traditional forms of science fiction and make it more relevant to the present day, Brunner had already struck out to reshape science fiction in his own way. *The Dreaming Earth* (1963, but serialised in 1961) depicts an overpopulated world with depleted resources, stricken by famine, where the population seeks refuge in drugs. *The Squares of the City* (1965), which follows a revolution in a fictional near-future South American country, has a plot based on a genuine historical chess game. *The Whole Man* (1964), the first of Brunner's books to be shortlisted for the Hugo Award, takes us into the mind of a man struggling to come to terms with his powerful telepathic abilities. *Quicksand* (1967), one of his own favourites of his books, has a woman from a parallel but very different Earth struggling to cope with a world in which nothing is familiar or understandable.

Brunner had long wrestled with his own views about the world and our place in it. Born in 1934 he was five years old when the Second World War broke out and his family moved to run a farm in Herefordshire. His youth was thus filled with an understanding of the soil, plants and the natural world, so it is not too surprising that when he turned to fiction—and science fiction had become his first love—he considered environmental issues. His first novel, *Galactic Storm* (1951), published under the alias Gill Hunt, was one of the earliest sf novels to give consideration to global warming.

He rapidly honed his writing skills because in a little over a year he sold a long story, "Thou Good and Faithful", to the leading American science-fiction magazine *Astounding SF*, edited by John W. Campbell, Jr., where it appeared in the March 1953 issue under the alias John Loxmith. Set on an Earth-like planet near the galactic hub, explorers grapple to understand how this world, otherwise unpopulated, is inhabited by robots controlled by giant computers. When the solution is discovered it reflects on humanity's way of life, with over-population and ruined ecologies. As one of the computers remarks about humans, "Your technical ability has left your social conscience behind." The feelings behind that comment are what drove much of Brunner's fiction.

Brunner was determined to be a writer—something abhorrent to his family who had expected him to take a role in the family chemical business, Brunner Mond—but National Service caught up with him and he spent two years (1953 and 1954) in the RAF. Once discharged, Brunner threw himself into writing, primarily for the British magazines which were prospering in the 1950s. His main markets were the two magazines edited by John Carnell, *New Worlds* and *Science Fantasy*. When Carnell added a third title, *Science Fiction Adventures*, in 1958, it allowed Brunner the scope to develop longer stories and series, which he could adapt for book publication, mostly in the United States.

He also became active in the "ban the bomb" movement, attending the first meeting of the Campaign for Nuclear Disarmament (CND) in February 1958, and eventually becoming a member of its National Executive Council. Brunner came to realise, though, "I could reach far more people by writing something, than by walking down the street with a banner." This was when he turned to his dystopian novels at least one of which, *The Squares of the City*, had been drafted by 1960. Brunner was of the view that if one was disciplined and cautious, and knew the facts, most people would act responsibly—something we may reflect upon during the coronavirus pandemic.

Elements of Brunner's outlook are evident in the stories reprinted here. The premise behind the three Society of Time stories is that the Spanish Armada was victorious and as a consequence scientific progress in Britain and the rest of Europe was limited. The slave trade continues. Though women are not yet treated as equals there is a movement for female emancipation. In this alternate world the ability to travel through time was discovered in 1892, almost a century before the series starts, but it was realised that any access to the past had to be rigidly controlled for fear of changing events. Hence the Society of Time was established to monitor and investigate any breaches. As Don Miguel, one of the licentiates of the Society, investigates an Aztec mask, which appears to have been stolen from the past, he begins to discover that the controls over time-travel are being broken.

The series ran in consecutive issues of *Science Fiction Adventures* in 1962 and an abridged version was published in the United States under the title *Times Without Number* in October 1962. The abridged version did no favours and Brunner later revised and expanded it under the same title in 1969. The original stories here, which have not previously been reprinted, still hold Brunner's verve at exploring a fascinating idea.

"Father of Lies" first appeared in the April 1962 *Science Fantasy* and may seem like a fantasy at the start, but as you progress you will discover that something more sinister and alarming hides behind the world that the protagonists discover. "The Analysts" is also from *Science Fantasy* (August 1961) and this is a puzzle story, focusing initially on plans for a house which don't seem to make spatial sense. It allowed Brunner to explore another theme that troubled him—the scale of intolerance in the world, especially racial and religious bigotry. The story uses some words and phrases in common use at that time though shunned now, but they serve to emphasise Brunner's concern over human attitudes and relationships.

These stories are all examples of Brunner writing at his most inventive, creating societies that reflect upon our own and give us pause for thought.

MIKE ASHLEY

THE SOCIETY
OF TIME TRILOGY

Spoil of Yesterday

I

D ON MIGUEL NAVARRO, LICENTIATE IN ORDINARY OF THE Society of Time and loyal subject of His Most Catholic Majesty Philip IX, *Rey y Imperador*, regarded himself as a man of modern and enlightened views. Among other radical notions he held the opinion that women should not be barred by prejudice from science, philosophy and those other fields which were traditionally the preserve of men.

He had therefore been pleased to receive the invitation to tonight's function, the more so as it was in the Marquesa di Jorque's own handwriting—a rare honour!—with the great sprawling signature across the bottom: "Catalina di Jorque." He had turned down an invitation to the reception of the municipality taking place on the same evening, where they were promising clowns, jugglers and pyrotechnics—part of the quatrocentennial celebrations, of course—in order to come here.

And what had he got?

The Marquesa had been a famous beauty when she was in her twenties and thirties; having lost her looks at about the same time as she lost her husband—and enjoying the late Marques's considerable wealth, because he also had been of advanced views—she had set up as a successful society hostess and was a well-known campaigner for female emancipation.

Yet and still, her reputation for erudition seemed to have been founded on nothing more than a habit of assembling leading lights in various fields and displaying them to each other. Tonight's function seemed to be typical. The invitation had said "a small gathering of intelligent people," and that was what had hooked Don Miguel; he preferred good conversation to the finest tumblers and fireworks in the Empire. Instead, he had found upwards of four hundred people— clerics, philosophers both pure and natural, musicians, artists, and a dozen other kinds of people.

That was well enough so far as it went. The trouble was that they all seemed to be slightly second-best. And after his arrival he had had to suffer the embarrassing experience of being shown around the hall by the Marquesa—as it were, a real live Licentiate of the Society of Time, exclamation point, in the same tone of voice as one would say, "It's a real live tiger!"

At length he had managed to slip away into a quiet alcove; now he was wondering how he could get out of the building altogether. Rather the municipality's clowns than *these* clowns!

His glass was empty, and he looked around for a slave bearing a tray of full ones. He caught the attention of a slender Guinea-girl with knowing eyes and active hips, and as he watched her move away after changing his glass, he sighed. There were so many better ways of wasting time!

The sigh must have been too loud; there was a chuckle from near where he was standing, and a deep voice with a humorous edge to it said, "Your honour is perhaps not accustomed to the Marquesa's entertainments."

Don Miguel half-turned. He saw a man of middle height, in a maroon cloak and white velvet breeches, whose ginger hair was fastidiously high on his head. There was something rather engaging in his freckled face. Don Miguel gave the semi-bow that etiquette demanded, and said, "Miguel Navarro. No, it is the first time I've been to one of these affairs. I'm seldom in the country."

"Arcimboldo Ruiz," said the freckled man. "You're the time-traveller, aren't you?" It was permissible for him to revert from the formal "Usted"—your honour—to the simple *you* now that Don Miguel had given him his name.

A little taken aback, Don Miguel nodded. Don Arcimboldo gave another chuckle. "Don't be so surprised that you've been identified. Once your acceptance of the invitation came through, Catalina couldn't keep from publicising the fact. She might at least have had the grace to inform you of the technique for getting through her receptions, though—or maybe she couldn't, because she probably doesn't know it herself."

"You *seem* to be enjoying yourself—" said Don Miguel doubtfully.

"Oh, I am! Perhaps you were misled by Catalina's reputation as a centre of intelligent activity. As you've probably worked out for yourself by now, Catalina is actually—shall we put it kindly?—overconfident of her own talents. No, the trick is a simple one. She serves excellent food and truly miraculous wine; therefore, come to her receptions for the refreshments, and take your chance on finding good company or not."

Don Miguel's face twisted into his crooked smile—always crooked, thanks to a certain Greek hoplite on the plains of Macedonia. "I had indeed arrived at that conclusion," he admitted. "Yet it seemed to me improbable, for how could so many people be deceived for so long?"

Don Arcimboldo shrugged, picking a luscious-looking cake off a tray borne by a passing slave. "Are we deceived? How much and how many of us are deceived? I think rather few. I think rather that we prefer to give Catalina her little meed of glory, and enjoy her food and her drink."

Another slave—the Marquesa di Jorque was wealthy, and had perhaps a hundred in her household—came searching through the crowd; this time a tall Guinea-man who towered above the heads of those he passed by. Catching sight of Don Miguel, he broke off his wandering and came hurrying up.

"Her ladyship requests the honour of your honour's company," he said, bowing low. He straightened, and stood like an ebony statue awaiting an answer.

Don Miguel pulled a wry face at Don Arcimboldo. "There's no way of getting out of it, I suppose?" he said.

"None at all, unless you wish to incur Catalina's wrath—which can be spectacular and public."

Don Miguel heaved a sigh and tossed off the last of his wine. "Lead me to her," he told the slave, and as he turned to go, added formally to Don Arcimboldo, "The meeting has much honoured me. May we meet again."

"The honour is mine. May we meet again."

The Marquesa was standing under a bower of hothouse creepers, trained on silver branches, deep in conversation with two men. One of them Don Miguel recognised—Father Peabody, whose official post was clerk to the Archbishop of Jorque but who was commonly known as "her ladyship's chaplain"; men whispered unkind things about his function in her household. The other, Don Miguel did not know.

"Ah, Don Miguel!" said the Marquesa when he bowed before her, and flashed him a look that had probably laid suitors low in swathes when she was twenty years younger. "I trust that I have not dragged you away from an interesting discussion! But we are speaking of a difficult problem and would welcome your expert advice. Let Don Marco propose it to you."

She gestured at the man Don Miguel did not know, a foppish person in a moss-green cloak and yellow breeches, whose sword-handle was so heavily encrusted with jewels it was obvious he never intended to use the weapon. He uttered his name in a high goat-like bleat.

"Marco Villanova, your honour!"

"Miguel Navarro," said Don Miguel briefly. "What is your problem?"

"We were disputing regarding the private lives of the great, Don Miguel. It is my contention—indeed, reason demands it!—that the greatness of individuals must be manifest as much in their private as in their public lives."

"We spoke, in particular, of Julius Caesar," said Father Peabody, rubbing his hands on the front of his long black cassock. "There is a man whose greatness is not in dispute, I venture to say."

He spoke with a broad flat native accent, and bobbed his head humbly after every other word as though conscious of his inferior family status.

"Well, as you speak of Caesar," said Don Miguel, a little more snappishly than he had intended, "I can give you accurate information. As it happens, I've spoken to him. And he was a perfumed fop. In his youth, he was guilty of abominations with men, and in his maturity his promiscuous behaviour was such that the gossip of all Rome centred on it. If this is greatness in his private life, you may maintain so; I would not."

Don Marco flushed and drew back half a pace, with a sidelong glance at the Marquesa. "It does not seem to me to be fitting to speak of such matters in the hearing of a lady!" he said.

Don Miguel answered him frigidly. "Her ladyship asked my expert advice; I gave it. I do not think dabblers, who turn aside from what displeases them—and history is full of unpleasant things—are qualified to pass opinions."

The jab went home; Don Marco's flush deepened still further. And the Marquesa added more coals when she gave a vigorous nod of confirmation.

"Indeed, Marco, that is what I want. For far too long, we women have been sheltered and pampered and secluded. This is not due to any weakness in ourselves, only to masculine prejudice."

She raised her sharp eyes to Don Miguel's face, and heaved a sigh. "But that we have in our midst a man who has spoken with Caesar himself! Is it not a *miracle*?"

"We of the Society of Time do not regard it as such," Don Miguel answered off-handedly. "It's an application of natural laws. A miracle, perhaps, would be to discover a means of flying to the moon. No one has suggested natural means whereby that might be accomplished."

"With—with respect," said Father Peabody, bobbing his round head in which his eyes were still rounder, "how was this feat accomplished? I understood, if you will pardon me, that the rules of your Society forbade interference, and limited the actions of time-travellers to simple observation."

Already Don Miguel had regretted his ill-considered boast; the cleric's sharp question made him regret it still further. He said stiffly, "True, father. I assure you that that rule is most strictly kept. All I can say is that the means employed are a secret of the Society, and used only with maximum safeguards."

"I may be only a poor stupid woman," said the Marquesa, and paused, as though waiting for automatic contradiction. Not getting it, she was forced to continue. "But to me it seems that interference with the past is out of the question. What, was, was, and how can it be changed, or interfered with?"

Don Miguel sighed. For all her boasting about her intellectual accomplishments, the Marquesa had just put a question that no fifteen-year-old schoolboy of average intelligence would have uttered; he would have been taught the answer in school, or pieced it together from the items in the news. Indeed, even Don Marco was a little surprised, and showed that surprise in his expression.

"The basic arguments, my lady, are rather a matter for the speculative philosophers than for a pragmatic person like myself. But I have some conception of them, and if you wish, I'll try and elucidate."

A shadow of discomfort as though caused by the realisation that she had let herself in for some heavy brainwork, crossed the Marquesa's face. But she composed herself and adopted an expression of polite interest.

"Do go on!" she murmured.

II

"First," said Don Miguel slowly, trying to cast his thought into words suitable for the Marquesa's intelligence, "there are in history certain crucial turning-points, are there not? Of these, some are due to yet earlier causes, and some are comparatively random. It's rare that we can fine down any event in history to a single essential causative element. The fall of Rome, for instance, was not only due to the invasion of a barbarian horde; it was also due to decadence among the Romans, and as such is the sum of vast numbers of individual acts and attitudes. Do you see?"

The Marquesa nodded, beginning to frown. Don Miguel assumed that she was not yet out of her depth.

"If we—I say *if*, for we have never dared!—if we were to tamper with the life of even a single Roman in the year 300, we might affect the entire course of events. We might rule ourselves out of existence! Rome and the Roman Empire might yet be standing!"

"I'm *fascinated* by the great empires of the past!" said the Marquesa with enthusiasm. "Especially by—"

She noted the pained look on Don Miguel's face, and broke off. "I was carried away!" she said self-excusingly. "Do continue!"

"You've followed me so far?"

"Ye-es—except that if we were so to change history, then how would history have been changed? I mean, without us having gone back to change it?"

Don Miguel sighed. "We wouldn't exist, you see," he said. "This would be *history*—all the history there was. And if the outside interference was marked, then we presume that some other agency would have caused it."

Father Peabody shook his head, a look of resigned wonder on his face. "Truly the ways of the Lord are inscrutable!" he said.

The Marquesa gave a sudden nod and smile. "I see!" she said, and then added doubtfully, "I *think*..."

Don Marco spoke up. "You mentioned turning-points of a different nature, where interference is less dangerous, I think. What are those, then?"

Don Miguel shrugged. "The classic example, of course, is one which we all know—the storm that broke the English defences four hundred years ago, doused their fireships, and in effect made certain the conquest of Britain. We could hardly interfere with the brewing of a storm!"

"But—was that storm really so important?" the Marquesa put in. "I mean, the Armada was so huge and so well-armed..."

"We have studied this matter exhaustively, I can assure you," said Don Miguel. "The most eminent strategists and naval authorities agree that encumbered as they were with occupation troops and supplies, the galleons might well have been worsted—especially if the fireships had got among them with a steady following wind."

"Wonderful!" said the Marquesa, shaking her head in admiration. "Tell me, Don Miguel, is it true that in this year—this quatrocentennial year—some specially honoured outsiders have been invited to witness the actual victory?"

"No, my lady!" Don Miguel looked at her sharply. "From whom did you hear such nonsense? The rule of the Society—that only Licentiates are permitted to travel back in time—is absolutely inflexible. The purpose of time-travel is serious historical research; it is not a—a carnival, a spectacle for sensation-seekers!"

"Curious!" mused the Marquesa. "I had heard—but no matter. Yet I find it in my heart to wish that the rule was not so rigid. I have such a tremendous desire to see these great past happenings!"

"We have brought back pictures of almost all the great events of the past—" began Don Miguel.

"Ah, pictures! Pictures are dull, flat, lifeless! What are pictures beside a view of reality? But your heart is hard, Don Miguel. I see that."

"I assure you, time-travel is no pleasure trip. The dirt, the squalor, the cruelty, the—the disgusting facts of life in earlier ages, in short, see to that."

"Ah, but dirt and squalor are still with us. Why, yonder in the market outside the city wall of Jorque itself, there are people with *lice* on them, who do not know the meaning of the word soap! I have no desire to view their ancestors—they were probably the same fifty generations ago. But I would greatly love to see the rich and beautiful things of the past. As I began to say"—she punctuated the sentence with an arch look of reproach, that belonged in the armoury of a far younger woman—"I am most fascinated by the empires of the past. The Empire of Mexico, for instance, with its wonderful gold-work and featherwork!"

"And its pleasant custom of sacrificing human victims by tearing out the living heart and displaying it to the victim," said Don Miguel sourly.

"Have you no romance in you, Don Miguel?" cried the Marquesa.

"It is not I that lack romance; it is the empires of the past."

"And yet—ah, but I called you to me to ask your expert advice, and I must accept what you say in that spirit." The Marquesa gave a delicate, lady-like shrug. "And I would ask you one further favour of the same. I have a mask—a golden mask, of Aztec manufacture—which I wish to show off to you."

Her choice of words betrayed satisfactory honesty. Don Miguel bowed by way of answer. "But I know little of gold and ornament," he said doubtfully.

"Oh, no matter! I am just proud of it, Don Miguel, and should like you to admire it also. You will excuse us," she added to Don Marco and Father Peabody, who stepped back obediently. A slave answered an imperious gesture and cleared a way through the press of guests.

"You will not think it disgraceful of me, I am sure," said the Marquesa briskly, "when I say that the mask hangs in my bedchamber. I feel that it is an insult to the dignity of women to assume that they cannot protect their own virtue if they happen to be alone in masculine company."

The Marquesa had practically succeeded in making the enlightened and progressive Don Miguel into a bigoted reactionary by her behaviour so far this evening; accordingly, he answered irritably, "And to men also, you must admit, my lady—by assuming that they are inevitably inclined to make improper advances whenever they have the opportunity."

The Marquesa looked blank; then she smiled. "True, true! I plead for the quality of the sexes, so I must confess you are right."

Through the head-turning, bowing throng they passed, down a corridor where their footsteps echoed on magnificent Moorish tiles, and into a room which their accompanying slave opened with a key from a chain at his waist. The room was large and luxurious, its great bed disguised as a bank of moss, its walls and ceilings festooned with the Marquesa's habitual creepers; an adjacent bathroom was revealed through a half-open curtain in one wall.

But after the first glance, Don Miguel saw nothing of this. His attention was riveted by the magnificent golden mask that hung on the wall facing the foot of the bed. Hardly daring to breathe, he walked up to it and stood gazing at it.

It was more than just a mask. It was a representation in beaten gold of the head-dress, mask and shoulder-plates of an Aztec warrior. The square, snarling face of the mask was nine inches deep; the head-dress was twice as high, and the shoulder-plates were fifteen inches square. It dominated the room with its rich yellow lustre.

"Is it not magnificent?" said the Marquesa happily. "I am so proud of it!" And then, when Don Miguel did not reply, she added anxiously, "Or do you not think so?"

Don Miguel reached up and touched it, half-hoping that it would prove to be a mere illusion. But the heavy metal was hard and cool to his fingers. He stepped back, his mind beginning to whirl as he noted the signs of genuine Aztec workmanship that identified it.

"Why do you not answer?" said the Marquesa interrogatively.

Don Miguel found his voice at last. "I can only say, my lady, that I hope it's a forgery."

"A forgery? What do you mean?" she cried in alarm.

"A forgery! For if it is not..." His mind quailed at the implications if it was not.

"But why?"

"Because this is perfect, my lady. As perfect as though the gold-smith had finished it today. Therefore it is not a buried relic dug up from the ground and restored. No restorer of the present time could so precisely adopt the Aztec style. A forger might—just—achieve a uniform pseudo-Aztec style over the whole of a work such as this, if he had long steeped himself in the period."

"But it isn't a forgery! It can't be!" The Marquesa was almost in tears. Don Miguel pressed on ruthlessly.

"In that case, my lady, I must take possession of it in the name of the Society of Time, as contraband mass illegally imported to the present!"

How much does that thing weigh? Twelve pounds? Fifteen?

When every single grain of dust gathered by a time-traveller in the past had to be re-deposited in its own age before return, what might that theft from the past not have meant in terms of changes in history?

"Where did you get it?" he pressed. The Marquesa looked at him with a stunned expression and ignored the question.

"You're joking!" she accused. "It's a cruel joke!"

"This is no joking matter," said Don Miguel harshly. "It's as well for you, my lady, that the first Licentiate of the Society to hear about this is under your roof as a guest, accepting your hospitality. Otherwise I can't guess the consequences. Why, anyone with the intelligence of a two-year-old ought to have jumped to the conclusion that something as perfect as that mask must be imported from the past! How did you get it—as a gift?"

"Y-yes!" The Marquesa was beginning to recover herself, and to understand what was being said. Don Miguel saw that he had been right in making crude threats to her in the name of the Society; the Society of Time had an almost magical reputation to most people.

"Then did you report the gift to the office of the Society in Jorque? Did you check that it had been licensed for import?"

"No, of course I didn't!"

"You probably thought it beneath your dignity to obey the law, I suppose. I won't insult you by saying that you didn't see the obvious—that you didn't know it was imported from the past. I'll try and make things easy for you—"

"Offer me no favours, traitor!" she said with a sudden blaze of spirit. Don Miguel let that pass.

"Who gave it to you?"

"Don—Don Arcimboldo Ruiz." She choked out the name. Don Miguel whirled, his cloak flying, and snapped at the slave who waited by the door.

"Get him! Get Don Arcimboldo! And quickly!"

He passed the time while he was waiting for the freckled man to arrive by inspecting the mask. Everything pointed to the same conclusion; the gold was as fresh as though hammered yesterday. Oh, there was no doubt!

"You desired my presence?" said Don Arcimboldo, hurrying into the room. He bowed in passing to the Marquesa, who had sunk on the bed with her face in her hands, a pitiful figure.

"Yes!" Don Miguel wasted no time on formality. "You gave this to her? Yes? Where did you get it?"

"Why, I bought it openly enough, in the market beyond the city wall!" said Don Arcimboldo, blinking. "Is something wrong?"

"Did you report it to the local office of my Society?"

"To check if it was licensed for import? Why, no! Why should I think of such a thing? It was offered openly for sale by a merchant who vends his wares regularly in the market—why should I assume it was unlicensed?" A look of awe spread across Don Arcimboldo's face. "Am I to take it that—that it's contraband?"

"You are," said Don Miguel curtly. "You probably acted in good faith—but God! That thing weighs more than twelve pounds; it's so magnificent it must have been famous in its own period to begin with, and it would certainly have come to my notice if the Society had licensed it. Besides, we don't license things like that for sale in a public market! We'd have given it to the University of Madrid, or the Mexicological Institute in New Castile." He sighed. "Well, at least you had sense enough to recognise it as an import. Who was this merchant? Where's his pitch? I must find out where he got it—and I'm afraid we're going to have to take possession of that mask and get it back where it came from just as fast as is humanly possible."

"But—who could have smuggled it in?"

"Just possibly, a corrupt Licentiate; we've had cases, but the Society doesn't publicise them. If not, my friend—then you can guess at the implications yourself. They frighten me out of my wits!"

III

With the passage of time, the fear had not diminished, but grown. It still held him in its clammy grip as he sat in the Chamber of Full Council of the Society a week later.

The atmosphere of the Chamber was rich with a sense of authority and ritual, like the interior of a great cathedral—which in many ways it resembled. It was panelled with fine dark woods inlaid with gold; most of its floor was occupied by four tables arranged in the shape of two capital L's, with a gap at diagonally opposite corners. These tables were covered with red velvet; the chairs were upholstered in the same material, except for one, which was still vacant. That was purple, the prince's colour, and it stood at the eastern end of the room, transfixed—like a butterfly on a pin—by a shaft of pure white light stabbing down from the ceiling. Another shaft of light, horizontally focussed, completed the cross.

Along the northern table, the General Officers of the Society sat waiting. Don Miguel could not tell one from another, for they sat in shadow, as did he. Behind them, their private secretaries stood dutifully at their masters' orders.

He himself was in the middle of the western side of the oblong formed by the tables; while on the southern side, facing the General Officers, were the prisoners—the Marquesa, attended by two of her personal maids, Don Arcimboldo, who was alone, and the merchant from whom Don Arcimboldo had purchased the mask. The Marquesa had been weeping. But Don Arcimboldo had an air of puzzled boredom, as though he was certain that this stupid misunderstanding would shortly be regulated.

And on the velvet-covered table before the vacant chair, the mask itself rested like a great golden toad.

Suddenly there was a ring of trumpets, and the room seemed to tense. There was movement behind the vacant chair, at the eastern door of the Chamber. A herald in cloth-of-gold strode forward and spoke in a voice much resembling the trumpets that had just sounded.

"His Highness the Prince of New Castile!"

The Commander of the Society: Don Miguel rose to his feet and bowed.

When he was told in a grunting voice that he could sit down again, the Prince had already taken his place. He was a round man with stubby limbs and a short black beard; a ring of baldness was spreading on his scalp. He wore the full dress uniform of a Knight of the Holy Roman Empire, and his chest glittered with the stars of all the orders which he as a Prince of the Blood had accumulated. The total effect was impressive; it was meant to be.

His face was partly in shadow because the light was from above him, but it could be seen that he was studying Don Miguel intently. Don Miguel felt uncomfortable, as he might have done under the scrutiny of an inquisitor.

At last the grunting voice came again, like a saw rasping into fresh oak-planks. "You're Navarro?"

"I am, sir," said Don Miguel, finding that his mouth was dry. He was certain that he had acted correctly in the matter and yet there was still the nagging doubt...

"And this bauble in front of me is the thing that all the fuss is about?"

"It is, sir."

"Hah!" The Prince leaned forward in his chair; behind him, an obsequious personal attendant moved slightly, ready for any emergency. The Prince caressed the golden thing with his thick fingers, that sprouted coarse black hair along their backs. Obviously, he liked it—or he liked the presence of so much fine gold.

At last he sat back and shot a keen glance down the line of the three prisoners before turning to the other side and saying, "Father Ramon, this is for you, I think."

Don Miguel watched to see which of the formless officers replied; whichever moved and spoke, that one was Father Ramon, the Jesuit, the master-theoretician of the Society and the world's greatest expert on the nature of time and the philosophical implications of time-travel.

"I have inspected the object," said a dry, precise voice from the officer who sat at the end of the table nearest to the Prince. "It is Aztec, of Mexican gold and workmanship—of that there is no doubt at all. And it has not been licensed by the Society for importation."

Don Miguel felt a surge of relief. At least he had been correct up to that point, then.

"The consequences of this temporal contraband cannot be assessed as yet," the Jesuit continued. "We are attempting to establish its provenance to within a few years; then we shall investigate the effects of its removal. If we find none, we are faced with a serious dilemma."

"How so?" said the Prince, leaning back and twisting a little sideways in his chair.

"*Imprimis*," said Father Ramon, and thrust forward a thin bony finger from the darkness to lay it on the table, "we shall have to determine whether we have in fact replaced it—and if we have replaced it, then we shall have to establish the time at which it was replaced, and the circumstances. And *secundo*, we shall have to determine whether— if it has *not* been replaced—whether we have in fact a case of history being changed."

Shorn of its emotional overtones by this cleanly logic, the problem seemed to Don Miguel nonetheless terrifying.

"You mean"—it startled him to find that he was speaking, but since heads were turning towards him, he ploughed on—"you mean, Father, that we may find its disappearance incorporated in our *new* history as an accomplished fact?"

The shapeless head turned towards him. "Your presumption," said the Jesuit coldly, and hesitated, so that Don Miguel had a while in which to wonder what "presumption" meant, "is—accurate."

Don Miguel breathed a sigh of relief.

The Prince shrugged. "It sounds as though the matter is safe in your hands, then, Father Ramon."

"I think so," said the Jesuit in a voice that implied a smile.

"I leave it to you, then. My business is with the associated troubles. For example—Navarro!"

The last word was uttered in so sharp a bark that Don Miguel jumped. He said, "Sir!"

"Navarro, what possessed you to arrest the Marquesa di Jorque, who was plainly an innocent party in this case?"

Don Miguel's heart sank so rapidly he could almost feel it arriving in his boots. He said stiffly, "I acted, sir, in strict accordance with the law." He was glad that his voice remained firm.

"Have you no sense, man?" said the Prince sharply. He gave the Marquesa a sidelong glance. "I have studied the informations you have laid, and there is no evidence at all that she acted otherwise than as an innocent party. I'm discharging her from custody here and now, and I require you to apologise to her before she returns to her domains at Jorque."

What?

For a moment, Don Miguel had the impression that he had actually uttered the word—in the presence of the Commander of the Society, an unforgivable breach of manners. But he had not. He licked his lips. To have to apologise for acting in accordance with the law? But this was ridiculous!

He grew aware that the heads of the General Officers were all turned in his direction; he saw that the Marquesa had suddenly recovered all her poise, and was giving him a triumphant glare, tapping her manicured fingers on the arm of her chair. What was he to do?

To cover his loss of self-possession, he rose slowly to his feet. By the time he was standing, he had decided what to say.

"I will not apologise to the Marquesa," he said, "for acting in accordance with law. I *will* apologise for not realising that she is an innocent."

An innocent. A simpleton, in other words. He hoped the distinction would penetrate.

It did. The Marquesa stiffened with growing fury; the countenance of the Prince began to purple. The air was thick with their reaction. But the tension broke suddenly—broke against a thin, rather high-pitched laugh. With amazement, Don Miguel realised that it came from Father Ramon.

"Commander, that is an apology exactly meet for the case," he said. "It is true, as our brother Navarro submitted, that anyone but an innocent would have questioned the presence of so magnificent a primitive artifact in the present day."

The Prince gave a tentative laugh. Then another, more convincing. Finally he threw back his head and roared. Other General Officers joined in, and to the accompaniment of their mirth the Marquesa hastened from the hall, her shoulders bowed and shaking—but not, for sure, with laughter. With humiliation.

Don Miguel felt he had gained an unexpected victory. He sat down again slowly.

"Good!" said the Prince finally. "Now to the main part of the business. What action have you taken, Navarro, to discover the source of this—this thing before me?"

Don Miguel spoke rapidly. "The merchant is present from whom Don Arcimboldo bought it—a certain Higgins, native of Jorque and of family in that town and province. He maintains and short of torture will doubtless continue to maintain that he in his turn acquired it from a stranger."

"Indeed!" The Prince turned thoughtful eyes on the merchant, who tried to sink in his chair; he was a middle-aged man without great personality. "And how was this, may I ask?"

The merchant turned from side to side, as though seeking a way of escape. Finding none, he babbled in the flat broad accent that Peabody exhibited also, and most of the people in the north of England. "Your highness, I swear! I swear it's true! I bought it from a stranger who offered it to me at the market—on the first day of November it was, as I recall."

"You often do business with strangers?" the Prince said.

"Never! Never in my life before! I cannot"—and his voice dropped to scarcely a whisper—"I cannot recall his name, or his face! I can say only that I must have been mad—must have had a brainstorm, your highness! For I'm a reputable man, and I've always traded in strict accordance with the law, and—"

"Enough!" said the Prince curtly. "Navarro, have you investigated the claim?"

"I have, sir. And it seems to be true as far as it goes. Hitherto, this man Higgins has been a law-abiding merchant, and I've spoken to several people who have sold him goods; he has been careful to ascertain that they have proper title to them, and to avoid handling anything imported without licence. He has had many extratemporal objects through his hands, and the office of the Society in Jorque has previously found him scrupulously careful."

"Yet this time he buys contraband from a total stranger, without investigation, and sells it to Don Arcimboldo who takes it in good faith, I'm sure"—this with a dip of the head in Don Arcimboldo's direction—"and gives it to the innocent Marquesa." The Prince chuckled again, reminiscently. "Surely he must indeed have had a brainstorm!"

"Sir." A flat word from one of the hitherto silent General Officers. The Prince glanced towards the speaker.

"Yes, Red Bear?"

The Director-in-Chief of Fieldwork, Don Miguel noted. They had really assembled the big guns for this case, then!

"I'm inclined to disbelieve that. I think Navarro was in a fit of pique against the Marquesa, and that this has coloured his investigation."

"How say you, Navarro?" the Prince demanded. Don Miguel felt his face grow warm.

"I admit," he said slowly, "that I was annoyed with her for showing off a Licentiate of the Society—myself!—like a performing animal for the benefit of her guests. But I deny that this was sufficient to colour my investigations."

There was a grunt from Red Bear. The Prince paused, as if seeking further remarks, heard none, and slapped his hand down on the table like a pistol-shot.

"Resolved, then! That the merchant Higgins be interrogated further! That Don Arcimboldo be discharged as an innocent party! That we meet now in private session to speak of what has passed! Clear the room," he added in a lower tone, off-handedly, to his personal aide.

Don Miguel sat back, feeling slightly weak, but conscious of an overpowering relief that—the attack from Red Bear excepted—he seemed to have justified his actions to the Full Council. And this, for a lowly member of the Society, a Licentiate with only five years' experience and four field trips to his name, was no inconsiderable achievement.

IV

As soon as the Chamber had been cleared, the doors had been locked with a great slamming of heavy bolts, and the lights had gone up, the assembled officers relaxed in their chairs. Don Miguel was surprised to find that with the lights full on the Chamber was just an ordinary room, large and palatial, but simply a room. And—more surprising still—when they threw back their cowls, the General Officers were just ordinary men.

He found himself relaxing with them.

The Prince fumbled out a large pipe and stuffed it with tobacco in coarse-cut hunks. Lighting it, he mumbled around the stem.

"Well, young Navarro, I don't mind telling you that you've created an almighty kind of chaos with this rash act of yours!"

A harsh laugh, as though to say "understatement!" came from Red Bear—who was a long-faced Mohawk with black braided hair showing oily-slick around his face.

Father Ramon—whose face was like a bird's, with the skin stretched tight around a beaky nose and little, very bright eyes—passed a thin hand over his bald cranium in a way that suggested he had acquired in youth the habit of running his fingers through his hair and still expected to find hair on his head. He said quietly, "Sir, that is a harsh way to speak."

The Prince shrugged, puffing his pipe like a bonfire. "I dispute that—though I should know better than to dispute with one of your Order, Father! What I mean is what I say. Navarro has caused us a good deal of unnecessary botheration."

The Jesuit looked worried. "Again, no. In my view he has acted well, aside from the element of innocence in connection with the Marquesa, where he has let himself be deceived by appearances. My son"—he turned to face Don Miguel directly—"I must say that you were as guilty as she of overlooking the obvious. The Marquesa di Jorque is not a woman of any great intellect. She has at most a certain low cunning, which enables her to gather about her people of superior intelligence, and to pass herself off as their equal. It is a harmless pastime enough, provided all the players understand the rules. I think you should have seen that she would never have thought, even for a moment, to report the mask to our local office."

"I accept your judgment, Father," said Don Miguel, and was glad that the strictures had been phrased so mildly.

"On the other hand, the question of the merchant puzzles me," continued Father Ramon. "Our brother Navarro has said that he objected to being displayed like a performing animal, simply because he was a real live Licentiate of the Society. There is here a far graver matter—that the work of the Society itself is being turned into a simple spectacle for sensation-seekers."

Like a spark and gunpowder, two facts came together in Don Miguel's mind and shot him forward in his chair. He said explosively, "Then it is true!"

The curious gaze of the General Officers turned on him. Of them all, only Father Ramon seemed to know what he was talking about. He said, "You have heard about this disgrace to us?"

"I—I know only what was said to me by the Marquesa herself: that it is rumoured that certain people have been taken in this quatro-centennial year to witness the victory of the Armada."

"Hah!" said Father Ramon. "If it stopped there! If that was all!"

"Then it is true?" pressed Don Miguel. "How could such a thing be allowed to happen?"

The Prince coughed. "Father Ramon, as usual I'll defer to your judgment—but is this wholly wise?"

"To give our brother the facts? Why, indeed it is. His action, heedless of possible consequences to himself, in this matter of the mask, indicates that he is uncorrupted and upright." Having thus justified himself, the Jesuit turned back to Don Miguel and resumed.

"As for how it is *allowed* to happen—it is of course forbidden. As for how it does happen—why, simply enough. Certain Licentiates whom I cannot yet name, but whose licences will not last long when they are

caught, have stumbled on a trick. They act after this fashion: they take
payment from those who wish to be treated to this spectacle, whatever
it may be—the victory of the Armada, or the games in the Coliseum
in the time of Nero, or the battle of the Guinea Coast, or the disgusting acts in the temples of Egypt—and they then plan an innocent field
trip, which is approved as routine by our brother Red Bear. This field
trip is always to a more recent time than their actual destination. They
then establish a time and place when their customers were alone and
unobserved; they go to that time and place, collect them, go to their
official destination, go back further and deposit their customers, resume
their fieldwork, collect their customers again, return them to the split-
second of their departure, and then return to base. Put so elaborately,
it seems difficult; in effect, it is not. Who can tell from which direction
in time a traveller approaches?"

Don Miguel nodded. "And is this corruption widespread?" he said
slowly.

"I regret that it is. We are at present investigating the finances of no
less than thirty Licentiates whose income is—shall we say?—remarkably high."

"Thirty!" Don Miguel's dismay and shock appeared in his voice. The
Prince, finding that his pipe had gone out, felt for means of relighting
it, and spoke in a gruff tone.

"It wouldn't be so bad if it was simple—uh—unofficial observation,"
he said. "I mean, we've all done this at one time or another. I've taken
my father on the odd trip myself."

"But that's different," said Don Miguel slowly. The Prince chuckled.

"Yes, kings get away with a good deal! So do—well, no matter."
He coughed again to cover his momentary embarrassment. "But the
habit of accepting bribes is hard to lose. And no one really accepts the

possibility of altering the past, except the experts. It seems that certain of these unofficial travellers have acquired souvenirs of their trips."

Father Ramon nodded. "Of which this great golden mask is probably one."

A chill passed down Don Miguel's spine. "Is that, then, not the only thing which has been brought in as contraband? Why, the possibilities are inconceivable!"

"It's the biggest that we know of," said Father Ramon. "I presume you're aware of the principle on which we permit the importation of extratemporal objects—of course you are, for you've already made field trips, I gather. Then you know how we limit ourselves to objects which the historical record shows to have been lost, such as treasure buried in a secret place by one who is killed without divulging his knowledge, or something which we know to have disappeared without trace, because the fact is to be found in contemporary annals. This is not an altogether reliable rule, naturally, since we cannot be certain that some of these items lost by 'natural causes' were not in fact lost through our intervention." He gave a skeletal smile, and shrugged. "But we trust in the divine plan, and rule ourselves by this precept.

"What would happen if we deliberately stole away something which history records as being in existence at a date later than our interference, we do not know, and I pray God we may never find out. In such a case as this, though, we may justifiably fear disastrous consequences. Oh, it may turn out that this mask was melted down, and the loss of simple mass—even so much of it, and even gold—might pass unnoticed. But if not; if we find that its mysterious disappearance is on record, we face a still graver problem. Should we assume that history has in fact been changed? Should we replace the mask where it disappeared from, in an attempt to change it back? Shall we find paradoxes developing afterwards, because the events which led us to replace this object no longer form part of the universal chain of causality?"

The smile with which he accompanied his words was in fact a pleasant one, but to Don Miguel it seemed more like a skeleton's grin. He said slowly, "My mind boggles at such possibilities, Father. I'm glad I do not have to involve myself in such deep philosophical problems."

"Nonetheless, we are giving you charge of a problem which is just about as deep as this one," rumbled the Prince. He swept the others with an inquiring glance, and received confirmatory nods. "We're charging you with discovering, first, the origin in our time of this mask—of identifying, if you like the unknown man from whom it was bought. And then, second, of returning it unnoticed if such is the decision of Father Ramon."

Don Miguel's heart pounded. "I—I feel unworthy," he said after a pause. The Prince snorted.

"Worthy or unworthy, Navarro, you've opened up the problem. You close it again!"

In its way, the assignment was a signal honour; it was also a terrifying burden. The more Don Miguel thought about it, the more he felt qualms.

He was not yet thirty. He had held the licence of the Society for a bare five years. His experience of fieldwork had been confined to a few trips—one, the last, on which he had spoken with Julius Caesar and contrived to settle a long-standing argument among historians regarding Caesar's motives for refusing the crown of Rome; another, on which he had suffered the blow from a blunt sword which had permanently twisted his smile.

And perhaps he might have accepted the task with equanimity, nonetheless, had it not been for the news Father Ramon had announced to him at this meeting. Thirty Licentiates of the Society suspected of taking bribes—this was hardly believable!

To Don Miguel, work in the Society had something of the air of a sacred trust. That was the principle on which it was founded, after all. Since Borromeo's epoch-making discovery in 1892, the right to exploit time-travel had been strictly limited to those judged fit to be placed in charge of it; in the Empire, this was the Society of Time, and in the Confederacy, it was an analogous body.

Don Miguel had accepted this fact as gospel. Now, though, thinking over what had been said, he realised that what he had taken for hard sense was founded basically on fear. Fear of what might happen if irresponsible people were allowed to make journeys into the past. It was that, and not a sense of responsibility, which had so rigidly restricted time licences.

And given this premise, then it followed almost automatically that after nearly a century of time-travel, people would grow blasé and tolerant—that their upright posture would sag a little here and there.

Yet this too entailed paradoxes. One of the most familiar justifications for the rule confining the purpose of time-travel to observation without interference was the argument that if this rule were not made and kept, then time-travellers from the future, visiting the past, would be noticed in the here-and-now. Therefore the rule was a good one; therefore it was to be kept.

And if it were not being kept...

Don Miguel had visions of whole areas of unrealised history being swept into some unimaginable vacuum, into the formlessness of absolute not-being. Worlds, perhaps, in which Jorque was York and an English monarch sat the throne of the Empire; in which possibly a Mohawk prince ruled New Castile and called his subjects braves and squaws. Worlds in which men travelled—to stretch the idea to its uttermost—into space instead of through time, by some undreamed-at miracle of propulsion.

Resolution hardened in him. The first line of attack on his problem, inevitably, would be to inquire further of the merchant, Higgins, from whom the mask had been bought.

V

The guards on the door of Higgins's cell inspected his commission; it was under the Prince's own seal, so they gave way respectfully and permitted him to enter.

The cell was large and spacious. In the centre, Higgins sat lolling in a chair, his head sideways on one shoulder, his mouth half open. He was fastened down with leather straps. At a table facing him, the two inquisitors charged with interrogating him were conferring in low tones; their faces were anxious and they frowned continually.

At Don Miguel's entrance, they glanced up, their faces pale in the shadow of their dark brown cowls.

"How goes it?" demanded Don Miguel, when he had explained his business and authority. The inquisitors exchanged glances.

"Badly," said one of them—the taller. "We greatly fear, Don Miguel, that he has been bewitched."

"How so?"

"We have used all the means that are lawful to unlock his tongue," the other inquisitor said. "We have employed liquors of divers kinds, and we have used mirrors and pendulums. We have established that he remembers purchasing the mask, but he cannot recall the face of the man who sold it, nor his name, nor any clue to his identity."

"But he recalls the date?" suggested Don Miguel. The inquisitor who had spoken first nodded.

"We have given orders that all travellers in or about Jorque who registered with the authorities at that time shall be followed up. But it seems hopeless; whoever brought the mask for sale would have been a wealthy man—perhaps a noble—and could too easily have avoided the demands of the law."

"The justification of the law lies in men's obedience thereof," said the other inquisitor in sententious tones. Don Miguel nodded.

"What kind of enchantment might this man have used?"

"There are many possibilities. A drug of some sort, one imagines. Or possibly he constrained Higgins to stare at some bright spot—a reflection on the mask itself, even—and then soothed him to oblivion with gentle words."

It sounded unlikely. But the inquisitors were experts in that kind of work themselves; he had to take their word for it. He sighed.

"Inform me of what passes," he said.

"We will. But we have small hope of reaching the truth."

If the interrogation of Higgins had reached a dead end, the only thing to do was to go back to Jorque and continue on-the-spot investigation. Accordingly, Don Miguel left Londres that same evening by fast coach, and next day presented himself at the local office of the Society—a great house set in spacious grounds not far from the Cathedral.

Here he was received by an old-young man with a pale face and a high, hesitant voice whose eyes fastened greedily on the Prince's seal at the foot of Don Miguel's commission. He was probably a failed Licentiate, Don Miguel diagnosed both from that fact and from his further behaviour.

"We have discussed much the problem which you are come to look into," said the old-young man fawningly, having introduced himself as Don Pedro Diaz. "We greatly admire the way you saw straight to its heart."

"Did I?" said Don Miguel dryly, thinking of the clouds of mist that still shrouded its solution. "You are too kind. I am come to know what has been discovered concerning the origin of the mask since I left Jorque the other day."

The other looked disconcerted. "Why, we have not sought further," he admitted uncertainly. "Was it not enough to have arrested the merchant, Higgins, and his clerks?"

"It was not enough," said Don Miguel shortly. "Take me to these clerks; I would speak with them."

But the clerks were of no help either; their story was that their master Higgins had himself conducted the purchase and the sale, as he often did when the other party in a bargain was a person of noble family. Don Miguel well understood this—it was sometimes necessary for a nobleman to sell family heirlooms or other valuables in order to replenish a shrinking coffer, and when this was the case he usually preferred to treat in private with a discreet merchant.

It seemed that Higgins had a reputation for being exceptionally discreet; he had handled many such transactions.

The clerks stuck to their story—that they had known nothing of the mask until their master was arrested.

Don Miguel sighed and left the cell in which they were incarcerated. Walking back through the fine grounds of the Society's office, he spoke musingly to Don Pedro who accompanied him.

"This market, now—the one where Don Arcimboldo said he purchased the mask. It's outside the city wall, is it not?"

"It is. The municipality banned markets within the city, save for freemen of Jorque, in the last years of the last century; thus the custom arose of going beyond the walls to trade. And now, indeed, marketing within the city is rare—all the richest merchants trade yonder."

"Good. I wish to view this market. Call a coach, and let us begone."

"At once," said Don Pedro eagerly, seeming overjoyed to be of service.

While they were waiting for the coach, Don Miguel turned to another subject that interested him currently. He said, "And of Don Arcimboldo Ruiz, now—what manner of man is he?"

Don Pedro spread his finely manicured hands. "He is of noble and ancient family, I believe; he has estates in the north, but prefers to live in Jorque, occupying himself with the pursuits of the wealthy and with the collection of rare works of art."

"So he's a connoisseur, is he?"

"Men speak highly of his expert knowledge."

"Then he'd have known how strange and rare the mask was." Don Miguel bit his lip. He recalled that Don Arcimboldo had stated straightforwardly his assumption that Higgins would not try and sell him contraband; this was reasonable enough, if he had previously done business with Higgins and found him honest.

And yet he might have questioned...

Don Miguel firmly repressed that line of thought. Don Arcimboldo had struck him as a sensible, level-headed person; he had revealed a healthy cynicism in his assessment of the Marquesa di Jorque, and there was no doubt that he would have had the sense to make inquiries if he suspected he was receiving contraband. More to the point, perhaps, he would not have made a present of the mask to the Marquesa if he had suspected it was contraband; he would probably have kept it secretly for his own collection.

Why had he given such a remarkable object to the Marquesa, though? If he was himself a collector, then...

A crease of puzzlement deepened between Don Miguel's eyebrows, and remained there all the time he was in the coach *en route* for the great market of Jorque.

They called it a market; in fact, it was almost a town on its own now, spreading out beyond the walls in an easterly direction. Wide well-paved roads ran between the plots of ground occupied by the merchants' stalls; these consisted of booths erected before and around solid stone-built warehouses. During the day, goods were brought forth under awnings and in glass-sided huts, where brawny men guarded them with clubs. At night, they would be taken back into the warehouses and secured firmly against robbers.

Don Miguel instructed Don Pedro to dismiss the coach for an hour, and set forth on foot through the market. He paused, apparently at random, to test the quality of nutmegs at a grocer's; to feel some splendid Eastern brocades in a draper's; to inspect a set of candlesticks in a silversmith's. As he did these things, he asked questions casually of the merchants who attended him. Don Pedro, blinking and uncertain, listened to what was said, and at last began to catch hold of an important fact. Somehow in each conversation, Don Miguel was contriving to introduce the names of Higgins and of Don Arcimboldo.

The hour passed. Their last call was at a bookbinder's, where gold-leaf glittered on fine calf bindings and the air within the booths was rich with the scent of leather and size.

Brooding, Don Miguel emerged and indicated to Don Pedro that they should walk together back to the place where their coach waited. Their course took them through the heart of the market; many persons of great wealth and standing were now entering it, since it was past noon, to visit their favourite merchants.

"Higgins seems to have been a very upright and much respected trader," said Don Miguel at length, while they stepped to the side of the road to allow the passage of a gilded coach.

"So it has been said," agreed Don Pedro, with a sage nod.

"Therefore he must indeed have been bewitched." Don Miguel cast a lingering glance after the gilded coach—for its passenger had been a rather beautiful young woman—and resumed walking. "And witchcraft is tricky. Don Pedro, I require a word of advice from you."

"You do me too much honour," said Don Pedro nervously.

Don Miguel did not comment. He said merely, "Don Pedro, if you were in Don Arcimboldo's place, why would you give a very rare and costly mask of solid gold to a lady who is—to be blunt—past the age of courting?"

Don Pedro's eyes widened. He said nothing for a moment. When he did reply, his voice was hesitant.

"Ah—I would not say such things of Don Arcimboldo—"

"Speak your mind!" rapped Don Miguel impatiently.

"Why, then, one would assume he stood to gain some small advantage or other. If he did not do it purely from motives of friendship."

After Don Arcimboldo's scathing denunciations of the Marquesa, Don Miguel felt that the latter possibility could be ruled out. He shrugged.

"So too would I say. Don Pedro, instruct your coachman to pass by Higgins's town house on the way back to the Society's office."

At Higgins's town house, Don Miguel descended alone from the coach and went indoors. He came back after twenty minutes, his face very thoughtful. During the rest of the trip to the office, he said nothing, responding only with grunts to Don Pedro's tentative essays at conversation.

There was a message waiting at the office, which had come by semaphore telegraph from Londres a few minutes before their return. It was a report from Red Bear's department, informing Don Miguel that the golden mask was almost certainly the work of a certain celebrated Aztec goldsmith called Nezahualcoyotl—Hungry Dog. And that placed its origin somewhere in the middle fifteenth century, most likely in the great town of Texcoco.

Another puzzling factor! If the mask was the work of so famous a smith that Red Bear's fieldworkers could trace and identify its origins in so short a time, then it was all the more unlikely that Don Arcimboldo would readily have given it away.

And especially since…

A great light suddenly broke in on Don Miguel. Facts came together and formed a pattern. A pattern that made sound sense. He slammed fist into palm and muttered an oath.

"What ails you?" demanded Don Pedro in alarm.

"Nothing!" snapped Don Miguel. "Nothing! But I see it, and yet I do not see it! If—Don Pedro! Send speedily to the office of the Inquisition in Jorque; demand for me a skilled inquisitor, to visit me and answer certain questions. Then a coach, to await my orders—for tonight I purpose to call on Don Arcimboldo."

"It shall be done," said Don Pedro, a trifle nervously, and hurried away.

Don Miguel conversed lengthily with the inquisitor who came in answer to his request, in private and alone. When he had finished it was near dark, and yet he refused Don Pedro's request to stay and take a bite to eat before his departure. Instead, he buckled on his sword, threw his cloak about him, and went into the night as though fiends were hot on his heels.

VI

Don Arcimboldo's house was a fine one, of recent building, in extensive and well-cared-for grounds. Inside, everything bespoke luxury and elegance; the same stamp that marked the Marquesa's house was to be seen here, in the many creeping plants and hothouse flowers that turned the rooms and halls into gardens, in the exquisite panelling and the many cases holding rare trophies—Greek, Roman, Egyptian, Etruscan, Aztec, Inca…

The majordomo who admitted Don Miguel presented his master's apologies, saying that he was at dinner but would shortly be finished and would wait on his distinguished guest; meantime, would Don Miguel have the grace to occupy himself in the library?

Don Miguel would, with pleasure. Wine was brought for him by a slender Guinea-girl—she must have been very expensive—who poured him a glassful and then retired to sit in the darkest corner among the bookcases, her white eyes and white teeth glimmering in the shadow.

Glass in hand, Don Miguel walked absently about the room. It was not merely a library; it was almost a museum, with many shelves of fine objects—gold, silver, jade, turquoise. Don Miguel passed his fingers caressingly along a pair of Moorish silver knives that caught the light on one shelf, before turning away abruptly and interesting himself in the books.

Don Arcimboldo displayed a truly catholic—but definitely not Catholic—taste. There was one case which would probably have sent Father Peabody into hysterics. Don Miguel caught the thought, reconsidered it, and decided that it was probably incorrect. Father Peabody's association with the Marquesa had probably cured him of any such tendency. Nonetheless, there were very many books here that were on the Index, for heresy as well as for other reasons.

He selected a finely illustrated edition of the *Satyricon* of Petronius Arbiter and settled himself in a superb leather chair, its back tooled all over with gilt, to pass the time until Don Arcimboldo should enter.

When he at length did arrive, he was full of apologies for having made Don Miguel wait. But Don Miguel waved the protestations aside.

"Of course not!" he said. "I should have sent word that I was coming. But I wished to speak with you, and I have not long to spend in Jorque before I must return to Londres—so it is rather I who should apologise. And I have not been bored. I have been admiring your excellent taste."

Don Arcimboldo dropped into a chair that was the twin of Don Miguel's, snapped his fingers for the Guinea-girl to bring him wine, and gave a deprecating chuckle. "I'm flattered," he said dryly. "But it is hardly a question of taste; rather, I am selfish enough to like to sur-round myself with beautiful things."

"You have certainly succeeded in that," agreed Don Miguel. "Tell me, did you acquire all these in Jorque?"

"Many of them. Our great market—have you seen it?—is a fine hunting-ground for rarities. Indeed, I bought many of the items here—the gold and silver, at least—from Higgins. By the way, what news is there in that matter?"

"You hold no grudge against me, I trust, for having acted a little—rashly," suggested Don Miguel.

"No grudge at all, of course. I see perfectly that you had to act as you did. The smuggling of temporal contraband is a very serious matter, I know; I've been looking into the question since I returned last night, and though my mind spins with some of the tenuous arguments of the philosophers, I am fully aware of the risks attached to it."

Don Miguel repressed a desire to frown. That choice of words seemed inapposite. Or apposite. He was very glad he had had that illuminating discussion with the inquisitor before he set out this evening.

The strong wine was affecting him a little, on an empty stomach. He waved aside the Guinea-girl when she came to offer him more.

"No, so far we have made little progress," he said. "It appears that Higgins was bewitched into forgetting the name and looks of the man who sold the mask to him. The best efforts of our inquisitors have not broken down the barrier in his memory."

He watched closely to see if there was any change of expression on Don Arcimboldo's face at the news; none was visible.

"But it puzzles me," said Don Arcimboldo reflectively, his hand caressing the cut-glass goblet in which his wine was served, "how anyone could have acquired the mask in the first place. As far as I can see, it would have had to be a Licentiate, would it not?"

"Possibly not," said Don Miguel, giving a shrug. "It is known that certain outsiders, not of the Society, have been taken into the past lately—having oiled sufficient palms, of course."

Don Arcimboldo raised his eyebrows. "Indeed! I believed that your Licentiates were incorruptible."

"It would seem not. Thirty at least are known to have accepted bribes." There! That was a direct jab. But in vain Don Miguel sought a sign that it had struck home.

"Almost, I find it in my heart to envy these outsiders," said Don Arcimboldo, and gave a grin which conveyed engaging frankness. "For I must admit I have yearned to walk among the people to whom the rare and beautiful things I so much admire were almost common-place—modern! But I fear that even if I were to overcome my natural revulsion against infringement of such a basic law, I would find it an expensive business to indulge that yearning."

Don Miguel found himself oddly at a loss. There was a ring of great sincerity in Don Arcimboldo's words. He said uncertainly, "I am glad that you say so. It seems to me in the last degree wrong that the marvel of time-travel should be degraded to a mere spectacle."

Don Arcimboldo shifted comfortably in his chair. "On the other hand," he said reflectively, "I suppose there is some reason to say that—provided, always provided, that the rule regarding non-interference is strictly kept—others than Licentiates might be accorded the privilege of visiting the past."

Don Miguel shook his head. "But who, except Licentiates, could one trust to—?" he began. Seeing the flaw in his argument, he broke off. Don Arcimboldo chuckled.

"Yes! Yes! On your own admission, Don Miguel, it has now turned out that even your Licentiates are not to be altogether trusted. Although, I have no doubt, they charge a very stiff price, and do their best to see that their—uh—clients keep the rules."

Don Miguel felt that somehow he had been bested in a subtle dispute. He rose nervously to his feet and began to walk back and forth on the soft, expensive carpets.

"Possibly," he said after a few moments of silence, "possibly in the end we shall be compelled to extend the scope of time licences. Possibly we shall find a means of bringing objects out of the past which does not entail changing history."

"As far as I can find out," said Don Arcimboldo, "changing history is highly theoretical—up to now. How can one tell whether history was in fact changed by the contraband importation of that mask, for example? One can't. Our idea of 'changing history' actually consists in changing the written record of history, does it not?"

"Partly. Not entirely."

Don Arcimboldo paused to see if the other was going to add anything. When he did not, he rose to his feet also. "Well, as I said, this is all too deep for non-experts like myself. Tell me, was there any special business about which you came to see me?"

Don Miguel debated for a moment with himself. His original resolution was fading; he was no longer so sure that he was right. He covered his hesitation by staring thoughtfully at a fine Saxon buckle of hammered gold, set with garnets, that occupied a shelf among the books on the wall.

Well, it was risky—but if he did not stake his hopes on this deduction, he might go on hesitating for ever. He said, "Yes, Don Arcimboldo. There was. I wished to ask you why you gave such an expensive present to the Marquesa."

Don Arcimboldo looked taken aback. He spread his hands. "Don Miguel!" he said reproachfully. "I think you have no right to pose me so personal a question."

"You leave me no alternative but to command you, then," said Don Miguel, and drew his documents from a pouch at his belt. "My commission is under the seal of the Prince of New Castile."

Don Arcimboldo scowled. "I suppose I have to answer, then. I think it is ungracious and unmannerly. Why do you wish to know this?"

Don Miguel drew a deep breath and turned to face the other. He said, "You must have had a reason for doing this. Because you were heavily in debt to Higgins, and you would not lightly have paid him for that mask, nor would he lightly have sold it to you."

Don Arcimboldo half-turned his head away, so that his face was shadowed. His voice was cold and distant. He said, "So you have been prying into my personal affairs."

"I was commanded to," said Don Miguel, and waited.

Don Arcimboldo picked up a delicately wrought silver chain from a shelf near him, and let it swing between his fingers as though absent-mindedly. He said, "Very well, then. Yes, it is true that I owed Higgins a good deal of money. But it is not true that he would not have extended me further credit. After all, Don Miguel, I am far from being a poor man."

"Are you?" said Don Miguel glacially.

"What do you mean?" Don Arcimboldo flushed and spoke in a harsh tone. The swinging chain did not vary its pendulum-like motion. "Think you that this around you is the home of a poor man?"

"Yes."

Don Arcimboldo sighed. "I yield, I yield. That also is a sort of truth. I will tell you, then, why I gave the mask to the Marquesa. I hoped that she would loan me a sum to rescue me from my temporary—temporary!—difficulties."

The chain went on swinging. There was silence. Don Miguel allowed the silence to stretch. And after a little while, Don Arcimboldo's self-possession began to crack. He looked first puzzled, then alarmed. When his alarm was acute enough, Don Miguel spoke out.

"No use, Don Arcimboldo! Before I came here, I spent an hour in talk with an inquisitor, who is expert in this work. I have taken an antidote which countered the drug you gave me in that very good wine. So you cannot lull my mind with your swinging chain and hypnotise me into forgetfulness—as you served Higgins!"

The last phrase came out like the lash of a whip. Don Arcimboldo let fall his hands; white-faced, he whispered, "I—I do not understand!"

"Don't you? I do. This is how it happened. You decided to join those fortunate outsiders who have bribed Licentiates to take them into the past. It was, as you yourself said, an expensive business. Yet you persisted. You ran into debt with Higgins—an undignified situation! He may have become eager for his money. Doubtless your original plan was to smuggle a valuable item of contraband back from one of your illicit trips and offer it to Higgins in settlement of your debt. Then you reconsidered. Higgins was an upright man— too upright to accept contraband. So you chose a subtler way out of your corner.

"You deluded him into believing that he had bought the mask from someone else. No wonder he cannot remember who it was! One cannot remember a nonexistent person, after all. But you did not get to his clerks, Don Arcimboldo. I have spoken to those clerks. Even the clerk who keeps the stock-list for his master does not know of the mask. And you gave it, then, to the Marquesa, knowing that she would show it off to all the world, and that sooner or later someone would deduce it was contraband. Then you could play the innocent dupe, and Higgins would suffer the penalty for trading in contraband—thus preventing him from dunning you further, of course.

"I was almost deceived. A few moments ago, indeed, I was ready to believe that I had made a mistake—until you made a worse one, and started to try and bewitch me with that silver chain. The inquisitor with whom I passed time this afternoon warned me about such tricks. Then I was certain, and am now."

Don Arcimboldo cast the silver chain violently to the floor. "It's a pack of lies!" he said harshly. "What's more, you'll never convince anyone else except yourself."

"That is a risk I'm prepared to take," said Don Miguel stonily. He jerked his sword from its scabbard. "I arrest you, by the authority vested in me, and desire you to go with me to face trial. You may have met one corrupt Licentiate, Don Arcimboldo—but learn from this that some of us take our rules seriously. After all, we are meddling with the very fabric of the universe."

VII

The vacant space between the crystal pillars hummed faintly; those present in the hall shifted in their chairs, wiping their faces occasionally. It was always warm in the neighbourhood of the crystal pillars when a traveller was about to return.

The Prince of New Castile seemed worse affected than anyone by the heat, and grunted and muttered to himself. Abruptly he could not stand it any longer, and snapped his thick fingers at the attentive aide standing nearby.

"Wine!" he said thickly. "The heat is awful."

"Yes, your highness," said the aide alertly. "And for the company as well?"

"Father Ramon? Red Bear? You want wine?" the Prince barked.

Red Bear moved his long Mohawk face once in a gesture of acceptance, but Father Ramon did not move. After a pause, the Prince waved to the aide to hurry.

"Think you it is well done, Father Ramon?" he snapped.

Father Ramon seemed to come back to the present from a very long time away. He sketched a brief smile, turning to look at the Prince.

"Well done?" he parried. "As well done as we may do, I suppose. At least we know that the golden mask has been restored; whether the restoration itself was wise and necessary or not, we can but guess."

Red Bear snorted. "If you had doubts of the wisdom of the act, why give me so much trouble over it?"

"We must always doubt our own wisdom," said Father Ramon peaceably. He raised a hand towards the crystal pillars. "I think the moment is at hand."

The technicians on duty around the hall had tensed to their positions. Now, suddenly, there was a clap like thunder and a smell of raw heat, and in the space between the pillars a shape appeared. A curious shape of iron and silver bars, that seemed to glow for a moment as energy washed out of their substance in the process of their turning back to right angles with normal dimensionality.

In the middle of the frame, a figure was seen to collapse.

Father Ramon jerked to his feet. "Be swift!" he ordered the technicians. "He has been long about his task!"

The technicians moved—some to dismantle the frame of metal bars, others to help Don Miguel to his feet and stumble with him to a couch that stood waiting. Slaves hastened to fetch restoratives and basins of clean water to rinse his face and hands.

Only a few minutes had passed in the hall since the moment when Don Miguel had shifted into the past. But it was plain that for him much time had gone by; his skin was burnt with sun to the colour of leather, and his eyes were red and inflamed with dust. The General Officers gathered anxiously about his couch, wondering how gravely he had suffered.

Not very, it transpired. For having accepted a sip of stimulating liquor, he waved aside further attentions and struggled to sit up. He passed his tongue over sun-chapped lips and spoke thickly.

"It is done," he said, and looked about him in wonder. His mind was still whirling with the memory of the great city of Texcoco burning in tropic daylight, as his body was still clad only in the breech-clout of an

Indian of that time. The slaves had started to wash away the painted symbols from his face, but had not completed their task.

The General Officers breathed a sigh of relief. Red Bear said harshly, "You are certain?"

"Indeed I am. I found the workshop of Hungry Dog without trouble, at a time when he was working on the very mask I had brought back. When it was complete, it waited in his shop for the great festival at which it was to be dedicated with sacrifices to the great god Tezcatlipoca. I waited until the time of that festival. And the day before it, a man came to the shop and went away with the mask."

"Was it Don Arcimboldo?" demanded the Prince.

"Perhaps."

"Aren't you sure?" The Prince leaned forward angrily, with reproaches boiling on his tongue-tip; Father Ramon laid a hand restrainingly on his arm.

"Don Miguel has done well," he said.

"How do you mean?" the Prince said, blinking.

"Why, if he had given himself away to Don Arcimboldo, then Don Arcimboldo would have recognised him on meeting him again. This did not happen. Therefore it was correct to hide from him."

"So I reasoned," said Don Miguel, laying his head tiredly in his hands. "Therefore, when I saw that the mask was gone, I replaced it. I stayed long enough to make sure that it was dedicated at the festival as planned. And—here I am."

The Prince breathed a sigh of gusty relief. "Is it now in order, Father Ramon?" he demanded.

"As far as we can tell."

"Good! Then I must go back to New Castile; had it not been for this affair, I had planned to leave Londres days gone. All else will be attended to, I take it."

*

He gave Don Miguel a curt nod, spun on his heel, and was gone from the hall with cloak flying and aides trotting at his heels. After a thoughtful pause, Red Bear also took his leave, and Father Ramon was alone in the hall with Don Miguel and the silent, scurrying technicians.

"How do you feel now?" said the Jesuit eventually.

"I begin to recover," said Don Miguel, and reached for another sip of the restorative. "My hurt is rather in my mind than my body. I was witness to the sacrifice to Tezcatlipoca less than a day ago, and I am still nauseated."

The Jesuit nodded.

"It sometimes makes me wonder," said Don Miguel in a hesitant tone, "what blindness we also may be guilty of."

Father Ramon gave him an odd sideways glance. "Go on, my son," he invited.

"Well—what I mean is this. For all their fine work in gold, their masonry, their social discipline, those Aztecs I have been among were savages, habituated to sacrificing men by the score in the most cruel manner. For all that they understood the motion of the stars and planets, they never used the wheel save to move children's toy animals. We are superior in some ways—in many ways, perhaps. And yet we may have our blindnesses. Although Borromeo showed us how we might rotate the dimensions of substances so that the worlds became flat and we could voyage back into time, although we live in a peaceful world free of much of the horror of war—nonetheless, what things may we not be using for children's toys, that later ages may marvel at and put to use?"

"Yes," said Father Ramon, looking unseeing at the frame of iron and silver which the technicians were now dismantling. And then he repeated more slowly, "Ye-es…"

"What is perhaps worse still," Don Miguel continued, "is that we—unworthy as we are—have the power to reshape the history of Earth! So far, we have managed to confine that power to a few fairly reliable individuals. But thirty corrupt Licentiates—if this figure was accurate—could in their overweening confidence wreck history back to the moment of Creation!"

He spread his hands. "How see you this, Father? It's a question for you, not for a layman."

Father Ramon seemed to draw himself together inside his habit. "We have free will, my son. Therefore it is up to us to do as we will with what we have been given. Only—"

Don Miguel broke in, suddenly incredulous. "But Father! Here is—oh, how have I never seen this before? With time-travel, would it not be possible for agents of evil to go back in time and undo the good consequences of the acts of others? Would it not even be possible for such persons to corrupt the great men of the past, deliberately?"

"You are astute," said Father Ramon soberly. "It has been debated whether indeed the influence of evil that we see in history may not be the working out of just such interference as you suggest—whether in fact the fall of the angels hurled out of heaven may have been a fall into the past, rather than a fall through space. But this is the deepest of all theological questions today."

"I'm glad you say so," said Don Miguel with a trace of irony, and wondered at his own audacity in being ironical with a General Officer of the Society. Yet for all his reputation as a philosopher living in the rarefied regions of metaphysics, Father Ramon seemed singularly approachable. He added, "I myself do not see how such a question could be answered at all."

"You mean—whether or not the good results of men's acts could be wiped out by temporal interference? Good, of course, cannot be destroyed, and it is heretical to think it can."

The edge of sharp reproof on the Jesuit's voice cut Don Miguel's self-confidence to ribbons. He said humbly, "But then, Father, that makes nonsense of the idea of deliberate interference for evil ends."

"Not altogether." The Jesuit rose to his feet, seeming to come to a decision. "When you are rested, visit me in my private office. I think you deserve some information you have not been given."

Father Ramon's bare office had two chairs in it—one hard, one soft. He was himself sitting in the hard one when Don Miguel entered, and indicated that the other was for visitors. Don Miguel sat down uncertainly, wondering what the knowledge might be that was to be imparted to him.

Father Ramon offered him tobacco and a pipe, which he refused with a shake of the head, and then leaned back, putting his fingertips together.

"Consider what makes an act of free will free," he said.

The suddenness of the question took Don Miguel aback. He stammered a confused answer which Father Ramon ignored.

"No, it lies in this. That all the possible alternatives be fulfilled."

"*What?*"

"Precisely that. If there is free will—and we hold that there is—all our acts of decision must in fact be fulfilled in just so many ways as there are alternatives. Thus to kill and not to kill and merely to wound more or less seriously—*all* these must follow upon a choice between them."

"But I do not see that! There—there is no *room* for that to be true!"

"No?" The other sketched his habitual faint smile. "Then think on this. You go into the past. You abstract a crucial object—shall we say, a bullet from a gun aimed by an assassin at a king? You return to the present with that object. A king may change history by living or dying. Would you return to the same present as that which you left?"

"I begin to understand," said Don Miguel slowly, his voice shaking.

"Then suppose you return and restore that bullet to its place. The king dies—*again*, so to speak. And the present to which you come after doing thus, is the original present."

"But this must have been done!"

"It has," said the Jesuit calmly. "We have been doing it for more than forty years."

"How about the rule of non-interference, then?" cried Don Miguel, feeling his universe reel about him. "Are the corrupt Licentiates not the only ones who are corrupt?"

"There is no corruption in this matter. Those Licentiates who have taken bribes and carried outsiders into the past were confident that they could undo any stupid act by their clients. Indeed, most of them have scrupulously undone them. He who was Don Arcimboldo's accomplice did not know about the golden mask, or doubtless he would have forbidden Don Arcimboldo to take it away. From fear, of course. We all fear the consequences of interfering with history."

"But if all this is true," said Don Miguel in a choking voice, "then what does it matter if we interfere or not? We ourselves may be only a fluid cohesion of possibilities, subject to change at the whim of someone who chooses not to keep the non-interference rule."

"True," said Father Ramon stonily. "That is a logical consequence of there being free will."

There was silence. Eventually Don Miguel said, "I suppose this might be foreseen by anyone who worked out carefully what kind of a universe Borromeo's discovery opened to us."

"We may give thanks that up to now, few people have thought the matter through." Father Ramon smiled again. "Well, Don Miguel Navarro! How do you like the universe we live in?"

"I do not," said Don Miguel, and was at a loss for words to describe the sense of impermanence, volatility and changeableness that the other's words had instilled in him.

"Nonetheless," said Father Ramon dryly, "this is how things stand. Go you now to Red Bear and report on your trip for him. And do not speak lightly of what I have told you. For if this truth were to become known to those who are not ready for it—why, the sky would fall!"

When Don Miguel turned and walked to the door, he was surprised to find the floor still firm beneath his feet.

The Word Not Written

THE QUATROCENTENNIAL YEAR WAS DYING IN A BLAZE OF GLORY. The weather had been kind, and New Year's Eve proved to be fine and mild, spiced with a wind whose nip was just enough to sharpen the step to briskness and put colour in the faces of the people. Bonfires had been lit at sunset in most of the main streets of Londres, and around them nut vendors, potato bakers and kebab men with their rapier-like skewers laden with alternate lumps of meat, kidney and onion cried their hot wares.

There had been a great mock battle on the Thames as dusk fell; people had flocked in their thousands to witness the finest reconstruction ever presented of the battle between the all-conquering Armada and the gallant but pitiful English ships, four hundred years ago.

Even yet there were a few diehards in the crowd who cried insults at the display, shouting that it was shameful to them and their ancestors. But most of the spectators answered with jeers, for they regarded themselves as subjects of the Empire regardless of what blood happened to flow in their veins. Soon enough the civil guards quieted the complaints, and the loyal shout that greeted the appearance of His Most Catholic Majesty Philip IX, *Rey y Imperador*, when his golden barge hove in sight, echoed across all Londres.

Smiling, bowing graciously from side to side, King Philip was rowed over the same water that shortly before had been full of the mock battle. Another barge followed, bearing the Prince Imperial, his

Princess, and their children, and behind that again came the barge of the Prince of New Castile. The King's barge had sixteen oars aside; those of his sons had twelve, and at one of the oars sweated and cursed Don Miguel Navarro, Licentiate in Ordinary of the Society of Time.

Whoever the blazes had thought up this delicate tribute to the royal family, he muttered to himself, ought by simple justice to have been pulling on the oars too. But it was fairly certain that he wasn't. He was probably simpering and dancing attendance on the King or the Prince Imperial.

Even if they were going with the stream, it nonetheless called for real rowing to keep up with the King's barge, as it had eight more oars and was anyway less heavily laden. As a gesture of loyalty the idea was splendid; as a job of work it was abominable.

The notion had started innocently enough. As Commander of the Society of Time, the Prince of New Castile was going to play host this New Year's Eve to his father, elder brother, and a raft of foreign dignitaries, chief among them the Ambassador of the Confederacy of Europe. It was certainly a great and signal honour for the Society to be chosen as the focus for the climax of the quatrocentennial year, but like a good many royal favours it had its drawbacks. Don Miguel was in no mood for merrymaking anyway, what with the aftermath of the recent revelations he had had from Father Ramon about the actual nature of his work in the Society, but at least among personal friends and at his own discretion he might have passed a pleasant enough New Year's Eve. As things stood, he was going to have to follow up this chore on the river with an evening of playing host to all kinds of noble idiots at the Commander's palace in Greenwich. He could tell that he was not alone among the younger Licentiates on the rowers' benches in thinking that this might prove unendurable.

Probably the crowds that watched the splendid water-procession from the embankments guessed nothing of all this. Probably, when the spectacle was over, they dispersed sighing, thinking of the magnificence of the royal occasion and envying those fortunate enough to be present. Conversely, Don Miguel and his companions sat scowling by their oars, envying the simple folk going off to spend New Year's Eve with their families or to join the revels which would make the streets noisy and bright until dawn.

"You'd think," he growled, selecting one of the many discomforts that plagued him, "that in a Prince's barge they'd at least pad the seats decently."

His opposite number on the other side of the boat, another Licentiate of about his own age whose name was Don Felipe Basso, curled his lip. "It's clear where you'd rather be tonight, Miguel!" he answered in a low tone.

"Macedonia was better than this," Don Miguel muttered. A surge of memory drew up the side of his face where his smile was permanently twisted by a Greek hoplite's sword-stroke; it had been on that field trip to the Macedonia of Alexander the Great that he had first made the acquaintance of Felipe.

"Don Miguel! Keep the time!"

From his post in the stern Don Arturo Cortes rapped the order in his shrill, acid voice. Seated in his most magnificent plum-coloured cloak and snow-white velvet breeches on a velvet and gilt chair, he was making the most of his task as overseer of the amateur rowers. He was one of the senior Licentiates of the Society below General Officer rank, and widely tipped to succeed the Mohawk, Red Bear, as Director-in-Chief of Fieldwork. Somewhere he had acquired a General

Officer's wand which he was using at the moment as a baton to beat time for the oars. It was typical of his overweening self-esteem to make such a presumptuous gesture.

Don Miguel bit back his answer—he was altogether too close alongside the tapestry pavilion in which the Prince was sitting to speak louder than a whisper without being overheard and perhaps ticked off—and leaned harder on his oar. But when Don Arturo's attention had wandered again, Felipe spoke softly.

"He doesn't seem to like you, Miguel."

"Who? Don Arturo? That makes us even. I don't like him either."

"A little faster still!" Don Arturo rasped now, rising to his feet with his wand conspicuous in his hand. "We're falling further behind!"

By the time the barge was gentled in to the wharf near the Commander's palace, Don Miguel's buttocks were bruised, his hands were rubbed sore by the oars, and his temper was close to flashpoint. Face like thunder, he sat on his bench and watched Don Arturo with his usual officiousness directing the disembarkation of the Prince. With part of his mind, however, he was wondering whether out of sheer self-interest he ought to try and counter the dislike to which Felipe had referred. It was obvious where it had its source—in the affair of the stolen Aztec mask in which he had recently got himself involved. Everyone seemed to think he had handled it rather well. Indeed, he was wearing tonight for the first time at any Society function the outward sign of the Commander's approval, the gem-encrusted collar and star of the Order of the Scythe and Hourglass which cynical old Borromeo had chosen as the Society's emblem.

It crossed his mind that if he had played his cards right he might have used this new honour as a way of escaping duty on the rower's bench. But it was not in his nature to think of things like that at times when they might be useful.

Don Arturo's reputation for being suspicious of any younger member of the Society who made himself too noticeable was being amply borne out by the way he had been treating Don Miguel lately. Simply for his own comfort, Don Miguel reasoned, he would be well advised to deal courteously with Don Arturo.

But he wasn't going to do it this evening. Not after the performance Don Arturo had given aboard the barge.

"Are you going to sit here all night, Miguel?" Don Felipe said, clapping him on the shoulder. "Have you suddenly found a liking for that badly padded seat?"

Don Miguel sighed and roused himself. "I suppose not," he said. He gave a rueful glance at his hands. "Why did I not bring leather-palmed gloves with me instead of my best white silk pair which the oar would have rubbed to shreds? Ah well—how long shall we have to wait before we find a drink here?"

The Prince was ashore now. The wharf had been carpeted with purple, and a pathway of the same material led up over the rolling green lawn towards the main portico of the palace. Either side of the carpet, huge immobile Guinea-men stood with flaring torches to light the way; candles in coloured glass balls had been hung like fairy fruit on the branches of the trees and glowed red, yellow, green, white among artificial leaves. Every window of the palace was ablaze with light except for the upper two floors where the servants and slaves had their quarters under the eaves, and the higher windows of the great central tower where the Commander's own time apparatus was lodged. Don Miguel had a sinking feeling that before the night was out someone at least would have been persuaded to take a royal or noble visitor up that tower and show off the gadgetry, involving the technicians in a day's frantic work tomorrow to re-adjust all the delicate settings.

The strains of a band playing the currently fashionable dance-music drifted down from the palace. There was a fad for the chanted melodic lines and intense drumming of the Mohawks, and as Prince of New Castile, of course, the Commander could have the finest of American musicians at call.

Distantly visible through the huge windows flanking the entrance door of the main hall Don Miguel made out the General Officers of the Society, waiting to greet the King, who by now was almost at the door. Red Bear himself, with his black braided hair, was instantly identifiable.

Surrounded by a gaggle of courtiers, the two royal brothers and the Princess Imperial went up towards the house. Their faces eloquent of their suspicion that these high-ranking amateurs might have done the valuable barges some harm, the Society's watermen were taking over the pot-bellied craft again, to paddle them back to the boathouses. Most of the temporary rowers had already started in the princes' wake.

"Move, you two!" Sharper than ever, Don Arturo came bustling across the wharf waving his wand. "Don't you see that the mooring must be cleared? There on the river is the barge of the Ambassador of the Confederacy—we dare not keep him waiting!"

Don Miguel shrugged and might have answered back, but Don Felipe sensibly warned him against it by closing his fingers hard on his upper arm. Together they stepped ashore, and the watermen hastily shoved off to make room for the new arrivals.

"Come on up to the palace now, Miguel," Don Felipe urged. "We don't want to get fouled up in the Ambassador's train as it lands."

"I suppose not." Don Miguel tore his dull gaze away from the looming, lantern-outlined shape moving with splashing oars down the river towards them, and started to walk up the lawn. "Are you expecting to enjoy this evening, Felipe?"

"Me? I can enjoy myself anywhere. But you look as though the hand of doom had been laid on you."

"I know where it's been laid, too," Don Miguel said ruefully, rubbing the seat of his breeches. "Ah, to Hades with it all! Let's make the most of it, what say?"

Don Felipe laughed and linked arms with his old friend, and hurried him up the slope towards the lighted palace.

II

There was a peculiar and unexpected air of confusion in the main hall of the palace, gorgeously decorated and remarkably warm—which had the minor advantage, from the point of view of most of the younger Licentiates, that the beautiful women present could show themselves off in their lightest and filmiest gowns. The confusion stemmed from the fact that guests were arriving from both sides: the river approach, and the roadway as well. Consequently every few moments a tall Guinea-man would lead a surge of notables one way or the other across the already crowded hall so that they could greet a newcomer as protocol demanded.

The sight of this swirl and bustle raised Don Miguel's low spirits a little. With such a shifting of people it was conceivable that he might be overlooked, and could slip away to some quiet anteroom and savour his mood of gloom in private with a jug of wine. He made a meaningless response to some comment of Don Felipe's on the quality of the women here, his eyes roving around for his best line of escape.

And then his name was called.

His spirits sank again as he turned and saw Red Bear making an imperious gesture to him on his way from the river entrance—where the Ambassador from the Confederacy had just come in—towards the opposite door. He could hardly ignore that. He moved in Red Bear's wake and Don Felipe came with him.

"I think we're going to be honoured," Don Felipe said softly as they hurried forward. "Do you see who that is who has just turned up?"

The majordomo at the land entrance had a fine voice, but the babble of conversation and the noise of the band made it hard to hear what names he called out. A group of three—a man and two girls—were pausing in the centre of the wide double doorway.

"I don't know them," Don Miguel was going to say, when Red Bear, greeting the trio, turned and made another imperious gesture at them. He and Don Felipe strode forward and bowed.

"Your Grace, I have the pleasure of presenting Don Felipe Basso, Licentiate in Ordinary of the Society"—you had the feeling that this formality and routine appealed to Red Bear, with his Mohawk background—"and Don Miguel Navarro, Licentiate in Ordinary, Companion of the Order of the Scythe and Hourglass. Don Miguel, Don Felipe: His Grace the Duke of Scania, Ambassador of the United Kingdoms of Sweden and Norroway. The Lady Ingeborg; the Lady Kristina."

His daughters, presumably. Bowing again, Don Miguel took a second look at them. They were very much alike in most respects, and also very much like the Duke—tall, slender, with the shining fair hair which on their father's fine head was turning to snow-white. Their eyes were large and blue, and their complexions were like milk. Their gowns were clearly designed by a master; without ornament or embroidery they managed to look dazzling and put the finery of most of the other women to shame.

"Honoured," Don Miguel said, and heard how much more enthusiasm Don Felipe was putting into the same word.

"Don Miguel, Don Felipe," Red Bear was saying, "I charge you with the duty which I'm sure you'll find a pleasant one of escorting these beautiful ladies for the evening."

There could be no doubt of Don Felipe's agreement. With a tremendous flourish he bowed again, grinning like a cat, and the Lady Ingeborg's eyes danced. Don Miguel, on the other hand, felt like a boor as he muttered some empty answer. It was not that the Lady Kristina, opposite whom he had happened to find himself, was not extremely lovely. It was simply that in his present mood the last kind of company he had been looking for was that of an emancipated girl. His near-disastrous brush with the Marquesa di Jorque had set him against female emancipation for the time being, and all his friends who had trifled with girls from Norroway had informed him that they liked—no, demanded!—to be treated as at home. He had never been in Sweden or Norroway, which formed a curious private northern enclave where the people determinedly minded their own affairs and ignored the rivalries of the Empire and the Confederacy. But he did know that under their system women were even entitled to vote for the members of the Thing, and this was almost alarmingly different from the usual way of running public life.

And that this was not all talk was shown by the fact that no other girls of such rank would conceivably have arrived at an affair like this without at least a duenna apiece and probably half-a-dozen ladies in attendance.

"I'm sure you'll be well looked after, my dears," the Duke said in excellent Spanish, smiling at his daughters. "Go ahead and enjoy yourselves. I've already seen several people I promised to have a word with tonight, so there's no need for anyone to look after me." He nodded at Red Bear.

Well...

The first steps were automatic: provision of refreshment, a few comments about how mild the weather had turned out, and something about the mock battle of the afternoon. And there it ran dry. For some reason Don Miguel's mind wandered off on the subject of his sore hands and the hard rower's bench, and he found himself at the tail-end of a long and impolite silence. Don Felipe and Lady Ingeborg were chatting with immense animation on the other side of a large pillar where they all four seemed to have wound up. He was standing like a booby.

It was something of relief when with true northern emancipation Lady Kristina decided to make good his deficiencies for him, and pointed at the star hanging on his ruffled shirt.

"Navarro," she said thoughtfully. "Of course. Aren't you the Don Miguel Navarro who was responsible for setting to rights that matter of the Aztec gold mask which could have been so disastrous?" She spoke Spanish as well as her father.

Somewhat uncomfortably, Don Miguel nodded. He said, "As a matter of fact—but how on earth did you know? It's not—uh—a matter of public record, exactly."

Lady Kristina gave a quicksilvery laugh. "Oh, your Empire-bred modesty, Don Miguel! Even if it wasn't explained in detail in all the newspapers, something which leads to the award of what you're wearing is bound to become a matter for gossip. And you must know that of all places an embassy is where gossip, particularly scandalous gossip, comes most quickly home to roost."

She gave a mischievous grin, and Don Miguel felt a corresponding smile come lopsided to his own face. He said, "In that case, my lady, I'm sure you have an absurdly exaggerated idea of what actually happened."

She shrugged the creamy bare shoulders that rose from her plain but exquisite gown. "Very probably. But I'm sure that if I were to ask you to tell me what actually did happen, you'd underplay your part in it grossly and persuade yourself that you were being honest."

The automatic, stiff, ridiculous words were already forming on Don Miguel's lips, triggered by the possibility that she was going to ask him to tell her about it, with the gushing flattery he would have expected from someone like—oh, Catalina di Jorque, for instance. He was going to say, "I'm afraid I can't talk about it. It's confidential to the Society of Time."

Barely in time he realised that she wasn't going to ask him to do anything of the sort, but was turning to find a place for the empty glass she held, and saying, "Well, if you're unwilling to converse with me, you might ask me to dance."

Somewhat disconcerted, he led her out on the floor. She was a very good dancer indeed. As they completed their first circle of the hall, they passed Don Felipe dancing with Lady Ingeborg, and over her beautiful shoulder Don Miguel saw his friend give a conspiratorial wink. Obviously Don Felipe had heard stories about northern girls— the so-called reformed religion of course had a lot to do with it, but it was probably mostly slanderous…

His mind made an abrupt jump. He stopped dead in mid-beat.

"What on earth—?" Lady Kristina began. She turned and followed Don Miguel's gaze. "Oh-oh!" she said under her breath. "Would you like to dodge out of sight?"

He did in fact want to dodge out of sight much too much to wonder why she should suggest it; automatically giving her his arm to lead her off the floor, he headed for one of the nearer side-passages leading away from the hall. It was not until they were safely around a corner that he completed his double-take and looked startled at her.

"Uh—I'm dreadfully sorry," he began.

"Why?"

"Well—to snatch you away like that. It was unforgivably rude. I must look an absolute boor."

She gave her quicksilver laugh again, this time throwing back her head and making the most of it. "My dear Don Miguel!" she exclaimed. "Let's work this out. Wasn't that just the Marquesa di Jorque that you saw arriving?"

He nodded.

"And exaggerated accounts or not," she pursued, "weren't you recently involved in something which showed to her detriment?"

He nodded again.

"And weren't you shaken to the core to find her suddenly appearing where you least anticipated her having been invited?"

He found his voice at last. "Yes my lady," he said ruefully. "I can only imagine that someone—some friend of hers—has wangled her an invitation to make up for the way the Society recently snubbed her."

"So you very naturally want to keep out of her way. Well, here we are. Shall we find somewhere to sit down? I presume these rooms are open for us. And by the way, stop calling me 'my lady'—nobody ever calls me that at home except peasants and artisans. My name's Kristina." She was opening the nearest door and peeping through it. "Yes, how about this? And let's have some drinks, too."

Don Miguel, slightly dazed, caught up with her at that point. He glanced around, spotted a Guinea-girl carrying a tray of wine past the end of the passage, and called after her. She came obediently and served them with a curtsey.

Kristina took six glasses off the tray and ranged them on a handy table, somewhat to the Guinea-girl's surprise. When the slave moved to go, she looked after her. As the door closed, she said, "I think they're beautiful. I wish I looked like her—so graceful. Don Miguel, I like you. You shock beautifully. It lights your face from inside like the candles in those glass globes they've put all over the trees."

She sat down on the end of a heavy-built padded sofa with gilt-tooled leather upholstery, and took the nearest glass of wine from the table. Don Miguel swallowed and tried to speak.

"Tell me," she went on, "you're plainly not enjoying yourself, and I hope that isn't my fault. If it is you only have to say so. But if it isn't, suppose you give me an idea—be honest, now—of what the rest of the evening will be like."

Don Miguel's defences suddenly crumbled. He sat down next to her. He couldn't help smiling, and the smile warmed his whole mind.

"To be completely honest," he said, "what will most likely happen is this. Red Bear, who has the Mohawk weakness for firewater, will probably decide at about nine or ten that he is a better drummer than the professional musicians. He will embarrass *everybody*. The Ambassador of the Confederacy will make slighting remarks about our celebrations, comparing them unfavourably with a winter carnival on the Neva. Everyone will drink furiously because the conversation keeps getting frozen in mid-run. Around midnight Father Ramon will arrive to celebrate Mass for the Society; those who are sober—and members of the Society had better at least *look* sober!—will heave a sigh of relief and go to chapel. And after midnight, when the King and the Prince Imperial can get down off their dignity, there might be some fun with the younger Licentiates and the Probationers who are here. Most of them aren't. They're out in the city enjoying themselves, except for whichever poor fellow is on duty at the Headquarters Office."

"I think I'd like to see some people who are enjoying themselves," Kristina said thoughtfully. "I suppose you have to be at this Mass at midnight, do you?"

Don Miguel nodded. "This is a great traditional occasion for the Society. All the members come. Even—" He bit the last word off short. That should never be mentioned to anyone, of course.

She took no notice. Rising with sudden determination to her feet, she said, "Miguel, let's go and be with people having fun, shall we? There's plenty of time to go into Londres and get back for your service at midnight, isn't there? How about seeing if you can find a carriage for us?"

Astonished almost beyond description, Don Miguel felt his jaw drop. Painfully raising it again, he said, "You know—that's an absolutely wonderful idea!"

III

There was no doubt about it, Don Miguel thought contentedly— this was a far, far better way to spend New Year's Eve than in the Commander's palace. Wandering among the crowds of merrymakers with a beautiful girl on his arm, doing idiotic things for no particular purpose behind the customary anonymity of half-masks bought from a pedlar, and laughing more and more often than he could ever remember laughing in his life before. He was naturally a serious person. It occurred to him that perhaps he was habitually too serious.

They had left their carriage shortly after reaching the north side of the river. They had sampled hot chestnuts and hot spiced wine from stalls on wheels, paused to watch a tumbler and juggler for a while, looked in at a display of animals from Africa on Queen Isabela Avenue, joined in the rowdy singing of a troupe of street comedians. Now at last they had come to Empire Circle, where five ways met. Here a bonfire was spitting and snarling as people threw fireworks into it; a band was playing raucous traditional tunes, and people danced in the roadway with an abandon that gladdened the eye.

It had turned much colder in the past hour or so, and Kristina, with only a light carriage-cloak covering her flimsy gown, ran forward to the fire to warm her hands at it. She tossed her hair back and looked laughing up at him, her eyes sparkling behind her black mask.

"Ah, Miguel! I hadn't thought that the people of these damp and misty islands knew so well how to amuse themselves!"

"Oh, it's their native good sense," Don Miguel said, smiling. "No matter how much our priests and prelates inveigh against these festivities, they go on nonetheless. Is it like this in your country?"

"It's colder in winter than it is here, but we do much the same things." She rubbed her hands together as they absorbed the radiant heat of the flames. "Why, Miguel, you look sad all of a sudden. What's wrong?"

He shrugged. "Nothing. I was only thinking—" He hesitated. Normally he would not have spoken of what was in his mind to a young girl, but Kristina was considerably different from other girls of twenty he had met.

"I was thinking," he continued slowly, "of other festivals I've seen, at other places and times. The Aztec feast, for instance, in honour of Xipe the Flayed God, where the officiating priests were dressed in human skins, and there was ritual cannibalism after the victims had had their hearts torn out."

"You've seen that?"

"Yes, I've seen that. And the *Ludi* in the Circus Maximus in Rome, where men died by the hundreds to glut the blood-lust of the crowd… So I was thinking: although the prudish and prurient so roundly condemn this New Year merriment, it is at least more innocent than much of what has gone before. Surely in this respect at least the world is changing for the better."

"And it made you look sad to think that this is so?" Kristina probed mockingly.

"No. I was thinking of death coming to so many people for the entertainment of so many others." Don Miguel shrugged and looked around for something to distract him. It was out of keeping to voice such gloomy thoughts here and now.

"Ah, but I'm warm again!" Kristina said cheerfully after a moment, turning away from the blaze. "It's the dampness with the cold now which eats to the bones. How do you suppose she endures it, for example?" She shook one arm free of her cloak and raised it to point across the circle.

For a moment he did not see what she meant, but a couple of youths standing nearby also caught the movement and looked up, and one of them whistled. "Look!" he nudged his companion. "Look there, I say. What do you make of that?"

His friend's eyes bulged. "Drunk, or mad, to behave like that!" he exclaimed. "Probably mad!"

"An interesting kind of madness," the first youth said.

Indeed, the subject of their remarks did appear to be out of her mind. For one thing, her costume—even for a night given over to fancy dress—was ridiculous. It appeared to consist of blue feathers pasted directly on to her smooth skin, on her hips and buttocks and on her belly as high as her navel. There were low red shoes on her feet; around her wrists there were bangles of various colours, and aside from that she wore only designs in yellow paint on her face, shoulders and breasts. She seemed to have emerged from the southward-leading avenue connecting Empire Circle with the river embankment, and was standing now in the middle of the roadway staring about her. She seemed both dazzled by the sudden brightness of the illumination here and dazed by her surroundings, for she stared wildly from side to side like an animal trapped and seeking a way of escape.

Ribald yells went up from the crowd and the noise of singing died as people turned to stare. Not far from Kristina and Don Miguel were a pair of civil guards; an indignant man of middle age, pointing furiously at the feathered girl, said something to one of them. Don Miguel did not catch the words, but the import was clear, for a grinning youth next to him bellowed, "Speak for yourself—some of us like to see 'em that way!"

It occurred to Don Miguel that the sight of someone so nearly unclothed was hardly fit for a duke's daughter, but the realisation was somewhat belated, for Kristina, her pretty face set in a frown of curiosity, was staring intently at the girl in the blue feathers. She said, "Do you know Miguel, I have never seen such a costume before?"

Something clicked in Don Miguel's mind. The word premonition flickered through his thoughts.

A group of drunken workmen at the edge of the crowd nearest to where the feathered girl was standing had made up their minds now that if she came out in public half-naked she could expect what they had in mind. Leering, they moved up to her, about five or six of them together. Tiger-wise, she paused in her frightened staring about and half crouched to confront them.

"Kristina," Don Miguel said in a low voice, "I think I ought to get you away from here."

"You'd do much better," came the reply as tart as lemon juice, "to make these civil guards go and help that poor girl before those men rape her!"

She glared at him through her mask. Taken completely aback, he missed the next step in what was happening, but a sudden cry drew his attention back to the edge of the circle. He saw to his amazement that one of the workmen was lying on his back on the hard ground, and the girl was in the process of hurling another of her assailants over her shoulder in a perfect wrestling throw.

"Oh, lovely!" Kristina clapped her hands, then caught Don Miguel by the arm. "Come on, let's go and cheer her!"

But the ferment of Kristina's earlier remark was working in Don Miguel's mind now. Never seen such a costume before…

What was he doing standing here like a petrified dummy? He started to shoulder his way towards the feathered girl as violently and quickly as he dared.

Ignoring the many complaints from those he pushed aside, he made his way to within a few paces of the girl, Kristina keeping up with him somehow. By now two more men had joined the first, bruised and cursing on the ground, and the girl was spitting insults at them. Her voice was almost as deep and strong as a man's. Listening, Don Miguel felt the hairs on his nape prickle.

The girl was small and thin, but wiry. She had—he could see now that he was close enough—black hair dressed in stiff wings on either side of her square head. Her complexion was olive-sallow. And the words she had uttered had sounded like—*like*, not the same as—the language of Cathay.

★

Don Miguel was as well acquainted with the costumes, behaviour and languages of the major civilisations of history as any Licentiate of similar experience, and better than most. He could make himself understood in Attic Greek and Quechua, Phoenician and Latin, Persian and Aramaic. He could also recognise the characteristic vowel-consonant clusters of many other tongues which he did not speak fluently. And what the girl had hissed at her assailants did not fit any language he could call to mind.

There was a slim chance that she was a legitimate visitor to Londres, perhaps a member of the Cathayan ambassador's suite. But he doubted that. He was suddenly so doubtful of everything about this girl that he did not believe she had a right to exist.

The horrible possibilities implied by his suspicion—it could not be called more than a suspicion—made him for a moment completely forgetful of everything else. Leaving Kristina to take care of herself, he strode forward.

The feathered girl spun to face him, taking him in her panic for a new attacker, and before he could even utter a tentative phrase in the Cathayan language, she had sprung at him.

Barely in time he reacted. She was not merely a wrestler—she was a killing fighter, fantastic though that was in view of her sex. Her first move had been to launch a crippling kick at Don Miguel's crotch; her toe landed on his thigh instead and caused him to lose his footing so that he had to go down on one knee, fending her off upwards, and she seized his right arm at wrist and elbow and attempted to bend the elbow-joint back so it would dislocate.

Pivoting on his prisoned arm and his knee, he swept his other leg through half a circle and kicked her feet from under her. Astonished, she lost her grip on his arm and fell sideways. He brought his leg back and laid its weight on her neck so as to hold her down for long enough to gather himself and throw himself on top of her. She made to sink her teeth into his calf.

Snatching his leg back from the pain, he managed to fall forward nonetheless, and pinned her wrists and one leg to the ground in an improvised but serviceable hold, half-sitting, half-kneeling. Then by main force he started to bring her wrists together.

She said nothing, but set her teeth and stared up at him, fighting to break his grip. During that long moment Don Miguel found time to hope grimly that there were no Probationers of the Society of Time in the crowd around, yelling crude approval at his success. If there was anything more undignified than a Licentiate could do than wrestle with a woman in the middle of Empire Circle, he couldn't imagine it.

All right, he was going to have to hurt her. There was no alternative, however much it went against his principles. He shifted his fingers on her wrists and stabbed down at the ganglia.

The shock went all the way through her. She forgot about resistance for long enough to allow him to seize both wrists in one hand and hold them, still applying the painful pressure. With the hand thus released, he sought the carotid arteries in her thin throat and scientifically began to strangle her.

In fifteen seconds she was limp; he gave her ten seconds more to ensure that she would not recover too quickly, and then sat back wearily on his heels. He wiped sweat from his forehead. Mingled now with the egging-on cries of the crowd he detected voices of complaint, perhaps at his ruthless treatment of the feathered girl; those people should have had to tackle her. But a nasty situation might develop unless it were checked at once. Where were those civil guards he had seen standing near the fire? As the saying went, when you needed a guard you never could find one—

Ah, here they were, the crowd jeering at them as they made their way over. He got to his feet.

"Make these people stand back!" he ordered crisply. "Get a hackney-carriage and help me to get this girl into it!"

The civil guards, taken aback, exchanged glances. One of them with bristling mustachios said, "Who do you think *you* are?" His hand fell to his sabre-hilt.

Don Miguel drew a deep breath. "Will you do as I say? I'm Don Miguel Navarro of the Society of Time, and this is Society business! Jump to it!"

The scar across his face made him look savage and very much to be obeyed. But it was the talisman-like name of the Society which made the guards blanch, and many of those in the crowd as well. There was a startled hush followed by a ripple of comment. Then the guards moved.

Don Miguel took off his cloak and laid it over the girl on the ground; she was stirring a little but had not recovered consciousness. Maybe he ought to tie her hands and ankles; he found a handkerchief and knelt to attend to the task. As he was feeling for a second means of tying her, something was dangled before his eyes. He glanced up. Kristina had somehow eluded the civil guards and was offering him the girdle of her gown. He took it with a word of thanks.

"Who is she?" Kristina demanded. "Why did you knock her out?"

"I don't know who she is," Don Miguel said grimly. "But if she's what I suspect, there's going to be the devil to pay tonight."

IV

In the dark padded interior of the carriage they sat mostly in silence, staring at the cloak-shrouded form of the girl on the opposite seat as successive scythe-sweeps of light from roadside lanterns moved over her.

Suddenly Kristina shivered and pressed up against Don Miguel. She said, "Miguel, what did you mean when you said you thought there would be the devil to pay tonight? You spoke so fiercely it was frightening."

Already Don Miguel regretted that he had spoken. After all he had nothing to go on but guesswork. He said, "If you don't mind, Kristina, I'd rather say no more until I've found out the real facts."

She looked round at him, lips a little parted as though about to ask another question, but deciding not to. Don Miguel sweated and wished that the driver would hurry. Guesswork or not, this feathered girl scared him. That costume was none he recognised; the words she had uttered were subtly wrong. Which could mean—which might mean... He choked off the thought.

The carriage wheeled with a grating of iron tyres on cobbles and came into the forecourt of the Society's Headquarters Office. Like the Commander's palace, it was set in its own grounds fronting the river, but unlike the palace it was all in darkness tonight except for a single yellow square of a window on the ground floor near the main door. Dropping from the step of the carriage as it halted, Don Miguel swore. Tonight, naturally, only the duty Probationer would be here—and just, just barely, possibly the man he needed to see more desperately than anyone in the world.

"Get the girl out!" he rapped to the driver. "I'll have the door opened."

The man nodded and climbed down from his high seat, while the horses shifted uneasily in the traces. Don Miguel started up the dark steps.

But the door opened before he reached it, and there stood a young man blinking diffidently in the light of a lantern in his hand. He was twenty or less, snub-nosed, blue-eyed, below Don Miguel in height but well enough built.

"Are you alone?" Don Miguel flung at him.

"Ah—yes, Licentiate!" the young man said. "I'm Probationer Jones, sir, on duty tonight. I believe your honour is Don Miguel Navarro. What service can I do you?"

"You are alone?" Don Miguel pressed. "No one else here?"

"Absolutely no one, sir," Jones asserted, wide-eyed. Don Miguel's heart turned over. He had expected—but no matter. It might or might not be true. He would have to see.

"There's a girl in my carriage," he said. "She ought not to be here— or anywhere, for that matter. I'm having her taken inside."

Jones gave a sigh. "Very well, sir. I presume you will require a suite in the quarters, and privacy—"

The look on Don Miguel's face made him break off, stuttering.

"Have you been required to do such services by members of the Society?" Don Miguel demanded.

"Uh—" Jones's embarrassment was acute. "Not I myself, sir. But I believe other students have."

"If anyone ever tries it on you, report him to your Chief Instructor. It's no part of your duties to act as a pander. Understood?" Without waiting for an answer Don Miguel swung round and saw how the confusion might have arisen, for Kristina was standing by the door of the carriage while the driver was still half-hidden in shadow as he wrestled to lift out the cloak-enveloped form of the unconscious girl.

"Show the driver inside!" he rapped at Jones. "Find a couch or something where he can lay his burden!"

"At once, sir," Jones said, and hurried down the steps, his face fire-red, to lend a hand.

"Kristina," Don Miguel said in a low voice, moving close to her, "I must apologise for this. I think perhaps I should arrange for you to return to the company of your father now."

"In any case," Kristina said, "it's gone eleven and you'd have to make haste to return yourself. But what—?"

"It is indeed!" Don Miguel remembered with dismay. "So in fact I've wasted time, idiot that I am, to come here at all. See you, I wished to speak with Father Ramon, and not realising how late it had become thought to find him still in his study here—Oh, what a kettle of soup we have to stir!"

He passed a tired hand over his face. "Get you back in the carriage, then. We'll return to the palace as soon as I've done one necessary thing."

He spun on his heel and dashed into the building.

When he came back, instead of climbing into the carriage, he scrambled on the driver's box and seized the reins. The horses whinnied and leaned on the traces, and Kristina gave a cry of alarm.

"I'm sorry!" Don Miguel shouted down to her above the grind and clatter of the wheels. "But as you saw, that feathered girl is dangerous. I dared not leave Jones by himself to cope with her, so I've paid the driver for his service in remaining there."

"Was that all you went for?" she cried back.

Don Miguel did not answer, but lashed the horses into a gallop. It was not all. He had needed to find out for himself that the great doors guarding the time chambers in the building had not been tampered with tonight. And they had not; Jones had told the truth, and he was alone.

He had imagined that perhaps some drunken Probationers, or some corrupt Licentiate, had secured access to the time apparatus unlawfully.

Yet it seemed his guess was wrong. And, the simple explanation having failed, he was left for the moment with no explanation at all.

A cold wind blew along the river now; their road followed the embankment. He shivered, and damned his impatience in abandoning his cloak.

Driving like a fury, he brought the carriage swiftly to the broad straight Holy Cross Avenue—the last portion of their route on the north side of the river. At the next bridge they would have to swing right and cross over. And there, at the approach to the bridge, something was going on. At first he took it for the expected crowd of people coming across from the south to attend Mass at midnight in the cathedrals of the city; it was not until the carriage was already among the pale-faced, terrified men, women and children that he heard the near-screams of the civil guards trying to keep order and realised that this was nothing so commonplace.

The whole roadway was flooded with people here; the windows of nearby houses were illuminated and the air was full of a confused moaning.

From behind him Kristina looked out as the carriage perforce slowed to a crawl. "What's happening?" she called.

"I don't know," Don Miguel answered curtly. "Guard! Guard!"

A civil guard on horseback breasting the flood of people as though it were a flood of water forged his way slowly in their direction, waving a gauntleted hand. When he came close enough, he called out, "You'll have to go around another way, your honour! It's impossible to get past here!"

Don Miguel stared, cursing the murky darkness which the lanterns barely penetrated. Some commotion under the bridge there: water splashing—

"What's happened?" he bawled.

"We don't know, your honour! Some say an invasion, some say rioting—but across the river there, it's total chaos!" He sounded frightened. "Men's bodies have been seen floating downstream, stuck full of arrows, they say! And there are fires!"

Shriller and more piercing than the general tumult, there was suddenly a scream from near the bridge, and people began incontinently trying to run. Ignoring the guard and Don Miguel, they surged past the carriage, making it rock.

The guard wheeled his horse and went off shouting, trying to restore some calm to the crowd. There was no hope of getting the carriage further forward, short of running down the people in the way of it, and Don Miguel jerked on the reins to bring the horses to the side of the road. Even to cover those few paces took a heartbreakingly long time. He set the brake and leapt down from the box.

Kristina was still peering pale-faced from the window. As he came close, she threw open the door and made to step down. He gestured her to stay where she was.

"I'll see if I can get one of the civil guards to escort you away," he said harshly. "This is inexplicable, but—"

"No, I'd rather not," she cut in. "I'm coming with you. The civil guards have all the work they can cope with, and I refuse to be abandoned in the carriage on my own."

Don Miguel bit his lip. What a time to be encumbered with a woman! But he shrugged and held the carriage door for her. With her leaning on his arm, he forced a way forward to the wide space at the approach to the bridge.

Here the confusion was fantastic. A small detachment of soldiers with horse-borne artillery had formed up at the side of the road; some of the men were assisting with crowd-control while the others looked after the horses. Men with spyglasses were staring across the river from the parapets of the bridge. On the other side blurs of red could be seen against the sky—the fires the guard had mentioned, presumably. Many of the fleeing thousands were half-clad, sick or aged and children among them.

In charge of the artillery troop was a young officer on a fine roan gelding. Kristina beside him, Don Miguel managed to get close to this officer.

"Miguel Navarro, Society of Time!" he introduced himself, cupping his hands to his mouth. "What's the chance of getting over the river to the Prince's palace?"

The officer stared down at him as though he were mad. He said explosively, "To the palace? You're lucky to be here, aren't you, rather than there?"

Don Miguel felt a cold hand touch his nape. He said, "I don't know anything about what's going on!"

"Nor do I, practically!" The officer's horse started at some alarm, and danced sideways three paces before he quieted. "But whatever's going on seems to have started at the palace. Haven't you looked across the river?"

He threw up his arm and pointed. Don Miguel turned, seeing for a moment only the same red smudge on the night as he had noticed already. Then landmarks fitted together in his mind. He said, "The palace is on fire!"

"That's right!" The officer laughed humourlessly. "One of my men reported a minute ago that the roof had fallen in."

"But the King's there, and the Prince Imperial, and the Commander of the Society, and the Ambassador of the Confederacy—"

The hand on his arm tightened. He glanced down at Kristina and saw that all the colour had gone from her face. Yes: her father and her sister, too…

"God knows what's going on!" the officer said savagely. "But it's the biggest disaster in a hundred years, no question of that. And the night on the other side of the river is alive with murderous shadows, killing and looting and burning."

From near the water's edge came a loud exclamation. "Someone out there! Swimming! Get him ashore!"

The officer saluted Kristina and dug his heels into his horse's flanks to go down and investigate. If this was someone from across the river, he might have more coherent news. Don Miguel hurried after the officer.

They arrived as the man was being dragged on to the bank. He had spent his last strength swimming; he collapsed immediately. Don Miguel saw with horror that each of his shoulders was stuck with a short, vicious arrow, the barbs buried in the flesh. It was a miracle he had got across.

"Miguel!" Kristina whispered. "Isn't it your friend?"

Don Miguel strode forward. "God's name," he said. "God's name, but it is. Felipe!"

He dropped on his knees beside the stricken man, but the officer, dismounting, waved him back. "Leave him till we've drained the water from his lungs, you fool!" he snapped.

Yes, that was sensible. Don Miguel moved aside and a medical orderly from the artillery troop came hurrying up with a case of medicines. Like a huge waddling white owl a Sister of Mercy came after him.

Aching, Don Miguel stared as they examined the arrows and made to extract them and dress the wounds. His sick preoccupation was suddenly broken by a rattle of carriage wheels from behind him, at the end of the bridge. A harsh voice called out to the driver, telling him to go around another way.

Then a dry, precise voice was heard, speaking from the carriage. "But I must cross here and now to go to the Prince's palace. I must be there before midnight."

Don Miguel's relief was so great that he almost swooned. He started forward, waving and shouting at the top of his voice.

"Father Ramon! Father Ramon! Praise heaven you're here!"

V

The Jesuit master-theoretician of the Society of Time got down from his carriage, bird-like head cocked as he surveyed the fantastic scene. He said, "I fail to see, my son, why my arrival in the middle of this to-do should so excite you, but something tells me that I shall not enjoy learning the facts. Enlighten me."

Rapidly Don Miguel summed up the catastrophe as far as he knew of it—the mysterious attackers beyond the river, the burning of the palace, the unknown fate of the royal family, the refugees streaming north, his being in the company of the Lady Kristina of Scania, her concern about her father, then last of all the astonishing apparition of the girl in blue feathers.

Father Ramon started. "Describe this woman!" he said sharply. As well as he could, Don Miguel obeyed, and was appalled to see the expression that came to the older man's face. It was as though the words were blows from an enchanter's wand, each one ageing him by another year.

"Do you think you know what her origin is?" he demanded.

"Yes, my son. I fear I do," the Jesuit said heavily. "And to judge from your reaction, it seems that you do also."

Don Miguel did not know whether to be relieved that his guesswork had been so accurate, or horrified for the same reason. He said, "But then—"

"Let us not speculate too far," Father Ramon interrupted. "How can we find with some degree of accuracy what has transpired at the palace?"

"Ah—just as you arrived!" Don Miguel said. "My friend Don Felipe Basso had swum the river, pierced with strange arrows but living when he came ashore. They are ministering to him—see, there on the bank." He pointed.

Father Ramon headed towards the white outline of the Sister of Mercy like a shot from a gun. Don Miguel glanced at Kristina; it was clear from her paleness and her trembling lips that she was using her self-control to its uttermost. He put his arm comfortingly around her and led her to Don Felipe's side.

Father Ramon was already kneeling there, head turned to the medical orderly. "Will he live?" was the crisp question. If the answer was negative, Extreme Unction must precede any questioning, of course. But the medical orderly, tossing bloody dressings into the river, nodded.

"He's tough as oak, Father," he said. "He'll live."

Don Miguel heaved a sigh of relief and bent close to Father Ramon's thin lips as they formed the crucial words. Don Felipe opened his eyes and tried to smile.

"You were lucky not to be there, Father," he whispered. "And Miguel—I thought you were… No matter. God's name, what madness can have taken possession of them all?"

"Speak on!" Father Ramon commanded sternly. "Without fear or favour I charge you to speak unvarnished truth in the name of God and the Society!"

Don Felipe closed his eyes again, but his lips writhed and in halting whispers he outlined the dreadful truth.

Partly, it seemed, it was the fault of the Ambassador from the Confederacy, who—as Don Miguel had sardonically prophesied—had compared the entertainment offered unfavourably with what he could see at home. Partly it was the fault of the Prince Imperial who according to rumour was known to be tired of waiting to succeed his long-lived father, and who had learned to pass away the time in unprincely ways. And partly it was the fault of Red Bear, whose notorious Mohawk weakness for liquor had sometimes caused trouble before.

At some time in the evening, a word had passed which broke a royal temper. A quarrel flared; the Ambassador from the Confederacy threatened to leave the country. In between the rowing parties came two dangerous conciliatory figures: Catalina, Marquesa di Jorque, and Don Arturo Cortes.

"The Marquesa spoke of the glories of the past," Don Felipe whispered. "Perhaps she meant well; perhaps she was trying to distract the obstinate minds. But she started the arguments anew, as to who were the bloodiest and fiercest fighters of all time. The Ambassador claimed the Scythian Amazons—his army as you know has a regiment of women infantry—while the King declared that Amazons had never existed. Then I saw Don Arturo speaking with Red Bear and the Commander, who as host of the evening was greatly put out by the turn of affairs. Then—but I don't know what happened then. All I saw was the terrible women with their bows and spears, swarming down the stairway leading from the centre tower. I stood and fought with those who could fight, but they came on like devils, and at last I was compelled to..."

His voice trailed away.

"My father!" Kristina said in a high thin voice. "My sister! What happened to them?"

But there was no answer. The medical orderly dropped to feel Don Felipe's pulse; after a moment he looked at Father Ramon. "We must get him away and let him rest," he said. "He is weaker than he was."

Unseeing, Father Ramon rose to his feet. Don Miguel took a pace towards him. "Do you know who these terrible women are? Can you fill in the gaps of the story?"

"I think so," the Jesuit said in a dead voice. "Amazons—yes, it pieces together. It must have happened like this. They wished—the fools, the fools! God forgive me for calling them fools, but what else can I say? They wished to decide this difference about the most valiant and dreadful fighters, and they trespassed where they should not have trespassed, beyond the bounds of our reality. Women such as you described to me, my son, are female gladiators from the court of King Mahendra the White Elephant, in an age where a decadent Indian usurper sits on the throne of a Mongolian empire governing all Asia and all Europe—a world further distant from ours than any which our researchers have ever explored."

It made sense to Don Miguel, thanks to his having been made privy to the best-kept secret of the Society of Time—the fact that its members had in fact deliberately altered key incidents of history to observe the consequences, then changed them back. But he wished that what Father Ramon said could have been as meaningless to him as it was to Kristina, who merely repeated as she looked from one to other of her companions, "My father and sister! What happened to them?"

He could only give her a comforting squeeze with the arm he put around her. To Father Ramon he said, "But—who can be responsible? Who can have broached this secret to the company? Not the Commander, surely!"

Father Ramon shook his head. "Not the Commander, my son. For all that he is of royal birth, he understands the danger of ignoring the rule of natural law." Don Miguel thought he was going to add something more, but he shook his head again instead.

"Then—who?" Don Miguel persisted.

"Don Arturo Cortes led the expedition to investigate this distant stream of history," Father Ramon said, and on the last word his mouth shut like a steel trap. There was silence between them, but the noise of the fleeing people continued, and now was mingled with the pealing of bells as midnight approached, and with gunfire.

The orderly and two soldiers were raising Don Felipe now, to set him on a wheeled invalid trolley. The movement seemed to awaken him, for he gave a sudden cry.

"Father Ramon! Where are you?"

"Here, my son," the Jesuit said, striding towards him.

"Father, I did not tell you the worst!" Don Felipe babbled. "I saw them kill the King! I saw them shoot the Prince Imperial full of arrows, and they speared men and women as they tried to flee! I saw a woman hurled from the head of the stairway to break her head open on the floor beneath! I saw—oh God, Father! I saw such monstrous things!"

"What?" said one of the soldiers helping to lift him. And before Father Ramon could stop him, he had spun round to shout to his officer. "Sir! The King is dead!"

A hush fell for an instant over all those within earshot of the cry, and was followed by a sound like a rising storm. "The King is dead! The King! The King!" Dying away across the sea of people like an echo, the words ran swiftly.

"Father Ramon, what can we possibly do?" Don Miguel said.

For a long moment, his bird-like head bowed, Father Ramon did not answer. At last, however, he stirred and seemed to brisken. He said, "Whatever we can, my son. Find a civil guard—have criers sent out to call in any members of the Society who may not have been at the palace to the Headquarters Office now; this should be easy, for they'll all be passing this way to attend our Society Mass. Then—have you a carriage?"

"By now I suspect it will have been commandeered by refugees," Don Miguel said. "In any case, it will be hard to make passage for a vehicle through this fear-crazed crowd."

"Then we'll take the horses from my carriage," Father Ramon said briskly. "It's many years since my aged bones spanned a horse's back, but needs must. To it, and quickly!"

Don Miguel had never before tried to ride at speed bare-back and controlling the horse with carriage-reins, at the same time trying to comfort a weeping girl seated ahead of him with her head buried in his shoulder. It was half nightmare, half farce, and about the only thing which could have made it worse would have been if Kristina had followed the Empire custom of riding sidesaddle instead of astride like a man. She would certainly have fallen off if she had.

One more window of the Headquarters building was lighted now, and the door stood ajar. As their horses stopped outside Jones came hurrying to meet them. One of his eyes was newly blacked.

"She got loose!" Don Miguel said in alarm, sliding to the ground and reaching up to help Kristina down.

"Yes, sir," Jones said unhappily. "And we had a terrible job tying her up again."

"But you managed it?"

"With the help of the man you left here, yes, sir. I'd never have done it on my own."

"Help Father Ramon dismount," Don Miguel ordered. It was some relief at least to know that the girl was still here. He helped Kristina up the steps and settled her in an armchair in the hallway, and saw as he was doing so that instead of turning through the door beyond which the driver could be seen keeping guard over the furious girl in blue feathers—tied now with good strong rope, he noticed—Father Ramon was heading into the interior of the building.

"Father! Don't you want to see the girl?" he called.

"Come with me, and be quick!" Father Ramon answered.

"Look after this lady," Don Miguel instructed Jones, and hurried after Father Ramon.

He caught up with him as he paused before the door of the vast library, hunting under his habit for the key. He found and inserted it, and marched forward among the high stacks of heavy, finely-bound volumes.

"What you are going to see, my son, you must not divulge to anyone, is that clear?" Father Ramon said. "But for the rule that no single member of the Society—not even the Commander—shall consult these files without a witness beside him, I'd not burden you with the dangerous knowledge of them. You've been burdened enough for so young a man already. But here"—and he halted before a securely padlocked stack with blank metal doors, fumbling out another, smaller key—"is where I must confirm my guess."

He opened the padlock and reached into the case, bringing out a fat, bright red volume of manuscript notes. Interleaved with them were accurate watercolour drawings. As directly as though he were merely looking for something he had already seen—and presumably he was—Father Ramon turned to one such picture and held it out to Don Miguel.

"Does she look like that?" he demanded.

Don Miguel nodded slowly. These feathers were green, and the painted designs were white instead of yellow, but the hair was the same, the complexion, the shoes and bangles.

"Then my worst fears are fulfilled," Father Ramon said. He slammed the book shut and thrust it back. "Then there is no doubt any longer. I must confess to you frankly, my son, that I am totally at a loss. This is without precedent!"

To hear Father Ramon, the expert of experts on his subject, say such a thing shook Don Miguel to the core. He said before he thought, "They must indeed have gone mad, all of them together! Why, but for the madness we would now be at the Society's Mass, and—"

"The Mass!" Father Ramon said suddenly. "Of course! My blessings on you, Don Miguel! That I could have been so blind and not have seen it before!"

Blankly, Don Miguel stared at him. And then, little by little, light and hope began to dawn.

VI

Don Miguel gave a start so violent that he almost fell. He looked about him at his surroundings with astonishment. It was not that he failed to recognise where he was—he could never mistake the robing cells in the antesection to the chapel of the Society, or the sound of the high clear bell which was now tolling somewhere outside.

Only—here? Now? And everything apparently normal?

He had not asked Father Ramon what was going to be done. He could read in the Jesuit's eyes the certainty that that was knowledge a man was better off without. But he had thought he knew. Fresh in his mind was the memory of the panic displayed by those junior members of the Society whom the criers had haled off the streets setting to work in the time chamber of the Headquarters Office under Father Ramon's direction. While they worked feverishly on the apparatus, he himself had been directed to take pencil and paper and work a computation in factors which Father Ramon had scribbled down for him. He tried as he worked to assign real-world values to the symbols and thought that most likely he was dealing with labels for human lives, for one by one he saw them cancel out, cancel out...

The problem reduced to an unassigned variable and a factor k, and he showed this result to Father Ramon, who stared at it for a long time before he sighed, closed his eyes for a moment with a fierce expression, and then gestured for him to take his place between the iron and silver bars of the time apparatus. The air grew very hot—

—and he was here in a robing cell, and the bell of the Society's chapel was tolling for midnight as it had done each New Year's Eve since the Society acquired this palace as the official residence of its Commander.

What had that unassigned variable equated to, for pity's sake? Don Miguel's mind raced. He was virtually certain that the factor k represented a *key* individual: himself, who by sheer chance had been spared from the holocaust, or perhaps Don Felipe, who by managing to swim the river despite the arrows in his shoulder muscles had carried the terrible news to those who could act upon it.

It was patent, of course, that the thing which had been done must be undone. He had never questioned this; nor had Father Ramon, it seemed. For one thing, the consequences of this night's madness would be a blot forever on the Society if left unrectified; for another, the death of the King and all his nearest heirs, and with them the Commander of the Society, was an effect out of all proportion to the act.

And yet the results of setting up a closed causal loop in local time had never, never been investigated. This event was—as Father Ramon had said to himself—without precedent.

Don Miguel's mind swirled like water in a rotated cup. He put his hands to his head and struggled to think clearly. He had been trained to some extent in casuistry, and he could see the dim outlines of a logical sequence here. Postulate: the terrible women gladiators who wrought the harm originated in a non-actual world—a world brought about through the experimental interference of Society members with their own past history. Therefore the consequences of their acts were also non-actual, or potential. Therefore the rectification of these consequences must be *not* non-actual, if this was a safe case to exclude the middle...

It came to him with blinding, horrifying suddenness that in fact, in the fact where he must now have found himself, all the nightmare so vivid in his memory had already not happened.

For a moment he had a glimpse of what it must be like to be a man such as Father Ramon, all his mind lighted by a logic as piercing as sunlight, driven by a terrible, inexorable honesty to conceal nothing from himself. And he felt sweat prickle all over his body as he knew why he was here, now, in the rectified situation, with the knowledge of his personal unique past.

The tolling of the bell had stopped, and from beyond the door of his cell came the slow shuffling of many feet, irregular in rhythm. The Society going in to Mass, he thought. For the most awful of all its formal occasions.

He calmed himself deliberately with deep breathing. When finally he thought he could walk without swaying, he took his own concealing robe from the wall, slipped it on, and pulled the hood far forward over his face. Then he opened the door and joined his brothers.

These, tonight, now, were all faceless men. Only differences of height and girth could give the slightest clue to their identity; the hoods hid their features, the sleeves hid their hands, the robes fell to the ground and swished around their feet. For a reason. For the reason which only members of the Society knew, and which made this the Mass it was.

Grey into the grey shadows of the chapel, lit only by the candles at the east end, whose thin beams played fitfully on the gilded coats of arms mounted over the stalls but were too faint to reveal faces at the distance of the nearest member. To the solemn music of the organ, the Society assembled.

Now, this year, there were three hundred and forty-six Licentiates and Officers of the Society. Accordingly there were, here in the stalls, three hundred and forty-six grey-robed men.

And one—or more—of these was not a present member of the Society, but a man who had died in its service.

Only the officiating priest, bringing the Host to the row of kneeling brothers, would be able to see by the light of the altar candles which of the worshippers was a stranger, and tell thus which of the present members was tonight—here words were lacking—celebrating the Mass with his brothers of an age yet to come.

And the priest was masked.

In his stall, Don Miguel thought of everything that was implied by that. He—after all, he himself—he here, now, as far as he could possibly tell, might not be at the Mass of the New Year's Eve he had so far been living through. For every year the organ played the same music; every year the dispensation was given that the service should be conducted in whispers, so that the stranger in their midst might not recognise an unfamiliar voice and thus be spared foreknowledge of approaching death. He might count the total of grey robes present to see if it differed from the number he expected—Don Miguel glanced round into the shadows, and shook his head.

No. No man would do that. No man would dare.

There was a shuffling. The grey robes rose, and the masked priest came forth before the altar.

When the service was over, it had come to him what he must now do. He filed out of the chapel with the rest of the Society and returned to the robing cells. It was of course here in the isolation of the cells that transference to the future would most conveniently take place in the event that he was selected to partake of another Mass on New Year's Eve. But he knew now that he had not in fact been selected—it was a definite relief to recognise this—and he thought he knew who had been chosen.

After all, it was not absolutely necessary for the time-transference to be operated from a robing cell. Why should it be?

A kind of grim excitement took possession of him now, and he stripped off his robe. He barely spared time to place it tidily on its peg before leaving the cell—ahead of most of the other members, who were probably spending a few minutes in contemplation alone before emerging.

There was a cold stone-flagged side passage running past the chapel to the priest's offices at the other end. He hurried down this, his heels clicking on the hard floor, until he came to the vestry door.

There he halted. Cold shivers traced down his spine. Suppose—just suppose—he was wrong. Suppose when he knocked it was another voice than Father Ramon's that called him in.

There was only one way to find out. He knocked. And an answering pounding of his heart began as he recognised the dry voice which spoke to him.

It *was* Father Ramon, no mistake. He turned the handle and slipped inside.

The Jesuit was alone in the starkly furnished little room, standing close to a table with one thin hand laid on its bare wooden top, his eyes bright and sharp in his bird-like face. He smiled on recognising his visitor.

"A good new year to you, my son," he said. "Is it to wish me one that you come calling when the year is still so young? I'd have thought you would be eager to return to the company of your colleagues in age." He broke off, searching Don Miguel's face, and then resumed in a more serious tone.

"Forgive me that I jest!" he said. "For I see by your look that you're on no light errand."

Don Miguel nodded warily. He said, "What I have to say may seem strange, Father. Indeed, I'm not sure beyond a doubt that it should be said at all. But will you permit me to establish that point?"

"However you wish," Father Ramon consented, sounding puzzled.

Don Miguel drew a deep breath. He said, "Father—if you can in conscience tell me—which one of us was absent from the Mass tonight?"

Stiffly, Father Ramon drew himself up. "I cannot possibly answer that!" he snapped.

"It was, I think," Don Miguel said, "Don Arturo Cortes."

There was a long pause. Finally Father Ramon nodded to a chair. "Speak your mind, my son," he said. "I am sure you have a reason for your visit, and I'll hear you out."

Don Miguel sat down, weak with relief, and wiped his face. He said, "Father, I swear to you that I've not—in this world as it is—seen the records concerned. But I know, and you know, that at the court of King Mahendra the White Elephant they have female gladiators who fight like madwomen. Don Arturo Cortes was in charge of exploring this bywater of history. I have not spoken with him about it. As you know, there is little love lost between him and me."

Father Ramon blanched. He said incredulously, "How—?"

"You showed me, Father. You told me. You told me so that I could tell you now and convince you that the rest of what I have to relate is more than delusion." Don Miguel had to wipe his face again.

"I—" Father Ramon said thickly, and hesitated. Then he turned and took down from a shelf a thick black-bound volume on the front cover of which a cross was inlaid in gold leaf. He laid it on the table between them and sat down.

Don Miguel nodded and placed his right hand on the book, and Father Ramon continued wonderingly, "You speak of secret things, my son. For good and sufficient reasons the existence of this potential world has never been advertised—you can imagine why?"

"Possibly because in that world the true faith is suppressed," Don Miguel guessed.

"Precisely." Father Ramon's face gleamed like oiled parchment over the underlying bones. "Tell me what you have to say to me now."

Already his fantastic mind must have reached the kernel of the matter, Don Miguel realised. Already he must know that he was compelled to the worst of all human predicaments: to judge his own actions with no knowledge of them whatever. He had to swallow hard.

"First, Father, you must write a message to the future. To close a causal chain you must instruct that when the day comes that Don

Arturo Cortes is called to celebrate Mass on New Year's Eve at another time than his own, they must fetch him from a moment earlier than usual. There is certain to be the opportunity, because this is what has happened—I think," he felt compelled to add. "He must not be permitted to speak with Red Bear or anyone else about the importation of female gladiators to entertain the Ambassador of the Confederacy."

Father Ramon looked stricken. He said, "I will do this. But tell me why."

So, by pieces and scraps, Don Miguel did so.

VII

When he had finished, Father Ramon sat for a long time in silence. At last he stirred, his face very white.

He said, "Yes. Yes, it could have happened. A venal and corrupt mind could operate so. And the result—the death of kings. You have performed a great service to the Society, my son. But you have been dreadfully burdened with a nightmare of knowledge."

Don Miguel nodded. His voice thick, he said, "I feel like a leaf tossed on the wind. Do I know what I have done—now, as things stand—this evening?"

"With caution and grace you'll discover that," Father Ramon said. "You need have no fear." He shot a keen glance at Don Miguel. "Do you wish to be free of your burden of knowledge? I could free you if you wish—what you remember is now clearly nonexistent, and I might lawfully absolve your mind of it."

Don Miguel hesitated. It would be quick and easy, he knew, using the humane drugs developed by the inquisitors for cases where a sincerely repentant heretic was prevented by memory of former errors and the attendant guilt-feelings from becoming a useful member of society. He was very tempted.

But suddenly a point occurred to him, and he said, amazed at himself, "No, Father. For you know it now. And I feel it would somehow be wrong for me to leave you in sole possession of the knowledge, sharing it with no one else."

"It is shared with God," the Jesuit reminded him gently. "But—I thank you, my son. It seems to me a brave thing to say." He drew back the black-bound book across the table and held it in both hands.

"I counsel you now, for your peace of mind, to return to the great hall. The longer you are still dominated by the memory of what did not happen, the longer you will be ill at ease. Go back, and see for yourself that the palace stands and does not burn, that the King lives, that your friend Don Felipe was not shot full of arrows. In the end, it will be like a dream."

"But—was it nothing more?" Don Miguel persisted. Father Ramon gave a skeletal smile.

"Tomorrow—later today, rather, if you wish, come to me and I will recommend you some texts in the library which treat of the powers of the Adversary and his limitations. It is possible for him to create convincing delusions, but not to create reality. And it is always possible for determined and upright men to penetrate those delusions." He rose to his feet. Don Miguel rose also, and then dropped to his knees and bowed his head. When the priest had blessed him, he looked up.

"And you, Father? What are you going to do?"

"Write the message to the future. Think again—you may know this but not speak of it—think again about Don Arturo Cortes, whose overweening vanity has come to our notice more than once, and possibly investigate a certain rumour about his conduct. And also, of course, I shall pray."

He walked past Don Miguel and opened the door for him to go out. "Go with God, my son," he said.

His mind churning, Don Miguel walked slowly along the cold passage which led back towards the adjacent palace. He could hear the sound of the band performing again, and voices singing with it, and much laughter.

This was real.

Yet—how *much* of what had happened had not happened? Had he spent this evening in Londres with Kristina, mingling with the crowds? Clearly they had not encountered the blue-feathered girl at Empire Circle, but what had they done? Why could he not remember what had actually happened to him? It must be—his imagination boggled at this but it must be accepted—that he had not existed for a period of time. In the world as it actually was, presumably he had to have lapsed out of existence so that he could remember the potential world on his return; otherwise he would have dual memories for some hours of tonight... Wait a moment: he was going to have dual memories in any case, because after midnight in the potential world he had been with Father Ramon and Kristina at the Headquarters Office, and in the real world he had been with Father Ramon at the same time...

Wrestling with the paradox was giving him a blinding headache. He snatched his attention away and found that he was now in a warm, brightly-lit, gaily-decorated corridor; he had regained the interior of the palace. Any moment now he might emerge into a room full of guests, and find Kristina there, and be unable to account for his disappearance. Or—and the notion shook him again—he might find that she and he had not slipped away together into the city, but had spent a dull and miserable evening facing each other formally and making polite small-talk.

Or conceivably, in view of what had happened, he might find himself already here.

No, surely not. Father Ramon would never have committed a gross and dangerous error like that in any world, potential or actual!

Cautiously, he headed towards the great hall. Slaves were coming and going with the traditional New Year breakfast on trays and trolleys, and with bowls of steaming mulled wine giving off a spicy aroma.

The great hall was only half full now. There was no sign of the King; but things seemed peaceful enough; the Ambassador of the Confederacy wasn't in sight, nor was Red Bear who had probably had to be sobered up forcibly to take part in the Mass; imagine a Licentiate trying to get away with that, but as a General Officer he managed it.

"Miguel!"

He glanced round. Coming towards him, smiling broadly, was Don Felipe.

"Miguel, where've *you* been all evening?" Don Felipe gave him a poke in the ribs and a knowing wink. "Don't tell me, let me guess. I'm sure you enjoyed yourself anyway. I've had the finest New Year's Eve I can remember!" He chortled.

"Quick!" Don Miguel seized his chance. "Put me in the picture about what's been going on since I—uh—"

Don Felipe's eyes grew round as O's. He said in a whisper, "Miguel, you don't mean you... *Really?* You lucky so-and-so! Ingeborg's fun, but she's a bit too young and bubbly, like sparkling wine—"

"Felipe!" Don Miguel interrupted sharply.

"All right, all right!" Don Felipe parodied repentance. "Speaking ill of a lady and so on... What do you want to know? I'm in a hurry to get rid of the drink I've had and go back to Ingeborg. Where did you lose touch?"

"Uh—" Don Miguel frowned. "There was some sort of disagreement between the Ambassador of the Confederacy and Red Bear, wasn't there?"

"Oh, that! Yes, it was pretty stormy for a while. And your old chum the Marquesa di Jorque didn't make things any easier. But the real fly in the ointment was Don Arturo. Luckily for the peace of everyone, he got mislaid at some point. Drank too much, I shouldn't wonder. Yes, look—he's over there, see? Looking as though the hand of doom had been laid on him."

Don Miguel followed the indicated direction. There indeed was Don Arturo, looking like death, pale as a ghost and trying as it were to restore his colour by drinking glass after glass of red wine.

"So what happened?" Don Miguel said slowly.

"Oh, the subject got changed to something more congenial and when the royals left at about half past eleven and the Ambassador too, there was laughing all round and handshaking and all kinds of friendliness. Perfectly calm and in order. Miguel, I *must* disappear!"

He vanished down the corridor, leaving Don Miguel to sigh with relief. It really was all right, then. For a moment he was puzzled by one point: if the other ambassadors and people had gone, why was Ingeborg still here—and presumably Kristina too? Then it struck him that they were of a heterodox faith, and of course had different observances. He didn't know whether to be glad or sorry as yet that he was going to see Kristina any moment, probably.

But before that, there was one thing he must attend to. He looked at the miserable face of Don Arturo.

That wasn't the result of too much drinking. That was the result of a very terrible experience. Don Arturo had lost—how long? Hours, perhaps, out of his New Year's Eve. He had gone to celebrate Mass at some other period of time, and he knew that he had not gone to the robing cell on his own two feet.

Oh, but that was an awful thing to have to endure! For what other conclusion could be drawn than that his death was on the way? He must be unique among members of the Society, past, present or future, in knowing what he had seen.

What justice was this punishment now that the effect of his disastrous actions had been swept into limbo?

Well, the casuists must be left to struggle with that problem, if they ever learned of it, as Father Ramon doubtless was struggling to find out whether his own actions in a world that never was had been justifiable or not. But there was one thing he, Don Miguel, could do.

He strode across the floor towards the unfortunate man and halted in front of him, his face set in a mask of pity. "Don Arturo!" he said. "Your hand, brother!"

For a moment Don Arturo's haunted eyes met his, not understanding. Then, in a convulsive movement, he let fall his wineglass with a crash and seized Don Miguel's hand in both his own. He said nothing, but his eyes were bright.

A prompt slave came to snatch up the fragments of glass and mop away the spilled wine. Don Miguel let go Don Arturo's grip, hearing his name called in a familiar voice.

"There you are, Miguel! Where've you been?"

Across the floor Kristina was standing between her sister and her father. She was waving to him. He could not ignore the command, but his heart turned over wildly. He walked up to them and bowed to the Duke.

"I'm sorry, Lady Kristina," he said. "I've been—uh—having a few words with Father Ramon in his vestry."

She looked slightly puzzled at his use of her title, and then seemed to find an explanation. "Oh! Oh, Papa doesn't mind people calling me Kristina, Miguel. He's just had to get used to it."

The Duke chuckled. "Indeed I have," he said. "I've even had to get used to her so-called progressive friends addressing me as Duke, pure and simple. Well, I'm not in favour of starchy behaviour anyway." He looked quizzically at Don Miguel. "You and my daughter seem to have been getting on very well," he added. "At any rate, I've hardly seen either of you all evening."

Kristina bubbled mischievously. "Miguel's been wonderful, Papa. We got dreadfully bored, so he found a way for us to slip out, and we've been in the city mixing with the people and having a marvellous time. You'd never think it to look at him, but he's got quite a sense of humour under that grim scarred face. Of course, Miguel, I suppose because you're really very stern the reason you wanted to see Father Ramon was to confess how wicked you'd been to enjoy yourself this evening."

"Kristina!" the Duke said sharply. "You mustn't make jokes about other people's religious faith!"

A strange light-headedness was taking possession of Don Miguel. Already the writing of the gruesome events on his memory, which he had thought to be indelibly etched, was fading as chalk-marks fade under a wet sponge until the words are as though they have never been written. He said, "Regret having enjoyed an evening with you, Kristina? Don't be silly. Let's have another dance—our first one was rudely interrupted."

He bowed his leave of the Duke and led her out on the floor. Taking her hand, he murmured to himself, "Everything for the best in the best of all possible worlds."

"What was that, Miguel?"

"Nothing. Just a rather bitter anti-clerical joke. It doesn't matter."

"Oh, explain it!" she urged him.

A look of sadness passing over his face, he shook his head. "Believe me, Kristina, I couldn't. Nobody could. Forget it, and let's just dance."

The Fullness of Time

I

"**Y**OUR PEOPLE," SAID THE LONG-FACED MOHAWK WHO MAN-aged the mines, "came to what you called the New World hungry for gold. You came looking for fabulous kingdoms—Cibola, Quivira, Norumbega, Texas. And so keenly were you disappointed when you found they didn't exist, you set about creating them."

He waved at the hillside opposite, where the mine galleries ran like holes into ripe cheese. Don Miguel Navarro followed the gesture with his eyes. Here where he sat with the manager—his name was Two Dogs—it was cool under the shade of woven reed awnings, on the verandah of the plain mud-plastered house which served as both home and administrative office. But there the fury of the sun lay full, and the Indian labourers emerging from the mouths of the galleries with their baskets full of crushed rock, to be tipped into the sluices for sedimentation, wiped their dusty faces, swigged water from leathern bottles, and seemed glad to escape underground again.

The heat of the air was such that the world felt silent, although there were always noises: the monotonous creaking of the pumps bringing up water for the sluices, the droning of flies, the cries of the overseers in a local dialect that Don Miguel did not understand. He was almost content.

"More wine?" Two Dogs suggested, raising the jug from the table between them.

"Willingly," Don Miguel agreed. "It's very good. You grow it locally, I understand."

Two Dogs nodded, pouring for his visitor and himself. "Our climate here in California is very good for vines. Take a piece of cheese also; the tastes mingle well." He set down the jug and offered the large baked-clay platter on which the cheese stood, stuck with a silver knife.

"Ye-es," he continued musingly after a moment. "You are indeed a strange people. We shall probably never understand one another."

Don Miguel laughed shortly. He said, "For people who lack mutual understanding, we get on well enough."

"Conceded. But because we serve one another's purposes, no more. And it could have been otherwise—we need only look south past the Isthmus to see what might have been."

Don Miguel stirred uncomfortably in his chair. It was always upsetting for an Imperial citizen to discuss the fate of the great civilisations of Central and South America, sacrificed on the altar of European greed. He said, "There has never been change without suffering—it's the way of the world."

"And as you people saw it, it might as well be the provincials who suffered," Two Dogs suggested.

It was impossible to be sure whether there was hostility in that even voice. Don Miguel stiffened imperceptibly.

"Isn't it so?" the Mohawk persisted. "As you conceive it, you look from the centre outwards; Europe is the heart of the world, and the other continents are its—outskirts. Of course, there's truth in this attitude. A great many local squabbles in Europe over the past five hundred years have created changes out of all proportion here, in Africa, and in Asia. And for my own people's sake, I should be grateful for small mercies."

The words seemed to dig into Don Miguel's mind like the touch of a claw. He felt little premonitory tinglings on the nape of his neck.

"Suppose your Empire hadn't won its great victory," Two Dogs went on thoughtfully. "Suppose Western Europe, like Eastern Europe, had split into petty principalities. Suppose you'd lost the Netherlands and never gained England. We might have had four or more different gangs of Europeans fighting over our hunting-grounds like dogs over a bone."

Don Miguel gave him a look of unconcealed respect. He said, "I see you've made a study of history."

"I have—as part of an attempt to understand the European way of thinking. But as I was saying: we'd likely have had you, and the French, and the Swedes, and the Dutch, and the English, all bringing their local differences to this continent and fighting over them. And we poor Indians might have been ground between them like corn between millstones." He raised his eyes to meet Don Miguel's and finished on a challenging tone, "Am I right? You can tell me, I'm sure."

"I?" Don Miguel forced an unconvincing chuckle. "Why?"

For a moment a flicker of uncertainty showed on the other's face, but he returned sternly to his attack. He said, "It should be better known that—having escaped being ground between your millstones once, by the skin of our teeth—we don't wish to see it happen after all."

What manner of man have I stumbled on—some revanchist fanatic? Don Miguel shook his head and said, "It's never likely to happen, so I fail to see—"

Two Dogs cut in. "Perhaps you thought, Don Miguel, that you were at the world's end here—well, it's true we're a long way from Europe. But we hear news eventually. On your way to California you passed through New Madrid; the Prince of New Castile happened to be in residence, making one of his occasional visits to the territory he nominally governs... and you remained a few days to pay your compliments."

"By the infernal fires!" Don Miguel said. "Isn't there anywhere on Earth I can get away from it all?"

"What in truth—in truth!—brought you to this hillside mining-town half a world from your home?" Two Dogs demanded.

"A need to be unknown," Don Miguel sighed. "Nothing more."

Two Dogs leaned forward on his chair, eyes bright. He said, "Then you don't deny it!"

"Deny my professional status? No, of course not. I'd simply hoped to have it overlooked for a while. Wherever a Licentiate of the Society of Time shows his face, people cluster like flies on honey, cackling and gibbering over the presence of this 'real live time-traveller.' I'm sick of it. I'd hoped that by coming all the way to California to spend my sabbatical leave, I'd be able to remain comfortably anonymous for at least a little while."

There was silence between them for a moment. Don Miguel's face, twisted savagely to one side by the ill-healed scar of a hoplite's sword-cut, looked in the harsh light as though it might have been copied from an idol carved by one of the Mohawk's Central American cousins. He hoped that Two Dogs would not press him for further details, because he would have to refuse them, and in the few days he had known the Mohawk he had come to like him well; moreover, even the act of refusal would reawaken memories that ached like deep bruises. He would have been happiest had he been able to forget altogether the things that preyed on him—that being out of the question, not having anyone around to remind him of them had seemed the next best cure.

But here, now, Two Dogs had gone to the core of his trouble as directly as a skilled engineer sinking a mineshaft to a lode of ore.

"I will not ask you to swear that," Two Dogs said after a pause. "Perhaps a European might, but I'll gamble on my estimate of you."

Don Miguel said stiffly, "I'm what I seem, and I'm not used to being taken for anything else."

"No, hear me out. We Mohawks realise that we owe to you our present standing, for without the alliance with the Empire which made us militarily capable of dominating so much of the continent, we'd be as we once were—one small tribe among many. Yet to be allied with the Empire is like being brother to a hotheaded adventurer. Any day a feud in which the brother has become involved may explode in the face of his family without their knowledge or desire."

Don Miguel studied the other wonderingly, but said nothing.

"Picture, then, my state of mind," Two Dogs went on, "when I learned that you, the pleasant visitor gratifying a wish for solitude and a curiosity about the Far West, were in fact a Licentiate of the Society of Time." He shrugged. "I was—disturbed!"

"Why?" Don Miguel made the word crackle like a fire-arrow.

For a long moment Two Dogs seemed to be struggling towards a decision. Suddenly he drained his wineglass and slammed it down hard on the table.

"I hadn't meant to come to this," he said, standing up. "And least of all I'd not meant to come to it here, now, with such a man as yourself. But I'll show you the reason, because—before God!—I can't endure the knowledge by myself any more!"

He started down from the verandah without further explanation, shouting at the top of his lungs for Tomas, his dour chief overseer. Some of the labourers on the other side of the valley heard, paused in their work and looked to see what madness had come upon their master. Don Miguel followed more slowly, not being accustomed to the strong sunlight. He caught up with Two Dogs when he had located Tomas and was giving him orders in the incomprehensible local Indian language, and asked for details, but the only answer he got was, "Wait, and you shall see."

Much puzzled, but eager to find some bottom in this, Don Miguel contained himself in patience while Tomas went in search of two burros with saddles fit for gentlefolk; then, his old but bright *serape* around him, took to the trail ahead of them, walking steadily with the aid of a staff.

The jogging was so unlike the motion of a horse as to make Don Miguel very uncomfortable; besides, it was nearing the middle of the day and the flies were troublesome. But a glance at Two Dogs persuaded him not to mention these facts; the Mohawk wore an expression like a man driven by demons.

The trail wound over the shoulder of the hill, becoming in places a mere footpath, but the burros found their way and Tomas went uncomplainingly ahead. On the other side, where the attention of the miners had not yet been directed, a smaller valley lay baking in the sun. Only the trail winding across it suggested human visitation; that apart, this land might have lain as it was since Creation Day.

"There!" Two Dogs said, causing his burro to fall back alongside Don Miguel's, raising his arm and pointing to a rocky slope ahead. Don Miguel saw nothing, and said so.

"Well, then, come closer!" Two Dogs snapped. As he urged his mount forward, Don Miguel wondered what could conceivably have disrupted the Mohawk's habitual placid calm like this.

Tomas reached the spot first, paused, turned, looked back with an inscrutable face, and tapped a nearby boulder with the end of his staff. Two Dogs leapt to the ground, leaving his burro to wander, and he and Tomas together leaned against the heavy boulder. Shading his eyes, Don Miguel saw it begin to rock back and forth, further—further—and suddenly it gave, rolling through half a circle and coming to rest in a cup of ground. Its displacement revealed an opening in the slope behind it. A dark, roughly square opening. The mouth of a tunnel—of the gallery of a mine.

Don Miguel felt horrified understanding dawn. He dropped from his saddle and came forward. He said, "What's this?"

Two Dogs shrugged. "We'd very much like to know," he said grimly. "Aside from being a mine-gallery, it's a mystery to us. Oh—and aside from *this*."

He stepped for a moment into the low opening, having to stoop to avoid the roof, fumbled on the ground, and turned to Don Miguel, holding out something in his hand. Don Miguel took it, stared at it, and felt the world tremble around him.

II

His Highness the Prince of New Castile, Commander of the Society of Time, ran his fingers through his short, black beard. He looked at the object on the table in front of him, and at last spoke.

"Well, since you seem to have a gift for turning up uncomfortable odds and ends, Navarro, I suppose I'll have to inquire what you make of this—this bit of scrap metal. I must say it seems to me an innocuous enough object for such a song and dance."

Don Miguel drew a deep breath and held it for the space of three heartbeats. He didn't need anyone to tell him that he was going out on a limb; he would have been far happier had he been able to consult with Father Ramon or another of the Society's theoreticians before approaching the Commander. But Father Ramon was on the other side of the Atlantic Ocean, and the Commander, fortunately, was here in New Castile. And the quicker some action was taken, the better.

He licked his lips, very conscious of the piercing eyes of everyone else in the Prince's audience chamber, especially of the eyes of the other Licentiates. He had previously experienced the double edge of his reputation in the Society, but here it was keener-cutting.

He said boldly, "I make of it, sir—though I'm open to correction—a breach of the Treaty of Prague."

Well… there was his bombshell. And it certainly went off to great effect: the Commander himself blanched and jerked back in his chair, while everyone else without exception paled and voiced wordless exclamations.

"By whom?" the Prince said sternly.

"By the other party to the Treaty," Don Miguel said. "I can draw no other conclusion."

"You realise that this is the most serious allegation you could possibly make?"

"I do," Don Miguel agreed fervently. "But having conducted such investigations as were possible to me without time apparatus, I found so much pointing that way that I was compelled to lay the facts before you."

The Prince put out one hairy-backed hand towards the harmless-looking chip of metal on the table, hesitated before completing the gesture, then drew his hand back as though from a sleeping snake. He said, "Sit down! Let's hear the whole story!"

The Treaty of Prague, Don Miguel had often thought, was the most fragile bulwark ever interposed between man and the forces of primal chaos. It was like a plug of wet paper in the mouth of a volcano—yet it was all they had.

At the time when Borromeo discovered how time might be rendered a direction like other directions so that men might make voyages along it, he—whom some called very wise, others very cynical—had clearly foreseen the uses to which fools might put his miracle. There were, for one thing, those in the Empire who wished to re-conquer Spain, the old heartland from which Christian civilisation had once more been driven by its virile Islamic rival, and who would not have been above sending back an army to ensure that change of history. This Borromeo feared so greatly that he came close, more than once, to destroying the results of his research.

But on reflection he decided that sooner or later someone else, without so many scruples, might stumble on the same discovery, so it was up to him to make the best of it. That was why he founded the Society of Time, as an organisation of responsible persons bound by oath to use their techniques wisely and honestly, to increase the sum of human knowledge but not to interfere with the past.

Nonetheless, what he was afraid of happened, and some lunatics began to agitate for the reconquest of Spain. For a while it looked as though madness would overcome sense. Then, however, the balance was swung. The Confederacy of Europe let it be known—discreetly, delicately—that they too had gained the secret of travelling in time. If an Imperial army went back to oppose the conquest of Spain, it would be met by corresponding forces determined to keep the *status quo*—for the Confederacy regarded the Empire as quite strong enough already without the retrospective addition of Spain to its lands.

It was whispered, but never proved, that Borromeo himself had leaked his secret to the Confederacy. At any rate, it was all for the best; the Empire came to its senses, proposed Papal arbitration and an agreement that neither of the two power blocs would ever interfere with history to the disadvantage of the other, and signed the Treaty of Prague. The Treaty was Borromeo's last legacy; three weeks after it was signed, he died of a chill caught in the mists of Poland, for it was a bitter winter that year.

But now...

"It's good steel," Don Miguel said, pointing to the object on the table. "It's the bit of a rock-drill—cracked in half. *We've* never mined that valley, I've established the fact beyond doubt. And history shows us no one who knew how to make good steel and who passed through California prior to our discovery of the New World. In company with Two Dogs, the manager of the mine, I searched the locality for several miles around. We discovered the traces of other mine-galleries, all of them caved in; Two Dogs was able to estimate that they had been collapsed approximately a thousand years ago. Moreover, once or twice at least the miners have been puzzled to find that a vein of ore ended unexpectedly—usually a very thick, rich vein, which should have continued far further. Such evidence points to the ore having been worked some considerable time ago."

The Prince exchanged a glance with one of his aides, and then indicated that Don Miguel should continue.

"I read it like this." Don Miguel licked his lips. "It's been known for a long time that those hills are rich ones. I think that the intruders decided to mine them at a time when we had not yet started exploiting the area. They went back in time to do so. Later, our undertaking crept close to the area they had chosen; they broke off their work, collapsed the galleries, and abandoned the project. Or maybe they didn't even go to that much trouble—after all, California is earthquake country, and in a thousand years you'd expect the galleries to cave in of their own accord. It may have been pure chance that preserved the one where Two Dogs discovered this steel drill-bit."

"You say it's been lying there for a good thousand years," the Prince mused. "Yet it's barely marked with rust."

"The mouth of the gallery was closed by this balanced boulder that I spoke of. Earth and grass-roots had made an almost perfect seal around it, and the interior of the cave was dry. In any case, the climate is equable."

For some moments the Prince was silent. His dark eyes searched Don Miguel's face. Then he said heavily, "You've made a case, Navarro. We'll get time apparatus out there as quickly as we can, and see if we can secure objective evidence." He rose to his feet. "Meantime, we'll also notify Londres, and bring out our most highly trained investigators. I'm not questioning your judgment, but—to charge a breach of the Treaty of Prague would be disastrous if it were unfounded."

"Sir," Don Miguel said with feeling, "I pray that I'm wrong. For how much more disastrous it will be if the charge is true!"

Before the discovery of humane drugs to unlock the gates of truth in the mind, there had been a torture—used even by the Holy Office—consisting in the placing upon the subject of a large wooden board, and in turn upon the board a succession of stones of increasing weight, so that in the end a stubborn man would be crushed like an insect beneath a boot.

For Don Miguel the next several weeks were like a period of that torture. And he was not the only one to suffer.

The first stone was the lightest. It was rumoured and had been for some time that there was more gold and silver circulating in the Confederacy than their known resources would account for. But it was not unreasonable to assume that new and so far secret lodes had been located—until suspicion began to gnaw as a result of the affair in California.

The second stone was heavier. A metallurgical expert compared the mysterious drill-bit with samples of other steels, and reported unequivocally: made in Augsburg! It was a type commonly used in the mines of the Confederacy, but hardly ever encountered elsewhere— certainly not in California.

The third and heaviest was a report from the men whom Two Dogs—at Don Miguel's urgent request—had set to searching the route between the site of the poachers' mine and the coast. It was unthink- able that a time apparatus belonging to the Confederacy could have been smuggled into California recently, but of course in operating the apparatus a spatial component could be included in the temporal displacement; any place on Earth where the gravitational potential was nearly the same was accessible from a given starting-point. Nonetheless Don Miguel doubted if this technique had been used—at least, not on the first trip. Jumping into the dark was far too dangerous. He suspected that the poachers would have shifted back while on familiar ground, and then would have voyaged by more conventional means till they located their target.

And the men sent by Two Dogs, following the most obvious route to the sea, came across a ship's timber buried in the sand, of a form not known to the aboriginal inhabitants of this land, and of an appearance that suggested it had been lying where they found it for some such period as a thousand years.

Weighed down by these facts, the members of the team hastened their preparations. The time apparatus was installed under the habitual conditions of secrecy—few people outside the Society ever saw an actual time apparatus, because it was so dangerously simple, composed only of bars of silver and magnetised iron in precisely determined relationships, and it might have entered somebody's head to make a model of what he had seen... with the disturbing consequence that the model might *work*.

Accordingly, a small town of canvas marquees bloomed in the California sun, and the labourers and their families went by incuriously for the most part, occasionally pausing and watching for a few minutes, but not often.

It was on the shoulder of the hill separating the valley where Two Dogs managed his mine from the valley where the time-travellers had established themselves that Don Miguel met his friend again for the first time after suspicion turned to certainty.

Don Miguel was plodding up the slope, head bowed, feeling as though the limping world were using him for a crutch, when he heard his name called and raised his eyes to find Two Dogs waiting ahead of him. The Mohawk's face was inscrutable, prepared for any news.

"Well?" he said as Don Miguel came up.

"They found them," Don Miguel said. "At 984. They worked through a summer here. They killed a Mohawk Licentiate who showed himself to them. With a gun."

Two Dogs showed no reaction. He said merely, "So your millstones are going to grind again, and we shall be between them."

"What do you mean?" Don Miguel said wearily.

"Is it what you suspected—poaching by the Confederacy?"

"Yes. No doubt of that. They've been seen, and heard talking."

The Mohawk nodded. "Then this is a breach of the Treaty of Prague—and what are you going to do about it? Fight a war? With each side taking the other in the rear of time?"

"I don't know," Don Miguel said. The heat of the sun and the terrible news were conspiring to make his head spin.

"You can't do the sensible thing, apparently," Two Dogs said. "That would have been simply to wipe out the poachers at the end of their stay here, when they had made changes exactly corresponding to the traces we found, which led to their discovery."

Don Miguel said sharply, "Why not?"

"Because—well, I was assuming that if you could, you would." Two Dogs hesitated. "It isn't that it hadn't occurred to you, is it?" he ventured.

"So far nobody's had time to decide on a course of action. But I don't see why we shouldn't do as you suggest—we'd risk creating a closed causal loop, but..." His voice trailed away, and he straightened his bowed shoulders. Clapping Two Dogs on the arm, he said, "My friend, do you have any of your fine Californian wine? I'm nearly dead of thirst, and I want to drink to your probably very practical suggestion. Don't ask me to pass final judgment on it, though—we'll leave that to Father Ramon, who's due here in a couple of days' time."

Two Dogs gave a slow smile. "Of course I have wine," he said. "But somehow I've lightened your depression already, I can see."

III

Don Arturo Cortes came, who still had the look of a man haunted by the ghost of himself, and who had not been a friend of Don Miguel's until he saw that ghost; Don Felipe Basso came and said that a certain Lady Kristina was sad at not having seen him again before she left Londres on her father being appointed Ambassador to the Confederacy; Father Ramon came, and unlike the other two showed no trace of the effects of the appalling journey, night and day from New Madrid in the huge cushion-wheeled transcontinental express-wagon which stopped only to change horses and pick up provisions. Don Miguel saw the last relay of horses as they were led away from the wagon on its arrival; they looked fit for the knacker.

These three, the very night of their arrival, gathered with Don Miguel, and the two experts who had had charge of the investigations here, of whom one was an Inquisitor. They met in one of the huge marquees set up by the Society over the hill from Two Dogs's mine. There was a breeze, and their shadows cast by flaring lamps on the white canvas behind them moved in eerie fashion as they sat around their table.

Don Rodrigo Juarez had conducted the expedition to the past personally. Since what had happened to Don Arturo Cortes, men had begun to speak of Don Rodrigo rather than of Don Arturo as Red Bear's probable successor in the General Officer's post of Director of Fieldwork. Don Rodrigo knew this, and saw that Don Arturo knew it also; the fact made his voice seem unpleasant as he reviewed what had been done.

"We found them," he said. "We saw them at work, and we heard them talking among themselves. To avoid anachronism we were clothed—unclothed, rather—as Indians such as we know to have frequented California in those days. A Licentiate from New Castile, a Mohawk known as Roan Horse, volunteered to show himself at their encampment. They shot him dead on his mere appearance. I agree with Don Miguel Navarro; we have a clear violation of the Treaty of Prague."

He sat back, jutting out his jaw. He was a large man whose mother had been Scots, and his gingery hair and lantern jaw were from her family.

*

All eyes turned to Father Ramon, who had been listening with total concentration to Don Rodrigo's story. Keenest of all to hear the Jesuit's opinion was Don Miguel, whose mind ached for it.

"No," said Father Ramon at length. "We have not."

"What?" All of them said it, except Don Felipe, who was keeping himself to himself.

"I said no." Father Ramon turned his bird's head slowly to regard them one after the other. "For various reasons. Not the least compelling is that a breach of the Treaty would be a total disaster, and we must avoid that at all costs. Luckily one has not yet been committed."

"But—!" Don Rodrigo began. Father Ramon's thin hand went up to interrupt him.

"Don Rodrigo, before leaving Londres I checked your qualifications. They're excellent. But they omit one important item. You've never attended the School of Casuistry at Rome; if you had, you'd have gone through a gruelling course of disputation on this very subject of a breach of the Treaty of Prague. Believe me, when the Vatican's experts framed that Treaty, they did not do it in a hurry, or in such a way as to leave loopholes."

"If there are no loopholes," Don Rodrigo snapped, "then why has no breach been committed by this flagrant act of poaching?"

"You should know why," the Jesuit said calmly. "In your position you should. Don Miguel's misunderstanding is forgivable; in the ordinary course of his career he would not be due to attend the School of Casuistry for another five years or so. Your colleague, however, I'm also surprised at." He shot a frown at the Inquisitor. "How say you, Brother Vasco?"

The Inquisitor shifted on his hard bench. He said, "I've reserved my judgment till I can consult a text I needn't name. I confess my memory of it had worn thin."

The Jesuit pursed his lips. After a moment he shrugged.

"On the other hand," he said, "Don Arturo *has* attended the School in Rome. And should by now be bursting with the right solution."

They looked at Don Arturo, their heads moving as if pulled by strings, and saw him pass his hand shakily across his face. "Solutions to the present problem I have none, Father," he said. "But I know one thing almost beyond a doubt."

"Which is?" Father Ramon prompted.

"There hasn't been a breach of the Treaty of Prague because such a thing is virtually inconceivable."

Don Miguel glanced at his friend Don Felipe, and received in return a look which said, "I'm out of my depth here." He turned back to Father Ramon.

"I—I must plead for myself, Father," he began, and got no further. The Jesuit smiled, as usual like a parchment-covered skull, and shook his head.

"Save your apologies, my son. They're not justified. An intent to break the Treaty is perfectly conceivable, and it appears that that's what you've chanced upon. Let me clarify the situation in terms which I think the judge of a Papal court would use." He raised one bony finger.

"*Imprimis*—the death of Roan Horse. He was an extemporate, was he not? His death had no consequence in the past; its effects began at a point in present time which is demonstrably later than the point from which he departed. It may also be later than the point from which the—the poachers, as you so conveniently name them, departed. This is not certain, but it's probable."

A second finger went up. "*Secundo*, there is a particular clause in the Treaty under which I am sure Don Rodrigo has been champing to frame an indictment. It states that neither party to the Treaty will act in such a way in past time as to cause a disadvantage to the other party affecting present time. It cannot be said that the abstraction in past time of a limited quantity of ore from this valley has been disadvantageous to us in present time—indeed, we haven't even extended our mining operations to that point yet."

Don Miguel was too full of an overwhelming relief to comment. Not so Don Rodrigo. He said aggressively, "But if they'd stolen the ore from the next valley, where we're already mining, this would indisputably have set us at a disadvantage! In fact, the mine manager tells me that they've found veins of ore which ended unexpectedly—and we've correlated this with the activities of the poachers! Much as it disturbs me to contradict an expert of your calibre," he added with bad grace, "I feel you're overlooking something."

"Nothing," the Jesuit replied. "Or rather, not I but all the experts in disputation who have threshed out possible interpretations of the Treaty." He lifted another finger. "I say further that, *tertio*, at the time when the poachers took the ore there was no property right subsisting therein."

Even Don Felipe gaped at the appalling casuistry of that remark. As for Don Miguel, he could not restrain himself from an explosive—but fortunately wordless—reaction. Father Ramon turned to him.

"I know what you're thinking, my son," he said. "You're thinking that if this is so, what's to stop us systematically rifling the prehistoric ages of the territory now occupied by the Confederacy, so that their lands will be poor and empty? I can answer that immediately. It wasn't done. And why should it be done? If we do it to them, they do it to us—and each of us winds up with the other's resources in any case, at the cost of infinitely greater effort."

He switched his penetrating gaze back to Don Rodrigo. "What you've forgotten, my son," he said with some gentleness, "is that the signatories of the Treaty of Prague wanted very much to prevent it ever being broken. The power to alter past time is so pregnant with terrible possibilities that no sane man could overlook them."

There was silence between them for a while. During it, Don Rodrigo began to blush like a woman, and seeing him Don Arturo smiled for the first time that Don Miguel could remember since that terrible New Year's Eve. It was embarrassing to Don Miguel. For the sake of breaking the silence, he said, "Something must surely be done, nonetheless!"

"Yes, that's clear," the Jesuit agreed. "May we have your proposal to begin with?"

Don Miguel stumbletongued. He said, "Why—why, I have no plan. Only a suggestion by Two Dogs which seemed to me to make fair sense, which was that we should pick the moment during their expedition at which the poachers complete their work so as to leave the correct traces which Two Dogs later discovered, and then step in. The death of Roan Horse suggests that we might teach a lesson which would not be soon forgotten."

"Agreed," Don Rodrigo said. Don Felipe looked cheerful and rubbed his hands together; this was his kind of game.

"No," Father Ramon said. "At least, not insofar as we are to copy what they did to Roan Horse. But we should certainly step in, and we should certainly learn who they are, and why they're there, and speak with them."

"Speak with them?" Don Rodrigo was scornful. "They shot down Roan Horse in cold blood!"

"I doubt if they will fire on an obvious extemporate," Father Ramon said. "Especially if he wears the cloth."

That took a moment to sink in. Brother Vasco was the first to speak. "Father, you're not thinking of going alone!" he exclaimed.

"No... By way of imprinting a small lesson on a certain party who has—not for the first time—overreached himself, I shall go in the company of... Don Miguel Navarro."

He did not switch his gaze until he had finished speaking. Don Miguel shrugged and smiled. He said, "As you say, Father. I confess, I'd not have started this wildcat rumour if I'd been better schooled in the legalities of the matter."

"Good," Father Ramon said, and glanced at his watch before standing up. "It's late. Tomorrow morning, then, I'll require the use of your time apparatus for us, and we'll settle the problem—God willing—once for all."

"What's been decided?" came the soft question from Two Dogs. He was sitting out late on his verandah, awaiting Don Miguel's return from the meeting. On the floor at his feet Conchita, his serving-maid and mistress, sat picking ethereal chords from her *cuatro*, a small four-stringed guitar. He had offered her to Don Miguel a couple of times when first he came to stay at the house, but this was so far from the customs of home that Don Miguel had refused automatically, and the offer had never been repeated. Subsequently he had looked again at Conchita, who was slim, berry-brown and graceful as a dancer, and regretted the fact. He could have welcomed the mere physical relief of her company as a key to the sleep which worry had so often denied him these past few weeks.

He sat down in the guest-chair wearily, and waited while Two Dogs dismissed Conchita with a gesture; she went like a shadow, silently. Then he said, "There's been no breach of the Treaty."

For a long moment Two Dogs didn't comment. Then he said, in a tight, controlled voice, "How's that possible?"

"You're too practical a man to follow the casuistry." Don Miguel shut his eyes. "I barely accept it. I'll just say that instead of what you proposed, we're going to pay them a sort of social call—Father Ramon and myself. What will come of it, lord knows."

Two Dogs laughed harshly. He said, "Indeed, indeed, as I said to you before—you're a strange people, and we'll never understand you. It seemed to me that you regarded your mines your gold, as we regarded our hunting-grounds in the old days. If outsiders came, and stole our game, we made war on them, and they didn't come back. Now here's this case where your beloved ore is filched, and you'll do nothing to restore it."

"We can't." Don Miguel felt suddenly extremely tired. "We found the traces of the poachers' work; we can't cancel it out, for then we'd never have found the traces. I didn't see it before, but Father Ramon made it clear; both parties to the Treaty of Prague wanted to make it impossible for a violation of that Treaty to lead to a war fought in time. So we shall settle it by calm discussion."

Again there was silence. Finally Two Dogs stood up. He said, "Well, I suppose it's a small consolation that your millstones won't be grinding us. I'll bid you good night, Don Miguel. And I'll wish you sharp wits in your discussion with the poachers—if I'm any judge, you'll need them."

He left the verandah, and it was not until he had gone to his sleeping-room that Don Miguel realised how peculiarly phrased his final comment had been. He got out of his chair, intending to pursue the matter, but Conchita had gone in with her master, which made the idea impossible, and anyway he was far too tired.

IV

As Don Miguel had expected, the valley had changed so little in a thousand years that it was not incongruous to see a mining encampment in the valley when they walked over the brow of the hill behind which they had arrived, choosing a moment when they were unlikely to be observed at once. There had been earthquakes, certainly; there were subtle differences in the outline of some of the nearby slopes. But you could recognise the identity of the valley at the two time-points.

He felt a stir of admiration for the magnificently simple stage-management of Father Ramon's plan. When they paused on the crest of the hill and let the poachers see them, the effect was instantaneous. Indians such as were to be expected at this moment of time would have called forth violent reactions but to see Father Ramon in his sombre habit, and Don Miguel wearing—at the Jesuit's insistence—the jewelled collar and star of the Order of the Scythe and Hourglass conspicuously glittering on his plain shirt: this was something to inform the poachers without words that their presence and their plans were known.

They waited, a light breeze touching their faces, while the impact of their arrival sank in. Don Miguel had his first chance to study the tented settlement, the mouths of the galleries, the sluices, and the rest of the equipment, all so like the mine which Two Dogs managed that he had to keep forcibly reminding himself that this was a thousand years away.

Work stopped. Harsh barking orders brought men out of the galleries to blink in the sunlight. Overseers—not a few of whom wore the uniform of the organisation which was the counterpart in the Confederacy of the Society of Time in the Empire—snapped at each other and their men.

★

Still the newcomers waited, for fully five long minutes in the baking
sun of late summer, until at last a man detached himself from the
ant-milling crowd and came up the slope to meet them, accompanied
by two of the uniformed overseers.

"Good day, sirs," he said in heavily accented Spanish. "I do not have
to ask the reason for your presence. Permit me to present myself: the
Margrave Friedrich von Feuerstein, Deputy Master of the Wenceslas
Brigade, High Brother of the Temporal College. I recognise your
honour as Father Ramon of the Society of Time."

The Jesuit inclined his head. "We've met before," he acknowledged.
"Though possibly you may not recall our meeting. In Rome—twenty-
seven years ago, as students in the School of Casuistry. My class was
departing as yours arrived."

"Why—that's so!" the Margrave said, and extended his hand.
"Strange that our acquaintance should be renewed here and now!"

Father Ramon ignored the offered hand. He said, "No, it's far from
strange. Are you in charge of this—venture?"

The Margrave hesitated a moment. Then he withdrew his hand,
folded his arms across his chest, and said challengingly, "I am!"

Father Ramon reached inside his habit and produced a rolled parchment. With his bird-claw fingers he undid the fastening and shook it
out; a heavy red seal swung on a ribbon from the bottom of it. He
seemed suddenly to speak in a voice other than his own, holding the
parchment up as though to read from it, but looking all the time at
the Margrave.

"This," he said, "is a copy of a Papal bull. Do I have to tell you that
it is the bull *De tenebris temporalibus*?"

The Margrave smiled. He was a large-jowled man with grey hair; the
smile made plump hummocks of his cheeks, on the crest of each of

which showed a red network of broken veins. He said, "I defy you to show cause for invoking that bull."

"We are not required to show cause." Father Ramon stared unblinkingly. "But in a Vatican court we're prepared to. You have twelve hours, present time, in which to remove your men, your equipment, and all traces of your presence up to that point which we decree, on pain of summary excommunication by the powers vested in us under the aforesaid bull. I read!" He snapped the nail of a forefinger against the stiff parchment so that it sounded like a beaten drum, and still without looking away from the Margrave began to recite.

"De tenebris temporalibus et de itineribus per tempus leges instituendae sunt. In nomine Deo Patri Filio et Spiritu Sancto dicimus et affirmamus—"

The whole world seemed to hesitate to hear the rolling Latin syllables ring out through the hot still air. *Regarding the shades of time past and regarding journeys through time laws are to be instituted. In the name of God the Father, Son and Holy Ghost we say and affirm...* Don Miguel felt his lips move on the familiar words which he had never before heard invoked.

"We say and affirm that the means of travelling in time is a gift bestowed by divine ordinance and therefore to be used only in accordance with divine law, subject to regulation, to conditions now or in the future to be laid down by Papal decree, and to the expedient judgment of those agents now or in the future appointed by us for the enforcement of those conditions. Let there be agreements between nations and before God for the employment of the means of travelling in time for the benefit of humanity and the increase of human knowledge, and let there be penalties imposed upon those who are tempted for evil ends to pervert and misuse the means of travelling in time."

The Margrave waited patiently until Father Ramon re-rolled the parchment with a crisp rustle, and then he said merely, "On what grounds do you base your orders? Can you show proof of evil?"

"Yes," Father Ramon said delicately. "But not evil of your doing."

The Margrave blinked. He said, "What then?"

Don Miguel could hardly believe his ears. He stared at his companion, who took notice and gave a faint smile. "Be easy in your mind, my son," the Jesuit said. "You'll see it all in a little while." And to the Margrave he added, "Is there somewhere we can speak together in confidence?"

"Yes! Yes, in my tent below. I'll see we're not disturbed there." The Margrave made to turn, but lingered for a long moment trying to read the expression on Father Ramon's face.

He failed, and led the way down the slope towards the mining settlement. Several of his overseers came up to him, demanding instructions. He told them to halt their work, and to wait for further orders. It was clear that they were puzzled by this, but glad enough of a rest, for the sun was scorching.

"Now explain yourself!" the Margrave said, when they had taken their places in his tent and were alone.

"I'd rather you began by explaining yourself," Father Ramon countered.

The Margrave shook his head sharply.

"Well, then, I'll explain you." Father Ramon put his sharp elbows on the table separating them. "I don't care, by the way, about the ore you've taken on territory which is to be Imperial ground by treaty with the Mohawk Nation a thousand years from now—doubtless, you've made some profit, or you expected to make some profit. That's totally beside the point. I want to show you the probable course of going ahead as you had in mind.

"It's no secret to anyone that the Mohawks are the Empire's uneasiest allies. But this doesn't make them friends of yours—a point you overlooked. Legalistically, there may be a claim to be made for freebooters' right in the ore you've taken. I doubt if there's one for Mohawk rights—they were nowhere near this part of the world... I correct myself: they *are* nowhere near, and indeed I'm not certain that they could be found to exist as a precedent tribal unit.

"Forget all that. Think of the predictable consequences of what you intended to do. You're perilously close to a breach of the Treaty of Prague—and if it weren't deliberately framed to be unbreakable in all reasonable circumstances, you'd have broken it already. Without prejudice, we're prepared to overlook the fact. We want to keep the treaty intact."

"Doubletalk," the Margrave said curtly, and Don Miguel found himself inclined to agree. What had the Empire-Mohawk alliance to do with this act of poaching?

"Are you prepared to act in breach of the Treaty of Prague?" snapped Father Ramon.

"Of course not!" The Margrave looked astonished. "As you yourself said, it's framed so as to be virtually unbreakable."

"But you think that the Empire-Mohawk alliance is not," Father Ramon said.

There was a long, cold silence. Finally the Margrave got to his feet. His voice had changed completely when he spoke again. It was heavier and somehow rang false, like a counterfeit coin.

"Very well. I'll clear the site and call the operation off."

Whatever had happened, it was effective. Don Miguel had still not figured it out when he found himself charged by Father Ramon to supervise the removal from this day and age of all the equipment used by the poachers, an order grudgingly acceded to by the Margrave, who told his clerks to provide fair copies of the equipment manifests so that Don

Miguel could check that everything which had been brought was going back. His head swimming with the itemised lists of picks, drills, sieves, flotation and separation equipment, chisels, crowbars, saws, hatchets, axes, guns, powder, shot, he spent the rest of the day on the task.

It was not until he and Father Ramon had watched the entire process through its conclusion, with the vanishing of the poachers back to the twentieth century, that he had a chance to utter his burning questions. In the gathering dusk, he turned to the Jesuit.

"Father, I simply do not understand anything about this—neither what the Margrave was up to, nor what was meant by your references to the alliance with the Mohawks, nor why the Margrave so tamely packed up and went home—!"

"I'm hardly surprised," Father Ramon said wryly. "I confess I hadn't expected to be shown so right. I didn't know, I only speculated, as to the reason for this ridiculous expedition by the Confederacy."

The last of the poachers vanished into the gloom; there was the inevitable wash of heat, like the opening of a furnace door, which accompanied temporal displacements. Father Ramon waited like a statue for long seconds. Then he said, "Have you the means of making a light?"

"Yes."

"Come with me, then."

He started across the now empty valley towards the mouth of the gallery which Two Dogs was to discover a thousand years from now and bring to Don Miguel's attention. It was closed by the counterpoised boulder, of course, but now it was freshly placed, and the shifting of the earth which later was to make it require the strength of two men to roll it aside had not yet occurred. Father Ramon set his shoulder to it, and gave a gentle heave; before Don Miguel could come to his aid, it had rolled and settled in the open position.

"Now—your light," the Jesuit said briskly.

Don Miguel struck it and offered it, but Father Ramon waved the offer aside. "No, take it into the gallery," he said. "Search carefully, along the walls and floor, right to the end."

Much puzzled, Don Miguel did so. He found nothing, except some traces left by the workmen—and as he was coming back, he saw what Father Ramon was implying.

"Well?" the dry voice said as he emerged. Don Miguel had a struggle to make his own voice equally calm and level.

"It's not there," he said.

"You mean this?" Father Ramon felt in a pouch at his waist and produced the cracked drill-bit which Two Dogs had originally given as the key to the whole affair. "I thought it wouldn't be there. Before my departure from Londres I made some inquiries of—well, of certain trusted agents. I'm prepared to state that this drill-bit was purchased in Augsburg the winter before last; I mean naturally in our present. And it was purchased by a Mohawk."

He tossed it up and caught it again; the light gleamed on the shiny broken edge of it. "Put the stone back, my son. I think we should return—and when we do, we'll make some inquiries of your affable acquaintance the mine manager. Two Dogs, isn't that his name? I think we'll discover that he's by no means a mere miner, but someone of a very much higher calibre, and infinitely more dangerous."

Bending to replace the boulder, Don Miguel turned the words over in his mind. He was about to speak, when another thought came to him. He said explosively, "But I knew it already! I had the equipment manifests in my hands, and I checked that the total of drill-bits returned to their time of origin was the same as the total brought here!"

"I know," Father Ramon said. "I watched that phase of the operation with some attention. Come, let's get away from here.

We've had a long day, and we're going back to the middle of another one."

V

It was always the strangest quirk of time-travel that a man might go back a thousand years to a later time of day, and feel below the conscious level of his mind that he had travelled forward, while by returning from a late hour to an earlier one he would feel he had travelled back. It was dizzying, as usual, to emerge from the dusk of the year 948 to the high noon glare of the day they had set out from.

Several Society officers were present to see them come back, headed by Don Rodrigo, who—possibly to atone for his ill-mannered speech to Father Ramon the night before—did not put his important questions immediately, but saw that they moved tiredly, and called for shade, wine and food for them.

That was very welcome. Don Miguel wiped his lips with the back of his hand and thanked Don Rodrigo with a nod, before turning, with everyone else, to listen to Father Ramon's report. Among those who had assembled for the news he saw several—indeed, as far as he could see, all—of the Mohawk Licentiates present at the site. Doubtless they wanted to know the fate of the poachers who had killed their colleague Roan Horse.

Don Miguel started as he realised that that episode had not even been mentioned to the Margrave.

"We got rid of them," Father Ramon said. "Almost more easily than I'd expected. The affair is closed."

So short a report was not what anyone was waiting for. Don Miguel saw an exchange of startled glances. One of the Mohawk Licentiates on the fringe of the group whispered to a friend nearby, and then turned away. For a moment Don Miguel let his gaze follow; then a surprised comment from the Inquisitor, Brother Vasco, called his attention back.

"Father Ramon! It's good to hear that they took their departure, but surely it can't simply be left at that."

"No, of course not." The Jesuit was irritable. "As far as people here are concerned, though, it's over."

"What about Roan Horse?" snapped one of the Mohawks, the same one that a friend had whispered to a moment back.

"We shall require recompense—but that must be obtained properly, from the government of the Confederacy."

A buzz of comment was going around now, like the droning of flies in the hot sunlight. The Mohawk spoke up again.

"That's scarcely good enough! What compensation can we accept for the life of a good Licentiate and a brave man?"

There was a chorus of agreement, and someone else said, "And what about the ore they poached, too? It can't be as simple as you say!"

It was then that the facts clicked together in Don Miguel's mind. The only reason he could think of for having overlooked the obvious twice in one day was that he was confused and tired.

"Felipe!" he snapped, bounding to his feet, and Don Felipe Basso whirled to face him. "Sword—quickly! And over the hill with me!"

He shoved his way unceremoniously between the watchers and Felipe, not knowing why but impressed by his friend's urgency, came after him.

"Wait, you!" the Mohawk snapped, and came towards them. "Where are you going?"

Almost Don Miguel unsheathed his sword, but as yet he had only suspicion to go on. Instead, he placed one palm flat on the Mohawk's chest and hooked a toe behind his ankle, sending him sprawling. The sudden commotion had drawn everyone's attention. Don Miguel saw Don Arturo starting forward, and barked at him.

"Hold this man! Hold his companions! Keep 'em here till we've gone over the hill—but one of them has left already, and we may be too late."

He gestured to Don Felipe and began to run up the hillside track. Behind him the noise of confused argument grew louder, but he dared not turn back.

He breasted the rise, and saw that indeed he was already too late.

Alongside the mud-plastered house where he had spent so many nights as the guest of Two Dogs, Tomas stood inscrutable in his gay *serape*. He was shading his eyes to look towards a cloud of dust on the road towards the sea—and in that cloud of dust could be seen two horses, not the stumbling burros of the locality, but horses of the finest racing stock, being ridden as though to outpace the devil himself.

"Miguel!" panted Don Felipe, coming up beside his friend. "What's this all about?"

"The birds have flown—and there's the whole continent and ocean for them to hide themselves." Don Miguel pointed. "Felipe, find Don Rodrigo—get men with good horses after those two! One of them is Two Dogs, who's been posing as the mine manager here, and he's probably the most dangerous man in the world!"

Don Felipe threw up his hands in a hopeless gesture, and turned back. His exclamation made Don Miguel turn also, and with sinking heart he saw that down in the valley there was flashing of steel, and some of it was coloured red in the sun. Red, too, was spreading across the dark habit of the bird-like figure seated in the chair in shade of the awning at the focus of the group.

"Father Ramon!" Don Miguel cried, drawing his sword. Together with Don Felipe, he launched himself down the slope.

"What we forgot," Don Miguel said uncertainly as he set aside the leathern water-bottle, "was that when we say Mohawk that's like saying Imperial. In the Empire there are people of Spanish extraction—English—Netherlanders—French..."

The others—all those who were in a condition to stand up and pay attention—nodded as though his words were pearls of perfect wisdom. If they knew how little he had actually learned, how much he was simply guessing, they would be less willing to lean on him as they had leaned on Father Ramon.

But Father Ramon was dead. And he was not the only one.

"So too," Don Miguel continued, trying to make everything crystal-clear, "Mohawk is a general term, convenient because it was our alliance with the Mohawk Nation that enabled that people to become the dominant power of this continent and subjugate the Crees and the Cherokees and the Choctaws and all the rest. Scores of them—scores of tribes! Some of them very resentful of the ascendancy which the Mohawks had achieved—others less so, and willing in the event to be regarded as members of a single super-tribe as we were willing to become Imperial citizens."

Don Rodrigo, his left arm in a sling, grunted. He said, "are we to take it that it's the resentment you describe which accounts for this fantastic day's happenings?"

"Partly," Don Miguel said, and was going to explain further when he saw the bowed, weary figure of Brother Vasco approaching through the wavery heat of the afternoon. "In a moment, though, we may be able to hear truth rather than my guesses, if Brother Vasco has been successful in his labours."

The Inquisitor came closer. In answer to an unspoken question from Don Miguel, he nodded.

"He's alive—the one who challenged you," he said. "They told me he was called Red Cloud, but—I gave him some of my relaxing draught and asked how he was named, as is customary."

"And he said what?" Don Miguel started to his feet.

Brother Vasco gave him a strange look. "He said his name was Bloody Axe," he replied.

"Let's go to him and get at the truth behind this," Don Miguel said, and strode towards the place where the injured man was laid.

The techniques of the Holy Office were refined more than they had been, as Don Miguel well knew; they were also more effective. It was eerie to see this man who consciously would prefer to die rather than utter the secrets he kept, yielding answers to every interrogation under the influence of Brother Vasco's draught.

Two Dogs? His real name, the injured man said without being able to stop himself, was Hundred Scalps, but he was commonly known as Broken Tree. At that, one of the non-Mohawk Licentiates drew breath sharply and said that he knew the name as that of a brilliant student at the Mexicological Institute some years before.

That fitted.

The information Bloody Axe gave them pieced together in Don Miguel's mind with the clues dropped by Father Ramon before he was killed to make a terrifying unity. Its roots were in envy, as usual in human affairs.

The Confederacy's expansion was barred—partly by the contrary expansion of Cathay, partly by the hostile winters which locked up so much of its potential northern territory. By contrast, the Empire's alliance with the Mohawk Nation gave access to a continent over much

of which the climate was equable, and whose resources were mostly
still uncharted, let alone tapped.

Some Indians, jealous of Mohawk supremacy, planned to make a
breach between the uneasy allies, using the Confederacy as a wedge.
They made an approach in simple terms to the government of the
Confederacy. They stated their feelings about the Mohawk-Empire
alliance frankly, letting it be assumed that they would ultimately
transfer their allegiance to the Confederacy. They asked for help.
The Confederacy might have given it anyway; a promise of payment was made which clinched the deal. The Indians offered to
pay by giving the Confederacy access to resources which they knew
about, but had not yet begun to mine for the Empire. Clearly the
Confederacy would have to take their profit at a time when nobody
was there to argue with them, and the Indians promised to conceal
the traces for them.

After much pondering, the Confederacy agreed. In law, it could be
argued that at the time when they proposed to take the ore, it belonged
to nobody, or if it did, it belonged to the ancestors of the present-day
Indians. It might not be possible, as they were promised, to conceal
the traces—but what did that matter? If the facts came to light, they
would drag with them for all the world to see the truth about the
Mohawk-Empire alliance. It would splinter, and it was to be hoped that
at least some of the splinters could be picked up by the Confederacy.

But it would be easier for all parties, of course, if the secret could
be kept.

The proposers of the plan, once it was accepted, took steps to
ensure not only that the loss of the ore was discovered, but to pin the
deed squarely on the perpetrators. Part of it was luck—the fact that
Don Miguel stopped off in New Madrid to present his compliments to

the Prince, and let it be mentioned that he was bound for a vacation in California, suggested an opportunity too good to miss.

And but for the fact that Father Ramon's agent knew of a Mohawk—or rather, a Mohawk subject—who had lately purchased some drill-bits in Augsburg, the result would have been as Two Dogs expected, especially when Roan Horse was killed. For this was only the first step. All over the continent there were other sites, waiting to be discovered. This one was genuine; the others were manufactured. The plan was that the Imperials should complain officially; the Confederacy would issue denials and promises that the same would not be done again... and then, time after time, evidence would be produced that it *had* been done. The same procedure would be adopted to fake these sites as had been used by corrupt Licentiates in Europe to take wealthy patrons on illegal sightseeing trips—one and the same journey would be used for a legal and a covert purpose. Since there was a sharp limit—four thousand four hundred and sixty years and a few weeks—on the operating range of time apparatus, by establishing the faked sites at maximum distance in the past it could be rendered impossible for anyone from a later point of departure to visit them and see that they were being prepared by Indians, not by miners from the Confederacy. And more than one drill-bit had been bought in Augsburg, and could be left if evidence had to be supplied.

In face of the Confederacy's denials, more and more indications of wholesale plundering would be found. Suspicion would mount—how much of our resources have been taken? Accusation would pile on accusation—there would be Papal adjudication, probably going against the Confederacy, so that the injured innocence of the Confederacy would turn to a cynical determination to be hanged for a sheep. So... violence.

Oh yes. The millstones across the sea were to be set grinding again, and from between them—so it went in the grandiose vision to which Two Dogs had dedicated himself—the unwilling subjects of the Mohawk Nation and the Empire its ally would escape into the freedom they desired.

Stunned by the subtlety of the plan and the narrowness of their escape, Don Miguel brought himself to put one last question to Bloody Axe. Suppose the plan was discovered and thwarted—as indeed it had been?

The answer struck cold and hurtful as that same axe-blade for which he had been named. "In that event… rather than endure the Empire's vengeance… we have sworn to bring it down around your ears, and all of history with it!"

VI

"We have to deal with a madman!" the Prince said.

Don Miguel nodded. "There's little doubt of it. I've not wasted a moment of the time since we discovered the truth—thanks to Brother Vasco's inquisitorial skill." He nodded at the Dominican beside him. "We have set on foot inquiries into the background of this man—Two Dogs was an alias he adopted on the old Indian custom whereby a child is named for the first ominous thing the father sees on leaving the birth-tent. He has been known variously as Broken Tree, Hundred Scalps, Storm of Rain, and several other aliases. As for Bloody Axe, who passed as Red Cloud when he became a Licentiate of the Society, his career is nearly as chequered. Almost sixty of the Licentiates granted their time licences in New Castile have proved to be associated with one or other of these two."

"We have to deal not only with *one* madman," Red Bear said. His long face was shiny with sweat, and his braided hair hung dull beside his head, as though tarnished with strain and worry. No one could question Red Bear's allegiance to the Empire and the Mohawk Nation—he was Mohawk for ten generations back. "We have to deal with madmen in the Confederacy! As you know, we've risked creating local causal loops a hundred times in the past few days, by operating time apparatus at maximum spatial angular displacement and minimal temporal displacement, so as to negate the time required to traverse distances. Already we have exceeded the safety margins laid down by Borromeo—but that's beside the point. What matters is that we got the news of the danger to diplomatic contacts in the Confederacy as soon as it was humanly possible—and some *fools* over there are hindering the co-operation of their Temporal College with us, thinking that for the Empire to fall about our ears as was threatened will be no bad thing for the Confederacy!" He spat with vicious accuracy between his feet. "Are they all out of their minds?"

"It seems like it," the Prince said. His face was grey—the first time Don Miguel had ever seen a man's face go that colour, through sheer unmitigated terror. One day, Don Miguel knew, he would probably look in the glass on rising from one of his sleepless nights and see that same greyness on his own tanned skin.

He half-turned to look down the long table at which the officers were congregated. This was no mere private meeting in the Prince's chamber of audience—this was the first full meeting of the General Officers of the Society to be held in New Madrid since the one called to establish the New Castile Chapter of the Society, better than sixty years ago. As Red Bear had mentioned, the limits of safety had been strained to bring the officers here—some of these people, indeed, might even now be where they had been, having returned from tomorrow. It was *that* much of an emergency. There had never been one like it. There might never be another such—never, until the Last Judgment.

"Father Terence!" the Prince said. "I'm not slighting you if I say that I turn to you as I'd have turned to Father Ramon your late colleague—may he rest in peace."

The man next to Red Bear shifted on his chair. He was most of the things that Father Ramon had not been—tall, heavily built, with a thatch of fair hair. He spoke with a strong Irish accent.

"Since Father Ramon went from us," he said, "of course no one has been able to match precisely the plans he doubtless had laid. I feel inadequate to take his place though I've worked with him for some years more or less closely. What's agreed is this: any attempt to create a closed loop by eliminating this Indian—Two Dogs, I'll say for convenience—by temporal intervention from this point will have incalculable consequences. I can only recommend it as a last resort. Moreover, his apprehension and execution at a point in past time will be unprecedented and a violation of all the canons of the Society. We must accordingly select—so long as we have the chance—a less dangerous alternative."

"Is there one?"

For a long moment Don Miguel thought he had gone too far in voicing his cynical thought. Father Terence flushed and bridled, where Father Ramon would have inclined his head and spoken with gentle reproof. He said, "My son, you've had greatness imposed on you by chance. Don't exceed the freedom it bestows on you!"

The story of that New Year's Eve when Father Ramon had condemned himself knowingly to an intellectual torture whose refinement passed imagining, as well as—incidentally—Don Arturo Cortes to being haunted by his own ghost and Don Miguel to being burdened by unique and impossible knowledge, came to the tip of Don Miguel's tongue. But now was not the time to speak of such matters. He held his peace and swallowed his pride.

After a pause and a glare at his interrupter, Father Terence resumed. "We analysed the studies which Two Dogs, under the name of Broken Tree, pursued while at the Mexicological Institute and previously at the University of New Castile. We took into consideration also the facts which Don Miguel Navarro laid before us regarding the secret society which he and Bloody Axe belonged to, and we've been able to make educated guesses concerning the point at which he would wish to attack the Empire's history."

"Guesses only?" stabbed the Prince.

"Bloody Axe was lucky to know even that this reserve plan existed. Its actual nature was privy to the members of an in-group of the secret society—Two Dogs was one of them, but we can't identify any of the others." Father Terence broke off and coughed behind his hand.

"We are fairly sure that they would attack at the most crucial known point of our history—the conquest of England. It isn't known what the course of events would have been if the Armada had failed to secure the seas for the transit of the forces from the Netherlands, but it can be argued logically that the Empire would have been swallowed up when Spain was conquered, having no prosperous alternative homeland to retreat to. As every schoolboy is aware, we barely survived the seventeenth century as it was."

"So what are your proposals?" the Prince prompted.

"Have all the obvious precautions been taken?" Father Terence countered.

Red Bear gave a snort. He said, "Oh, we've placed loyal men in charge of every time apparatus we have, but what's the use? Doubtless there are men associated with Two Dogs who can build him time apparatus good enough to serve his needs—or if not, then he can wheedle those idiots of the Confederacy into granting him passage!"

Father Terence hesitated. He said, "Well, then—our recommendations. We propose that every available Licentiate and Probationer whose loyalty is unquestioned shall forthwith be set to patrolling the causal paths leading to the sailing of the Armada and the conquest of England. If we fail to locate Two Dogs there, we'll have to resort to direct interference. But the consequences are unpredictable."

There was a dull, unpleasant silence. Finally the Prince said, "And that's all?"

Father Terence shrugged. He said, "Yes. That's all."

The Prince turned to Don Miguel. "You had something to say, Navarro?"

Don Miguel put the same question to himself. Yes, he did—but it was compounded of his personal acquaintance with Two Dogs, of all the indefinable impressions acquired while he was staying under the same roof. It didn't fall into words.

At last he shook his head, and the Prince slapped the table with his open palm. "Red Bear!" he said. "See to it—and in the name of God, man, find this lunatic before he ends us all!"

And it could happen... They knew it in theory. Don Miguel had spoken with Two Dogs, thought of him as an acquaintance ripening to the status of a friend, and *knew* that this was the sort of man who could bring history tumbling—the fanatic, the dedicated maniac of great intelligence and perverted idealism capable of committing the ultimate blasphemy of believing that he was uniquely right.

His own moment of notoriety was fading. The spotlight had turned on him because he chanced to have been on the scene when the crisis took fire. Now was the time for the organisers, the General Officers, the Don Arturos and Don Rodrigos, while he could once more resume his position as a mere Licentiate of the Society, with some experience and more credit than most of his age, but that only.

It would take a little while to arrange for this concentrated onslaught of the Society on this single perilous period of history and, since even the simple presence of so many extemporates was itself dangerous, many calculations had to be worked out, many special techniques tested, before they could depart. He himself, along with Don Felipe, would be among the first to be sent, to the very closest arrival point: the time of the Armada's sailing. Possibly they would find all well. Possibly not. The second alternative didn't bear thinking about.

Which was why, that evening, he met with Don Felipe in the drinking-shop which was currently popular with the younger members of the Society in New Madrid, and showed him a letter he had written.

"To Kristina?" Don Felipe said, his dark eyes darting back and forth between the folded paper and Don Miguel's face. His friend nodded.

"I've written also." Don Felipe felt in the pouch at his waist. He showed a letter that might have been the twin of Don Miguel's, except that the superscription was to the Lady Ingeborg. "But what's the point?"

"The point?" Don Miguel shrugged. "In the writing itself, I suppose. How do you imagine it will happen if it does? A fading, or an instant obliteration?"

"We'll never know." Don Felipe's face darkened for an instant. "There's one thing, though," he added after a moment in a more cheerful tone.

"What?"

"According to the experts, a potential soul is not subject to retribution, but is classed as Limbo-fodder. Which means that if Two Dogs succeeds, we can kick ourselves for not having taken advantage of our potential state."

"Do you find that funny?" Don Miguel said.

"No. No, honestly I don't. But I think after a few drinks I might— and what better medicine for the ending of a world is there than laughter?"

So they called for liquor, and spent this final evening reminiscing.

Don Miguel had never before been to the Iberian peninsula, either in present or in past time. But this was by far the best-researched area of Earth, and for various reasons the time prior to the departure of the Armada was thoroughly explored. So his briefing had been excellent—condensed, precise, comprehensive.

And when he walked out into the month of June, the year of 1588, he could say to himself, "Now the Armada is assembling; despite the efforts of the English who have raided its ports and tried to burn its ships, work proceeds apace. The Duke of Parma will have a force of more than a hundred ships; he'll muster six thousand sailors and twenty thousand soldiers, and waiting in the Netherlands are as many more to conquer England."

Put into such concrete terms, and knowing that down in the harbour here such vast preparations were going ahead, made it all unreal. How—after all—could one man change the course of this single historical event? Short of commanding the weather, so that the English and not the Spanish fleet was favoured, surely nothing could be done!

And yet… pestilence aboard the ships? Poison in the water-barrels? Something like that might have the right effect.

He tested his command of the archaic language by inquiring the way to the waterfront, which he knew; he passed without question, and shortly found himself among all the last-minute bustle of preparation. The last detachments of soldiers were going aboard; the last hogsheads of pickled meat and barrels of water and biscuit, the last wagonloads of shot. Unnoticed, he wandered along the quays until he saw a wineshop, and there turned in. Gossip would take root here if anywhere.

There were few clients. Five minutes' conversation with the landlord told him why—now that the fleet was due to sail, of course, his custom was aboard.

"Here's to their good fortune!" Don Miguel said, raising his mug. "What say you?"

"I'll drink to it," the landlord answered. "But—though the true faith will triumph—I'm not sanguine of this venture."

Don Miguel halted the mug en route to his lips. He said, "Why so, then?" And heard his voice shake.

"Why so?" The landlord gave a coarse laugh. "With a commander who's sick at the least lurching of his ship?"

Don Miguel said faintly, "His Grace the Duke of Parma..."

"Parma?" The landlord eyed him strangely. "Parma's in the Netherlands, man! Medina Sidonia's commanding this fleet, and a worse sea-commander could hardly be picked in all of Spain!"

VII

It was at that moment that Don Miguel Navarro became the first man to know that a universe was crumbling about him, except always for Two Dogs, and Two Dogs desired that it should be so.

The Duke of Parma... in the Netherlands. This was not history. The Duke of Parma, Spain's finest commander of the century, took the Armada to sea! Medina Sidonia—who was he? A nonentity, an entry in the footnotes of history books! And the Netherlands were secured permanently for Spain and its inheritor the Empire by that brilliant, unorthodox master of strategy, the Scottish Catholic Earl of Barton, who when the Armada broke the English resistance at sea was prepared with his hundreds of flat-bottomed barges to break the resistance on land as well.

Don Miguel said after such a pause that he thought he had heard the grinding of Earth on its axis, "And the Earl of Barton? Does he serve with Parma in the Netherlands?"

"The Earl of Barton?" The landlord shrugged. "Perhaps—I've never heard the name." He gave Don Miguel a curious glance. "Where've you come from, that you ask such questions?"

"Ah—I've been travelling." Don Miguel emptied his mug and got to his feet carefully. "My score—how much is it?"

The landlord rubbed his chin and mused for a long moment. All at once Don Miguel could not bear it any more. He snatched a piece of gold from his purse and flung it to the floor, then spun on his heel and took his departure at a headlong run, although reason told him that running could do nothing to speed his purpose.

He headed back away from the shore, making for the house which was the location for his return, his mind pounding faster than his feet. Yes, this was what he had wanted to say to the General Officers—that Two Dogs was subtle, that he would do nothing so open as poison the Armada's provisions! The Earl of Barton: what was known about him? He claimed to be related on the wrong side of the blanket to the Scottish royal family—but so did scores of others. He appeared from nowhere in the Netherlands when Elizabeth ascended the English throne; from then on he made his name by sheer military brilliance, and when Parma was recalled to command the Armada he finished the Duke's work in sixteen weeks of whirlwind campaigning, making sure for ever of the Netherlands.

That was the point at which Two Dogs had struck. Not here.

Now what was the Society to do? Lord Barton had come from nowhere, and to track him back to his origins would be impossible! *Already* it was impossible, for the man they were tracing could not exist.

For a second that fact stopped Don Miguel in his tracks, like a physical blow. He grew briefly aware that the townsfolk were staring at him, wondering what made a finely dressed gentleman race through their streets as though chased by devils, and at once ignored them again.

Was the Society to watch over the birth and childhood of a thousand royal byblows in Scotland, to find out which life Two Dogs had cut off? He could think of no alternative, and groaned because it all seemed so hopeless.

Then it occurred to him that he was still here and aware, and that therefore at this moment (he tried to bring back the laboriously-learned technique of five-dimensional thinking in which he had been schooled) the actual future existed and the potential future was unrealised. Accordingly there was hope even yet. The killing of the Earl of Barton—he didn't doubt that Two Dogs would have made his work definitive—had created a period of suspension, and it was in this period that he now existed. If he could get back to the twentieth century armed with his knowledge—if he could make the Society find the Earl of Barton—they could still thwart Two Dogs and restore history to its true form.

*

He began to run again, like a madman, and within ten minutes found himself before the house where the Society kept its temporal watch. The watchman on the gate leading up to it had passed him out shortly before, and was a Probationer he knew; he read Don Miguel's anguished expression and let him by at once.

The empty house was eerie, and the great dusty room where he waited for the pickup was looming and dark after the bright summer day outside. He fumed with impatience while the sense of blazing heat grew around him, indicating the onset of temporal displacement, seeing the melting of his surroundings as time was rotated to become a direction through which he could travel, seeing the distorted shape of the cage of iron and silver take on relative actuality as it contained his body and drew it forward into time.

A terrible relief weakened him. So at least he hadn't been forestalled in the carrying of his knowledge! The trip was going to take some "time," because of the considerable angular displacement involved in the return to his starting point in New Madrid which inside the cage affected him as though it were ordinary time. He had a chance to calm himself and order his thoughts.

It must work this way. Two Dogs had gone back and killed the Earl of Barton. Owing to the tangential relationship between elapsed-past time and elapsed-present time, the results of this deed had not echoed down to Don Miguel's own present before his departure for the year 1588. But in 1588 the effects were already established, and it was conceivable that they might have durated through to the twentieth century "while" Don Miguel was absent from it. If they had, though, it was to be assumed that this temporal pickup would not have taken place. With luck, Two Dogs had not departed until after Don Miguel; in this case, there was quite a considerable margin of actual time in the twentieth century in the course of which the work of tracing the Earl of Barton and ensuring his survival might be carried out.

If, on the other hand, Two Dogs had departed very soon after he was last seen, there was so little time for such a gigantic task that success was unlikely.

Don Miguel sat down on his haunches on the floor of the cage, and realised to his astonishment that he had become quite calm now he had had a chance to think things over. It seemed so unnatural for a single man to be able to wipe out the real course of history! Besides, hadn't Two Dogs spoken of his people being ground between the millstones of the rival European invaders if the Empire hadn't won its greatest victory? Would he desire that fate for his people?

Don Miguel shuddered. Yes, he thought. A man like Two Dogs might think it better that the Indians should go down provided only that the Empire went with them, and that the Europeans who came to his homeland should be torn indefinitely by their quarrels and never achieve the greatness of the united Empire.

Had he not, though, been too pessimistic in thinking that the task of tracking down Two Dogs would be impossible? A major figure of European history like Lord Barton must have been the subject of some research by the Society—they would not be hunting in the dark, but would have clues to guide them, and in a little while the natural order would be restored. The fools in the Confederacy who felt that the collapse in past time of the Empire would bring them advantages in the present would see reason; the members of the Temporal College would work together with the Society of Time to ensure…

Abruptly the growing cheerfulness in his mind was cut off. He stared at the frame of iron and silver which surrounded him, misty and deformed as always while in transit, and thought: it should be growing clearer as I come closer to the present. Instead, it's growing fainter. Or is it a trick of the eyes?

He dared not touch the semi-solid bars to confirm what his eyes reported—that way, he would die quickly. There were vast energies trapped in the configuration surrounding him.

He stared, wondering what lay beyond the bars: reality, or some unimagined nightmare, and while he stared, he found out.

There was a wrenching. It acted on his bare consciousness, so that he perceived it as pain, and as blinding light, and as a sound which shook his brain in his head; as a burning fire, and as a headlong falling into illimitable abysses, one beyond the other without number or end.

That was the most terrible thing of all: that they were endless, and yet after an eternity, they ended.

He had sight and hearing, touch and the awareness of his body. He looked, listened, felt air and warm sunlight, knew he was physically present, knew he had weight and substance. And while his mind still echoed with the dying reverberations of the crash of a universe, he was not ashamed to scream.

But that, said a small voice far distant in his mind, is a foolish thing to do. It can be understood what has happened. Think! Think that in less than one short century after Borromeo, the world you thought of as being real spawned not only Two Dogs, but others beside. Think of the New Year's Eve when a king was killed because men played with the power to master time. Think of the greed that made men steal from the riches of the past, and what had to be done to set right the consequences. Think why in your world that you imagined to be real no one had come back from the future to intervene in the future's past...

True. Oh, God's name! True as daylight, and never understood! If a span of a century less some years had brought about so many abortive interferences with the past, why had not the future, with its incalculable toll of years in which time-travel would be possible?

Because there *was* no future. Not rooted in that past. Don Miguel Navarro drew a deep breath into a throat made sore by his foolish screaming and said the words to himself.

A picture was coming to him now. He could visualise the path of history in each of those innumerable potential worlds where men had gained the power of time-travel as a series of loops. Every loop was like a knife; it severed the chain of causation and created a new reality. (Was there indeed any reality more real than any other?) At last the temptation to put the past to rights would lure one man at least to make the entire path of history unstable. The very events that led to the discovery of time-travel would be wiped out, and a new universe would form.

Perhaps this was what had happened to him. He could almost grasp the concept, but not quite. If he had crossed the margin of the spreading ripples from the Earl of Barton's death on his way to the past—as he clearly had, for when he came to 1588 the effects were established—then they would probably have durated to his starting-point as he was returning to it. In fact, he had been trapped between actual and potential "during" his journey... and here he was.

Where, then, were all the people he had known? Felipe, who had drunk with him last night, as it seemed; Kristina, who had made him the unwitting instrument of just such a loop in time as he was considering now—and who might have been more than a charming companion; the King, the Princes, the General Officers, the Margrave, even Two Dogs himself? Were they abolished from the total scheme of things, while he by a freak was left in possession of his knowledge and his life?

Only such a man as Father Ramon could answer that question—
and even in the universe which Two Dogs had brought crashing down
about their ears, Father Ramon was dead.

Passive, he began to study his surroundings. He was in a sort of
park, apparently; people were coming towards him, drawn by his
screaming, no doubt, for they hesitated while they were yet some distance away. They were dressed in extraordinary clothes; he saw young
women as well as men among them, their legs bare to the knee, hatless,
clinging shamelessly to the bare arms of their male companions. But
behind them he saw a city: towers of a tallness he had never dreamed
of, and there were sounds he could not identify, but which seemed to
have their source in the sky overhead.

He looked up. Something far vaster than a bird was passing, stiff-
winged. A mystery.

Now the people were getting bolder. A young man of about his
own age came striding forward, and addressed what was presumably a
question, in words completely beyond Don Miguel's comprehension.
He countered with a question of his own.

"Donde estoy?"

The man frowned. He said, *"Español!* Ah—you are in New York!"
He spoke slowly and clearly, as to an idiot, and Don Miguel suddenly
understood. Nueva Jorque: New York. A derivative of English, the
language which only peasants spoke in his universe—here, the tongue
of this fantastic city. He hunted through his limited recollection of the
parent dialect and formed his second question.

"When? Please—which year?"

The man blinked in astonishment. Either he didn't see the point of
the question, or he hadn't understood Don Miguel's accent. But on
reflection, of course, he could see that it didn't matter. It must be this

universe's year 1988 or 1989, assuming that he'd come to a New York which corresponded to the New Madrid he had known before, because if he had fallen short of his year of destination he would have fallen short in space too, and drowned in the Atlantic.

Only time would tell whether that fate would be preferable to the one which had actually overtaken him.

Now, seeing he was not dangerous, the other curious onlookers were approaching to study him and pass startled comments. Their surprise suggested that in this world time-travel was unknown; if it were known, it would supply a ready-made explanation for the arrival of a stranger out of thin air. The thought brought with it a sense of peace—a security which he could never remember having felt since he first learned how dangerous Borromeo's legacy had become.

Let them explain his presence how they would, then. He would never explain it. He could describe the operation of time apparatus; he could build one in a week, given the iron and the silver. He would not. He swore that silently to himself. Whatever this world was like, it was not for men to usurp the divine prerogative and alter the established order of what had gone before.

The young man facing him was beckoning to him, inviting him to accompany him somewhere. Don Miguel gave a slow smile. For better or worse, without chance of change, this was his reality now.

Don Miguel Navarro, formerly Licentiate in Ordinary of the Society of Time, now the most isolated of all the outcasts the human race had ever known, walked forward, into the real world.

FATHER OF LIES

I

CALMLY, MILES CROTON APPLIED THE BRAKES AND BROUGHT THE car to an easy stop. Then he backed up a few yards, one eye on the rear-view mirror, but his main attention on the thing in the field beside the road. He reached out to draw from beneath the dashboard a microphone on a spring-wound reel of flex, and with a fingertip tapped out a call-signal on the activating button: dit-dit-dit-dah-dit, dit-dit-dit-dah-dit.

"What is it?" said Colin's voice from the speaker grille under the dash.

Narrowing his eyes a little, Miles peered forward. "A dragon," he said. "About seven miles from the village."

"How's the road at that point?" Colin said.

"Still good. Metalled surface as far ahead as I can see, which is only about a quarter of a mile. Going by the weathering effects, it was made up in the twenties or thirties."

"Not much traffic," Colin said.

"None at all, looks like. Hedges probably meet across the middle of the road in summer. They're getting fairly thick already, and it's barely April."

"Uh-huh. And this dragon?"

There was a scratching, rustling sound from the speaker. Miles had a momentary vision of serious-faced Colin making his shorthand notes on the pad before him, even though the conversation was of course being recorded.

"Big," he said. "I caught sight of its back a couple of times before I realised what it was. It's standing under a clump of trees, partly shadowed. Not much detail. About ten feet high at the shoulder, thirty to forty feet long, plus the tail. A sort of anthracite black, dingy except where the light catches it. Flexible neck. Mouth looks big enough to swallow me up, car and all."

"Breathing fire?" Colin said.

"Not that I can see."

"Wings?"

"Sort of bat-like wings, folded close to the sides, with a kind of pleated effect that makes it hard to see details." Miles lifted the thirty-five millimetre camera hanging on its short strap against his chest. He focused as he talked. "I'm trying for a picture of it, but it's badly sited for a clear shot, and I don't want to get out of the car."

He took his picture, advanced the film and took a second one.

"I heard the clicks," Colin said. "Okay. What are you going to do—drive on?"

"I'm not sure. I think maybe I'll hang around till it moves away. It looks very—well, disturbing."

"Seven miles from the village, you said?"

"By my reckoning. I agree it's improbable, but what *is* probable in this lunatic corner of the world?"

"So far from the village it's not likely to be dangerous," Colin said. "Still, that's up to you. What—?"

"Hold it," Miles broke in. "It's moving. Damn! This road is only about ten feet wide, and now I can't say whether it's coming to look at me so I ought to swing the car, or whether it's just going for a walk and I'd better not rev the engine and catch its attention."

He heard the sound of Colin's heavy breathing from the speaker grille. Without looking away from the dragon, he felt for the cushion of the passenger seat and tilted it forward; his fingertips rested lightly on the cool smooth stock of the repeating rifle which was concealed underneath.

Ignoring the flimsy barrier of a seven-foot thorn hedge in the first flush of spring growth, the dragon tramped out of the field. For a heart-stopping moment its stupid, vast-mouthed head faced him up the narrow road; then it turned with majestic deliberation and began to walk in the other direction, its tail leaving a muddy streak on the ground between its huge muddy footprints.

He took two more pictures before he spoke again to mention these prints to Colin. "That much detail this far from the village," he said.

"I see your point," Colin said. There was a faint rattling sound; he was indulging his inevitable habit of rapping his pen between his teeth, up and down. "How about your gun? Is it still working?"

Miles froze for a second; then he gave a laugh which was more nervous than he meant it to be. He said, "Damn you for reminding me. But I'm glad you didn't speak up earlier. I was sitting here with my hand on it while the dragon was looking at me. I wonder if I got those pictures, even."

"If your engine is still running, you probably did."

"That makes sense," Miles agreed, somewhat relieved, and prodded the accelerator with his toe. The answering rise in the note of the engine was very reassuring. "I wish we could run an aerial survey of the whole area some time."

"We will. Some time. When we can stretch the funds. Well, what are you going to do?"

Miles leaned forward. "That looks like—yes, it is. The dragon just took to the air. It must be about half a mile ahead. God, what a sight! It's got wings on it like I don't know what."

He stared, fascinated, at the bulk of the monster flapping leisurely upward over the peaceful countryside.

"Still more than six miles," Colin said practically. "He's expanding, isn't he?"

"It looks like it," Miles confirmed. "I certainly won't be able to go beyond that point in the car. I'll follow the road as far as I can in safety, and then I'll swing it around and leave it ready to come back to. I'd be much happier if I knew where the road led to, I must say."

"It probably runs past the ogre's cave," Colin said. "We know that much from Hugh's reports, and so far our mapping indicates that spatial relationships are normal over most of the area."

"*Most* of the area," Miles muttered. "Okay, I imagine it's safe for me to go ahead now. Keep listening."

He laid the microphone on top of the dashboard, where it would pick up his voice if he spoke loudly, and engaged gear again. Eyes and ears alert, he rolled forward. By now the dark shape of the dragon was little more than a blot in the sky.

As he had guessed from the apparent distance at which the monster had risen into the air, he was able to go little more than another half-mile before he rounded a bend and found that the road was running out on him. For a few hundred yards more there were visible patches of metalled surface, but the muddy potholes grew larger and larger, and undoubtedly they joined up into one rough, rutted dirt track not far away. He stopped and swung the car.

"Colin?" he said. "Get a fix on me here, if you can. It's almost the end of the road."

"Will do," Colin said, and after a moment whistled. "It's growing!" he went on. "You're definitely more than six miles out."

"I wonder if I ought to go on after all," Miles said slowly.

"It's entirely up to you," Colin answered. "I don't think anyone would blame you for turning back."

Miles pondered. Finally he said, "No, I'll go ahead for a bit, anyway. See if I can establish one or two landmarks."

"As you like."

He turned off the engine, leaving the ignition key in place, and got out of the car. He listened for a moment, hearing only the breeze rustling the leaves, feeling the warm spring sun, before he went around to the back and fetched his big-bitted woodsman's axe. It was comforting to have something infallible in his hand. He swung it through a whistling arc, and then checked its flight, and froze.

He walked forward after a moment, to the place where the big potholes started to mar the road, and stared down thoughtfully for fully half a minute. Then he returned to the car and picked up the microphone.

"Colin? I've got to go ahead. What do you make of this? There are tyre-marks on the road past this point."

"Tyre-marks?"

"Perfectly distinct. Fresh. I can even recognise that it's a Dunlop tread."

"You're right—you will have to go on," Colin said after a pause. "But don't do anything damned silly, will you?"

"I'll try not to. I hope Hugh was wrong about the location of the ogre's cave."

"So do I, in that case. Well—best of luck, anyway."

"Thanks."

He put back the microphone and closed the door of the car. Thoughtfully he matted his beard a little with his fingers, rumpled his hair, and set the helve of his axe on his shoulder. Then he began to walk circumspectly along the road.

As he had expected, it decayed rapidly to a mere track. It sloped slightly downwards, which fitted with his tentative estimate of the lie of the land—there was a fairly wide brook somewhere near here, and the general direction of the road suggested that the two must cross. There might be a bridge, but he doubted it; more likely, there was just a ford.

And—yes, there it was. The ford. And in the very middle of it a baby-car stuck up to its axles in mud, with the driver's door open.

He lifted his axe from his shoulder and balanced it in both hands, his mouth setting in a grim line. There was a row of slippery stepping-stones paralleling the course which the road took across the brook. He went out along these after a thorough survey of the neighbourhood which revealed no sign of anybody, and stood in mid-stream studying the car.

No sign of violence, as far as he could tell. The driver must just have given up and gone to look for a telephone or a farmer with a tractor to haul the car out. He hoped devoutly that he had gone back the way he had come, rather than continuing ahead.

Then he noticed a dim gleam on the car's dashboard, and craned forward. The instrument lighting was on. So, when he took a closer look, were the headlights and rearlights. In the morning sun he hadn't detected their last faint glimmering when he approached. He reached inside and turned off the switch. That was disheartening. It implied that the car had stranded here in the dark, and the driver would have left the lights on to warn anyone else coming this way of the obstacle it made. In which case, not being able to see how badly the road ahead had deteriorated, he might have gone on instead of turning back.

There was no sign of footprints on the farther side of the ford, but the track was grassy there, so that meant nothing.

Frowning, he went on.

Like most of the area around here, his surroundings had a curiously constricted air. Although there was open sky above, he felt closed in.

The hedges were high and untended; when there was a gap, it revealed little more than a glimpse of a field beyond, with new season's grass growing among the stale dry stalks of its dead predecessors. Beyond the field there would inevitably be trees. They closed off any chance of a view beyond. It might have seemed accidental that there was no sense of distance or landscape. Miles knew better.

Consequently he kept himself alert for any hint of noise, and when he heard the distant shouting his first reaction was to poise his axe in his hands and cock his head to estimate its source.

Over there, on his left. Some distance off, as yet.

He hurried forward to one of the rare gaps in the hedge, and scrambled through, paying no attention to scratches. In the field he had entered an oak-tree stood by itself, and, dropping the helve of his axe through his belt, he swung himself up on one of its lower branches. From here he had a good view of the source of the shouting.

Not far away, a group of people in dirty ragged clothes, led by one finely-dressed young man on horseback, were clustered around a rocky outcrop on a steep slope. There was a cave in the base of the rock—big, dark and yawning—and close by a post had been set up. At this post most of the ragged people were busy doing something which their bodies concealed from him.

It was the young man on horseback who had begun the shouting, pointing up into the sky towards a dark, moving shape which grew moment by moment. The dragon, of course. Then...

Yes, he was right. The people busy about the post finished their work and took to their heels, and the young rider slapped his horse on the withers and broke into a canter ahead of them. As they departed, Miles saw clearly what the post was for.

If he had had another few seconds to think it out, he would probably have guessed even before he saw.

Stripped of all covering except an astonishing mantle of bright brown hair, there was a girl tied to the post, ready for the dragon's return.

II

Colin Graves tilted back his chair, crossed his legs, and tiredly ran his fingers through the curly black beard to which he was not yet used because it was so new before lighting a cigarette from the packet on the table beside the transmitter and the tape recorder.

Then he looked round at his companions and said, "Well?"

"We oughtn't to have let him go in alone," Myra Wilson said in a subdued tone. She was a round-faced girl whose glasses gave her an air of owlish silliness which she seemed rather to like.

"Hugh's been in alone," Colin said.

A little self-consciously, Hugh Baker shifted on his chair. He was sitting the wrong way round as he usually did, his big bare arms with their dusting of fair hair resting on the chair's back. He said, "True enough. But—hell, I'll be honest: if I'd known what I was in for, I wouldn't have been so eager."

Colin drew on his cigarette again and stared at the map on the wall—the inch-to-the-mile Ordnance Survey map with the curious errors which had started all the trouble. He said, "I think we're all crazy. Know that?"

"Of course we're crazy," Myra said. "Give me one of your cigarettes, will you? I've run out. Barry said he'd get me some, but he's being a hell of a long time."

"Probably run into some trouble," Hugh said. "He wasn't sure what he was looking for, remember. And the records may be incomplete."

Colin tossed the packet across to Myra before getting up and studying the curious map more closely. At last he took a red pencil from his pocket and drew a neat curve on the map—a curve beginning and ending at the junction of grid lines and not following them. He added a cross and a series of dots.

"He left the car about there," he said. He tapped the cross he had drawn. "So the road is good nearly as far as we estimated. According to what you found out, Hugh, the ogre's cave was on the edge of the area, right?"

Hugh nodded. Ripples went through his full Viking beard; he had two years' start on the others. He said, "The far edge from where I went in. I'm sure that was what was meant."

"What do you make of those tyre-tracks?" Myra said. "We weren't expecting that."

"I suppose people must have stumbled into the area occasionally," Colin frowned. "But not out again, presumably. Strangers who weren't going anywhere in particular—looking for a picnic site, or something like that."

"There can't have been many of them," Myra said. "This is not tourist country, even nowadays."

"We get in," Hugh said. "Without trouble."

"Ye-es." Colin tipped ash into the wastebasket alongside the radio table. "I'd give a lot to know the exact mechanics of this exclusion-principle. That's a fair amount of territory, you know. And there are quite a number of people in it. You'd think there'd be *some* contact."

"We've been over all this before," Myra said, thrusting back her hair from her forehead. "And we've got exactly nowhere. We need more data. And more people."

"That's what I meant when I said we were crazy," Colin answered.

"Seven of us tackling a thing like this. This is a vast—fantastic!—enigma which needs better resources than a bunch of amateurs can bring to bear."

"We know," Hugh said. "Save your breath."

There was the noise of an engine outside; Colin turned to the window. "That's the jeep," he said. "One gets you six he's forgotten something even after all this time. He's waving—go down and give him a hand with the stuff. I'd better stay here and listen in case Miles comes through."

The others nodded and went out, leaving the door—as usual—ajar. It couldn't be shut; it was warped with long exposure to the wind and rain. Nobody had lived in this creaking, musty cottage in living memory, but it was quite habitable now that the roof had been patched and the weak spots in the floors made good with nailed-down boards. And it was the only possible choice for the job in hand.

At least it was better than being under canvas—marginally better. Colin thought of four miserable weeks he had spent watching Loch Ruin for its hypothetical monster, two years ago, and of the three weeks when it had rained during that time.

On the other hand, it was considerably more comfortable not to find what you were looking for. If they had actually tracked down the Loch Ruin monster, which was supposed to have sunk several boats with a dozen people in, they could have done nothing with it.

Here they'd found much more than they'd bargained for.

"Tiger by the tail," Colin said under his breath, and turned the pages of his shorthand book to check that the impersonal words were really there: the statements Miles had made about the dragon.

Now Barry and the others were coming up from the hard-standing where the jeep was usually parked, laden with such necessities as canned foods, paraffin and cigarettes. They were talking excitedly as they entered.

"Barry thinks he found it," Hugh said as he shouldered back the door protesting on its rusty hinges. "Go on, Barry—tell him about it."

"I hope it's reassuring," Colin said dryly. He flicked ash off his cigarette. "Me, I'm getting a mite tense."

Barry unloaded his armful of goods on the table and started to sort them as he talked. He was a nervous, intense, small man; he was already going bald although he was only in his mid-twenties, and his voice tended to peak occasionally in a childish falsetto when he was very excited. He was excited now.

"I went to the County Records Office," he said. "I had a long talk with the chief clerk, and I also saw the county surveyor for a short while. I know what the village is called, I think."

"Go on," Colin said, hooking his foot round the leg of his chair and swivelling it so he could sit with his back to the radio.

"I said we were staying in this cottage and were interested in knowing something about it," Barry said. "I made it clear this was just idle curiosity, of course. They were very obliging and helpful and gave me access to all the records they had—which are pretty inadequate, of course. But this cottage was built just about when I estimated it must have been, in 1836, and at that time it was in the parish of Didswater. By the way, it hasn't been occupied since 1914, apparently—later than we imagined."

Colin made a mental gloss on what Barry was saying. "Just about when *I* estimated"—that had turned out to be right. "Later than *we* imagined"—that turned out to be wrong.

He said nothing.

"Well, the parish of Didswater has vanished. It just isn't mentioned in any records they could show me later than 1845. That fits, doesn't it?"

"Well enough," Colin said. "But where does it get us?"

"What do you mean?" Barry said, instantly on edge.

"Exactly what I say. Does knowing the name of the village tell us what we're up against?"

"Will you let me finish, then?" Barry said, flushing.

"There's more to it than that, I gather," Hugh said, transferring canned foods from a case he had carried up from the jeep and stacking them in rows on a wobbly shelf in the corner.

"Sorry," Colin said. "I'm a bit worried about Miles, that's all."

"Yes, Hugh and Myra told me." Barry took the chair Hugh had been sitting on and perched on its edge facing Colin. "What *may* get us somewhere—as you're pleased to put it—is this. The lord of the manor in 1845 was a certain Lord Davinside. Here's where it starts to fit together. You know I suggested there might be some Arthurian connections here?"

"Ye - es."

Barry gave him a sharp look, but went on. "Well, it so happens that among the papers which Tennyson left when he died is a curiosity. It's called—" He paused impressively.

"The Davinside letter," Myra said into the pause. "Of course. That's fascinating, Barry, go on."

Undecided for a moment whether to be annoyed at having his revelation deflated or to be flattered at the compliment, Barry hesitated. Finally he shrugged and got to his feet.

"What's that?" Hugh said. "This letter, I mean."

"An oddity. No one's ever been able to account for it." Barry spread his hands. "It's dated 1842—which was the year Tennyson published *Morte d'Arthur* and some other Arthurian poems—and it's a piece of apparently mock-medieval invective against him and his work. Why he kept it is anyone's guess, but it's usually believed that he hung on to it as something amusing to show his friends. And let me throw you one more fact which seems to me to tie in here. 1845 was the year they planned the route of the Metropolitan and Provincial Railway, and they wanted to take it across Lord Davinside's property, and they sent down two surveyors who trespassed on his land without his permission, and he personally hunted them off with a pack of hounds."

He gestured at the map pinned to the wall. "As you can see, the railway makes a big loop around the area. The detour must have cost thousands."

Hugh and Myra nodded thoughtfully. Colin stubbed his cigarette. He said, "That's very interesting. But it still gets us nowhere."

"What do you mean?" Barry said slowly.

"I think we're behaving like idiots," Colin said. He got to his feet. "Let's face it! This isn't any longer something we can treat as a sort of undergraduates' vacation project, like the Loch Ness survey and the Loch Ruin survey. You were right, Barry—there's a hole in the map here. There's a place where time seems to have gone backward instead of forward. There's a piece of the countryside where for generations no one seems to have ventured—the roads tail away into rutted tracks, the local farmers never seem to go that way when they're out shooting, and people tell stories about legendary beasts in the villages rounda-bout. Shamefacedly.

"Right—Hugh's been in, and seen it, talked with people who still use a dialect that vanished from the rest of England centuries back. He's seen a castle, and heard about an ogre, and now today Miles has called up to report a dragon. We know enough to know that we don't know enough. If I'd had any sense I'd have advised Miles to turn back before he saw the tyre-tracks which persuaded him he had to go on. We're meddling with something unbelievably big."

"Unbelievable is the word," Barry said. "Who, *pray*, do you want me to hand this over to? Are you going to call a policeman? Or the army? They'll laugh at us. We agreed that we were going to work at this for months if necessary, piling up incontrovertible data. And we can do it—if you don't betray the confidence I placed in you when I asked you to help with it."

"Barry's right," Myra said. "This mustn't end up in the sillier newspapers as a scare story. It's too serious for that."

"Yes," Colin said. "I only wish we'd started to take it seriously before. If we had, we wouldn't have let Miles go in by himself. I wish to God he'd come back!"

III

For an eternal moment after he saw clearly what they had been doing over there at the post by the mouth of the cave, Miles felt the universe around him shudder and grind into a new alignment. He recovered from it to find himself shaking and sweating all over, with the echo of a soundless question dying in his mind.

What the hell am I doing here?

Up till this very instant, when he found himself on the limb of an isolated oak, the weight of a woodsman's axe dragging at his belt, his body crudely wrapped in garments carefully tattered to pass muster among the people he might encounter, he had been acting with a sort of bravado, not engaged in what he was doing, but merely going through the motions.

Even the sight of the dragon, which he had taken so calmly, was little more than a pin-prick of reality on his sceptically armoured mind. The facts involving him were only as real as the words in which they were presented to him. There was going to be a weighable, measurable explanation, and in the certain knowledge of its eventual arrival he did not need to worry about the evident impossibility of what was happening.

But now—!

God damn it, he thought, *those were real people down there!*

He strained his eyes after the fleeing rabble, but already the rider who led them was out of sight and only the slowest of the others was not yet gone among the trees and bushes the other side of the rocky outcrop. And, of course, the girl lashed to the pole before the cave.

Whatever peculiar corner of legend this was dragged back from, the purpose was clear. This was the ancient practice of maiden-sacrifice; that black, awkward, limping-cross shape in the sky was a dragon—and this, *here, now*, was Miles Croton.

Here. Now. He had never thought that such simple little words could hold such an oozing weight of terror.

To stay and watch and try to persuade himself that dragons were creatures of myth was unthinkable—or rather, it was thinkable, for he considered the idea, but in the same instant as it came to him he discarded it and labelled it unactable upon.

The jolt with which his heels met the ground was another jar of reality upon insulated optimism; his crude, fancy-dress buskins reported the presence of flints faithfully to the soles of his feet as he started away from the oak where he had been watching. Breaking into a mindless run he fumbled the helve of his axe up past his belt, and cast a frightened glance at the dragon before plunging through a gap in yet another skin-rasping hedgerow and coming in plain sight of the cave.

The bound girl stared and screamed. As though all his awareness had been filed to a keen point, and had etched every detail microscopically sharp in the world about him, he saw the line of her throat tauten just before he heard the sound, and would have spared precious breath to shout back at her but that he realised he would probably not be understood. And to charge towards her, axe raised, was an act terrifying enough without adding an incomprehensible yell.

The space separating him from her seemed to grow as he covered it on pounding feet, yet at last it was done and she was through with screaming, her face pale and vacant, her eyes fixed on him like a rabbit's on a snake. She was bound with crude thongs of hide passed round her neck, her waist and her ankles; perhaps—had not the dragon threatened to stoop early to its cave—her captors would have been merciful enough to draw the uppermost one tight before leaving her there, so strangling her, as the executioner was said to have piled wet wood on the fire of a repentant heretic burning at the stake, so that the smoke choked before the fire roasted.

He gave another wild glance upwards to see the dragon looming enormous now, and swung the axe against the pole—once, twice, three times, and the thongs were severed and white chips showed on the dark wood.

The girl cried out and would have fallen, but he changed hands on the axe-helve and caught her wrist, praying that she would not faint; she found her balance, and enough presence of mind to realise that she had been set free, not attacked again. The only thing it occurred to him to do was to return the way he had come. He pointed with the axe, shouting something fierce and empty, and dragged her forward.

Halfway across the open field they were suddenly shadowed, and a vast hissing noise like the escape of steam from a boiler deafened them for a second. That past, there was a heavy thud which shook the ground; the girl cried out again, and Miles stumbled turning to look behind him and thinking that his axe against that dragon was a straw in his hands.

But the beast had settled at the mouth of its cave, and the carcass of a scrawny ox engaged its attention; it wasted only a second or two on snuffing at the wooden post and the ground about it before sinking its fanged jaws into the animal and beginning to feed. Incontinently Miles dragged the girl forward again, thrusting her through the hedge whose thorns marked her pale gold skin with red claw-marks.

At the foot of the oak which he had jumped down from only minutes before he paused to take his bearings, and she collapsed to the ground, panting and weeping. He spoke briefly to her in the laboriously-learned accent he had practised with Barry and Colin in what now seemed to be another world than this, but she looked at him vacantly and went on gulping air. Clearly he had not learned his lesson well.

He let his eyes linger on her for another moment—she was beautiful he saw now, from her wave of waist-long hair and large, soft-lipped mouth to her small feet, mud-stained and cut about one heel by a flint, so that she limped. Then he stared at the enclosing, constricting thorn-hedges which limited his field of view, trying to decide which gap had brought him from the track at whose beginning he had left his car.

That one, surely. Yes—but the brook must lie in a hollow, and beyond that gap the ground could be seen to rise. A hint of new fear began in his mind.

But before it could take form, the girl had raised her head and spoken piteously to him, fighting the words past her lips as her need to gasp for air allowed her.

"Where is this place?" she forced out. "Who are you? What happened to me?"

Hardly believing his ears, he stared at her. Then he saw that her skin was clean except where mud had splashed up on her legs, and that it was all of a pale golden shade, all of it, and probably she was about twenty years old and it occurred to him that she was almost as tall as himself, and her flat, muscular belly and her firm small bosom were— the word was *modern*. Once again things that had been mere wordplay turned in his mind and became real and relevant.

But before he could speak, she had raised a shaking arm and pointed at his chest. She said, "A—a camera, for God's sake! What are you *playing* at?"

He looked down in astonishment. Of all things to have forgotten! It must have been catching sight of the tyre-tracks which drove the camera out of his mind, and since then, even when it was bumping against his chest while he ran, he must subconsciously have ignored the information on the grounds that his whole get-up was unfamiliar to him.

A camera; his matted hair and beard, his axe, his belted smock and his tattered homespun breeches, and his rough, handmade buskins—he must be an appalling sight, Miles thought. He dropped on one knee beside her.

"You're the driver of the car that got stranded in the ford," he said.

"Am I?" she said. "Oh, my God! Am I? I don't know who I am or what's happened to me, except that I'm sure I must be out of my mind." She put both hands to her temples and swayed where she sat.

"No, you aren't crazy," Miles said in an urgent voice. "I can't explain it all now, but I can get you out of here—I have a car about a mile up the road. Here!" He began to pull off his smock. "Put this on! You'd better have these boots, too."

She pressed her hands over her eyes and seemed to calm herself by sheer will-power. "No, I can walk," she said. "I'm used to going without shoes. I just cut my heel on a sharp stone, that's all. It's nothing much."

★

She took the smock curiously and pulled it over her head, dragging her hair in huge handfuls through the gaping neck-opening and pouring it down her back like a gleaming brown river. Then she tried to get to her feet. He steadied her with one hand, the other still clinging to the axe.

"Who are you?" she said.

"I'm Miles Croton. Are you sure you can walk all right?"

She nodded. "Which way?"

"Over there," Miles said, pointing, and refraining from adding that he was not absolutely sure. "That gap in the hedge."

She set her teeth and started to walk, favouring her cut heel. Alert for any sound of danger, he followed her at a few paces' distance, axe held in both hands. Everything was quiet again. A bird was chirping somewhere, acid-sweet in the hedgerow. He had hoped to catch the sound of the brook, which would lead them back to the ford and a definite landmark, but he could not hear it. Damn the ill-luck which had compelled him to rush away from the track without a chance to mark his trail properly! And damn his city-bred carelessness, too!

He thought of stories about greenhorns in the African bush, who contrived to lose themselves within a hundred yards of camp. He was beginning to understand how this was possible.

Still, that was certainly the oak he had climbed. If the worst came to the worst, they could try every gap in the hedges surrounding this field, and one of them would give on to the track. And he could follow his own footprints back to the ford, perhaps.

As the girl was coming up to the gap in the hedge, he called on her to wait and let him go ahead. He had the intention of merely glancing through to check that the track lay beyond. Instead, the instant after he had peered past the thick-growing thorns, he darted back, his heart pounding.

"Quick!" he said, and caught her arm. "Over to the tree!"

"What—?"

"Quick!" he whispered, and dragged her after him. "Get behind it—no, better, get up in it and hide among the branches if we can!"

Again she tried to ask why, but she read his face this time and changed her mind. One-handed he hoisted her up on the lowermost branch which he had used before, and followed her with the agility of panic. Then he swung round and stared at the gap in the hedge, so innocent-seeming, and so deadly.

"What did you see?" she whispered—it seemed natural to whisper, though they were alone in the middle of the field.

"Get in close to the trunk," Miles answered in the same low tone. "Maybe he'll miss us."

"One of the madmen who tied me up?" she suggested, obeying with a shiver of fear.

"Worse," Miles said. "I heard there was an ogre in this area some-where—I damned nearly walked into him. My—God!"

He thrust her around the bole of the tree, feet insecure on unlevel branches, and tried to press close to the bark himself. Fascinated, he stared at the apparition coming into the field.

He heard the girl stifle a cry; glancing aside, he saw she was biting the back of her hand to control herself. He gave her an unconvincing smile of encouragement.

Yes, that must be the ogre Hugh had heard rumours about on his venture into the other side of the area. Like a tree! Eight feet high—nine perhaps, naked with a horrible animal nakedness, its... *his* skin showing dirty pinkish-grey through a matting of hair like that on the back of a wild pig except on the head, the belly and the legs, which were thickly covered with a darker, closer-set growth. His wide nostrils snorted over a loose mouth full of ugly yellow pegs of teeth; on one shoulder rested a club made of a whole branch broken from a young tree, gnawed short enough to wield at the point where it grew thin. If a gorilla weighed five hundred and fifty pounds at full growth, Miles thought, this thing-man must weigh eight hundred. You expected the earth to quake at every footfall.

He thought of the gun he had left in the car. It was no use to bring a gun, they had decided. Beyond a certain point in this area, a car's engine ceased to fire, a camera ceased to take pictures, radio communication failed—and so, they had worked out, a gun would probably refuse to fire. They had settled on the axe as the best compromise; a sword required skill.

Then, though, it was an intellectual game, word-chopping. Now...

The ogre paused. He snuffed the air. His monstrous head turned towards the tree. After a moment, he started to walk forward.

Wild thoughts chased through Miles's mind; it wasn't true, he would have to wield the axe one-handed so as to keep his grip on his precarious perch, it was too heavy to swing with one hand, anyway could he get enough force behind the blow to kill and what would he be killing—a man, or a beast? Out there, somewhere, behind the cunningly plotted screen of hedge and copse and hill, was a world without ogres or dragons with tidy civilised towns and the rule of scientific law. If thinking could have taken him back, he would have gone in that moment.

Ponderous, monstrous, intensely horrible, the ogre tramped forward on vast splay feet, the dull animal eyes under the receding brow sorting out Miles from the sparse-leaved tree-branches and assessing him as prey.

Miles snatched his gaze away from the ogre for one instant, to glance at the girl pressed close to the tree-trunk, her face milk-white with shock and disbelief. He had nothing to guide him in what he should do. This kind of thing should have happened to Hugh Baker, he thought—not to Miles Croton. Hugh, with his powerful build and quick, aggressive responses would even revel in such a challenge as this. But for himself, he was city-bred, living in his brain rather than his body. This was nightmare to him.

But *something* had to be done. Leisurely, the ogre was approaching. He sought for a foothold secure enough to give him room for the axe to swing, raised it, kept it poised where he could bring it crashing down. Sweat crawled into his aching eyes.

The movement of lifting the axe had not gone unnoticed. The ogre—though hardly seeming intelligent on a human scale—had some cunning of his own, and walked a little sideways, staring up from out of axe-sweep range. He caressed the helve of his tree-branch club, muttering a crooning chant of anticipation that raised the hairs prickling on the back of Miles's neck.

Then, though, impatience got the better of him. Instead of trying perhaps to go around the tree, or leaping up to snatch at the end of the branch on which Miles was balancing himself, in which case his tremendous weight would have bowed it and even perhaps torn it away from the trunk, he started forward with his club still on his shoulder, one hand lifted to clutch Miles's feet.

The girl screamed. Possibly the ogre had not noticed that there were two people in the tree; at any rate, his attention was distracted for one precious moment. Miles swung the axe.

His aim was bad. Instead of the keen-edged blade meeting the upraised arm, it overshot, and only the wooden helve made contact. Still, he had put all his force into the downward drive, and the ogre yelped with pain, leaping back and putting his hurt wrist to his slobber-lipped mouth. Miles lost his balance with the wild-swinging weight of the axe; he thought for a heart-stopping second that he was going to fall to the ground, but flailing his arms brought him back to stability, the axe-head serving as a prop against the wide, flat upper surface of the branch on which he stood.

The ogre's dismay gave way almost at once to savage rage. He gave a hoot of ear-splitting violence; dropping his hurt arm to his side, he raised his club in the other and strode forward to break Miles's legs with it. That was his clear intention, at least. The first blow Miles dodged, and then the second, but only at the cost of losing his footing and landing astraddle of the branch with painful suddenness. The jar blinded him with tears, beyond which the stinking, shrieking shape of his adversary was only a wavery outline.

He cried out with alarm and swung the axe randomly, and at the limit of its sweep there was a sudden soft resistance, a biting-in sensation, a howl of mortal agony. The helve was torn from his grip and he tumbled forward to the ground.

Again the girl cried out. Miles dashed the tears from his eyes and rose to an unskilful parody of a wrestling crouch, not knowing whether he was going to die but expecting to with a remote part of his mind.

Slowly his vision cleared. A few paces away on the soft spring grass the ogre was lying in a puddle of spreading gore; the axe, smeared with blood from blade to helve-tip, was beside him. Whimpering, his expression as pathetic as that of any animal in pain, the ogre was trying to staunch the river of blood pouring from a great gash which started at his shoulder and bit deep into the swelling muscles of his chest.

As Miles got slowly to his feet, the ogre groaned. With one hand—the hand on the side opposite the wound—he picked up the other, staring at it stupidly as though it did not belong to him any more.

Clearly the lucky stroke had severed the shoulder muscles so badly that that arm hung useless.

Sick, Miles knew what he had to do. He moved cautiously to seize the axe. Trying not to notice that his hands were slippery with the blood all over them, he raised it and walked forward.

It was curiously like chopping at half-rotted wood.

Eyes wide, moving unsteadily, the girl came down to stand beside him and look at the corpse.

"What—was it?" she said. "Some sort of—ape? Escaped from somewhere?"

Miles shook his head. Turning aside, he looked for a tussock of clean grass and wiped his hands on it as best he could, and then tore up clumps from further afield to wipe the axe.

He said, "No. It was an ogre. Not escaped, but—hell, I can't explain just one thing about what goes on. I'd have to explain everything."

The girl said nothing for a moment. Then she went on in a subdued tone. "I thought it was going to—but it didn't. How did you manage to keep your head? Or are you used to this kind of thing?"

There was a sharp note of false sarcasm on the last words; Miles looked up at her, and could read the struggle going on between hysteria and calmness, as it showed on her face.

"Let's move," he said abruptly, rising and taking her hand. "Let's get to hell away from here."

Like scuttering rabbits making for safety in their burrows, they fled across the field to a gap in the enclosing hedge. This time some subconscious clue must have guided him, Miles thought, for when he clambered through between the grasping thorns he found he had arrived where he had hoped—on the track which he had followed from the outside world.

Determinedly they stumbled along, the girl favouring her cut heel and picking soft places to tread, he warily glancing about him and ready at any moment to unshoulder the axe which had now saved their lives. It seemed incredibly peaceful here—sunshine, birdsong, hesitant spring foliage and even flowers marking their way.

Yet behind any hedge, any tree, death might lurk. Or something worse.

At last he heard the dim splashing of water. The ford must lie just ahead. He caught his companion's attention and gave her a skull-like grin; it felt skull-like.

"We're coming to the place where your car got stuck," he said. "It isn't far now."

"Thank God," the girl said.

They hurried their pace without noticing. It was the keen anticipation of coming in sight of the ford and the car which was their undoing, Miles knew afterwards. He allowed his alertness to diminish. When the ambushers leapt on them from an overhanging tree, a few yards before they rounded the last bend in the road before seeing the ford, he had no chance to do anything but utter a muffled cry.

Then a brawny arm was around his throat and he was fainting.

IV

Day-long, the tension in the cottage mounted. They waited at the radio, staring at it sometimes as if they would will it to crackle to life with a call from Miles. They smoked unceasingly till their throats were harsh and their mouths sour. A dozen times they called Isaac and Enid at the other base, on the far side of the frightening blank area, knowing that the act was ridiculous—Miles had had no intention of trying to make his way right across, but only to venture a mile or two inside and then return to his car.

Later on in the afternoon, Myra got a scratch meal together and passed round mugs of strong instant coffee, sickly-thick with condensed milk and much sugar. The distraction was welcome. It was at least a quarter-hour before Hugh stirred and said what had already been said twenty times since the morning in the same weary tone of voice by all of them.

"What in hell can have *happened* to him?"

Colin lit another cigarette; after the first puff he rubbed it out on the tiled floor. He said, "The dragon could have eaten him."

Myra paused in measuring out another cup of coffee and stared at him. "Colin! You're not serious!"

"Why the hell not?" Colin said angrily, rising to his feet. "God alone knows what goes on inside that area. If a dragon can be real enough to be visible, it can be real enough to eat somebody. Or the ogre which Hugh heard about could have beaten his head in for him. Or he could have met someone who thought he was a devil. His car could have been seen by someone—"

"Nonsense," Barry said with asperity. He was that much less perturbed than his companions. He seemed to be totally armoured against worrying about Miles as though his discovery of the morning about the possible origin of this phenomenon had constituted a complete day's work for him and he had no mental effort left over for anything else.

"Why nonsense?" Colin said. "Go on—tell us!"

Barry flushed. He said, "He left his car on a stretch of metalled road—or so you told me, anyway! That means he was well away from the village."

"Seven miles," Colin nodded. "And yet he'd just seen a dragon."

He bent forward, bringing his head close to Barry's face. "Now you figure this," he said. "Suppose that—whoever's responsible for the phenomenon—suppose he learned from our earlier intrusions into the area that someone was coming after him. Suppose he's decided to push outwards, how about that? Can you think of any reason why he shouldn't?"

"Of course I can," Barry said scornfully. "Why should he bite off more than he can chew? If there *is* in fact any person responsible."

"So it's an accident of nature now," Colin said.

"Will you two stop *wrangling*!" Myra said violently. "It's not getting us anywhere."

"Right," Colin nodded, and moved back to his chair.

Hugh shifted uneasily on his own seat. He said, "If he's not back by nightfall, we'll have to go after him, you know."

Barry swung round to look at him. "Are you crazy?" he exclaimed, his voice peaking on its inevitable crest of falsetto. "Go in there at night?"

The others looked at him. He grew aware of their stares, and froze for a moment; then moved, jerkily, like a puppet on ill-controlled strings.

"What else?" Hugh said at last. "Leave him? Abandon him?"

"I think Barry would do that," Myra said. She sounded surprised, as if the possibility was brand-new to her.

"Damn you," Barry said huskily. "That's a foul thing to say."

"Then why do you think we shouldn't go looking for Miles?" Colin said.

"I—" Barry checked himself and swallowed. Sweat stood out on his face. He started again. "I think it would be stupid to go looking over strange country after dark. Either we wait till morning, or we'd better go right away."

"We go right away, then," Colin said, getting up.

"Agreed," Hugh said, copying him. "We'll leave Myra here by the radio, in case. Colin, we'd better both go—and Barry drive. We might need a getaway man."

Barry didn't move. His face was pale. He said, "I think it would be better—"

"Not to go," Hugh cut in sarcastically. "So do I. But so long as Miles might be in danger, we're going, understood? You got us into this, remember?"

"Now look here!" Barry flared.

Myra cut him short. She said, "It's getting late. Don't waste time arguing!" Shouldering past Barry to get to the radio, she added, "I'll tell Isaac what we're doing right away."

"Come on," Hugh said to Barry, jerking his head at the door. After a moment, trembling a little, Barry stood up and went out in company with him.

Waiting while Myra got through on the radio and told Isaac, Colin watched the jeep from the window. There seemed to be some sort of trouble, apparently, for after only a few moments Hugh came striding to the cottage and flung back the door.

"The damned thing won't start!" he said. "Has Barry been out of sight of any of us so he could—?"

"Stop it!" Colin said. "No, he hasn't. Calm down. If it won't start, that's because—"

"Colin!" Myra said from behind him. "Something's happened to the radio. I can't even get the carrier hum."

"Are you sure?" Colin said, turning to her.

"Absolutely. Damn it, you heard Isaac yourself only a minute ago!" She raised a pale face to him.

He fiddled quickly with the dials. It was true enough. The set was completely dead; the speaker sounded as though it had been stuffed with cottonwool.

"What's wrong?" Hugh said, looking from one to the other of them.

Colin delayed his answer for a moment, staring out of the window at the jeep. Barry boasted some mechanical knowledge; he had the bonnet open and was peering inside.

He said, "Hugh, when you tried the jeep—was it just that it wouldn't fire, or was the starter out of order too?"

"Everything. Like a flat battery," Hugh said. "Not even the ignition light worked."

"Well, there's one reason," Colin said. "We picked this cottage because it was the closest habitable place near the edge of the blank area. At a guess, it's now the closest inside the blank area. We've been found out, and he—whatever he is—has moved against us."

He looked at the ground outside. The shadows were growing long already.

"Miles! Miles, it's me, Vivien! Wake up! Oh, in heaven's name why don't you *wake up*?"

The urgent, frightened whisper came to his ear from very close, on a hiss of warm breath and underlined with a touch from a tress of soft hair which was pleasant on his cheek—so much better than the prickly coarse straw which was under him, like a yogi's bed.

He came awake then, all of a piece, the diffuse discomfort localising into a sore throat and badly bruised ribs as well as the hardness of the ground and the roughness of the straw. The air was full of a sweet-ish, heavy smell. He fumbled after it for a moment and then placed it. They must be in a cow-byre. And indeed, a moment later, he heard a champing noise from somewhere nearby, and after that a slopping, spreading sound.

He tried to sit up, and the pain from his bruised ribs made him wince. He bit back most of his grunt of complaint, but enough escaped for Vivien to move quickly sideways on her knees beside him and put her arm behind his shoulders to steady him.

"Are you all right?" she said softly.

"I—think so," Miles said. And added, inanely, "You didn't tell me your name was Vivien."

"Vivien Hill," she said.

He pulled up his knees and folded his arms around them, staring into enveloping darkness. On all sides of them were black walls, chinked with wan strips of silver where—yes, it must be moonlight leaking through. Barely enough reached them to see each other's outlines dimly in the murk. One strip was longer than the rest, and vertical. An ill-fastened door, Miles reasoned. But ill-fastened only comparatively. They would be securely enough penned, and well guarded into the bargain.

"You can't see anything," Vivien said. "I've looked out of all the holes I can reach. There's just night, and stars, and half a moon, and you can see a few black trees and a building with no lights showing, twenty yards away. And there are noises from the other side of the wall behind you."

"Cows," Miles said. "You can hear them chewing the cud." He put his hand out to touch the nearest wall, and his fingers reported the rough surface of unplaned, crudely-split planks, some of them with the bark still on. He felt further, and a thick upright post with something hanging down from it—a hide thong, or a rope worn smooth—met his inquiring hand.

"This could be the bull-stall," he said. "In which case, it's substantial." He hoped he sounded reassuringly matter-of-fact; actually, he had never lived on a farm, and knew nothing about farming practice of the twentieth century, let alone those of the quasi-archaic world they found themselves trapped in.

Beside him, Vivien stirred. She put her hands up to press her temples. In a faraway voice she said, "Very interesting. I'm in a bull-stall. It stinks and it's cold and there's nothing but horrible scratchy straw and this—this *thing* I'm wearing is a piece of rag and everybody seems to be an escaped lunatic up to and including *me!*"

Alarmed, Miles turned to her. She went on, "What I want to know is just this—quite simply this. I'm in a bull-stall—fine, wonderful! *Why* am I in a bull-stall? Why did they set on me when I came away from the car? Why did they strip me and tie me to that post? What goes on—? Oh, for the love of God will you tell me *what goes on*?"

She clutched at him with sudden wildness, and her eyes caught a gleam of light from a chink in the wall and showed large and frightened, inches from Miles's face.

All he could think of to say was what came to his mind on picturing what she must have been through. He said, "You're tough, aren't you? Anyone else would probably have broken down by this time."

"I'm going to," she said raggedly. "Any moment now."

He drew her close to him, putting his arm round her to comfort her; closeness brought with it after a few minutes some welcome warmth also, for the night was cool. He said, "I'll try and explain. It's complicated, but—well, let me start like this. Where were you going? What were you doing by yourself on the road out there?"

She passed one hand across her forehead tiredly. She said, "I—I used to come up this way sometimes, two or three years ago. With a friend of mine who lived near here. There was a place we used to go with a stream and lots of trees and you could swim and lie in the sun. I've been in towns all the winter and I wanted to get out in the country for a weekend, that was all. So I drove to the place I knew, and there were people camping there, so I went looking for somewhere where there wasn't anybody. It was late. I chose a road which looked as if it didn't lead anywhere."

"And you got stuck in the mud at the ford," Miles said.

"That's right. I hadn't passed any houses for miles, so I thought of going on, but I found the road was bad—so I spent the night in the car, and when it was getting dawn I saw somebody coming, I thought, and went to talk to him, and I couldn't understand him, and he called some other people—I don't know where from—and they tied me up and put me on a horse and took me to a horrible squalid village with more of these mad people—"

Her voice was beginning to waver towards tears. He cut her words short. "All right," he said. "Now I'll tell you how I got into this—not just me, but a bunch of us. Seven of us. The others are still outside, and tomorrow they'll come looking for us and they'll get us away."

He hoped he sounded confident; he wasn't convincing himself.

"Anyway," he hurried on, "what happened was this. We were all at university together, and some of us were involved with the Loch Ruin project—did you hear about that?"

"I—think so," she said. "You went to look for the monster that was supposed to be bigger than the one in Loch Ness."

"That's right. Not me, actually, but some of the others. Well, there was this man Barry Higlett who was involved. Nobody likes him very much, but he was very persuasive, and he had a peculiar discovery he'd made about a map of this area. He'd been out here—he's made a hobby, you see, of looking into strange rumours like the Loch Ruin monster—and he showed his data to some of us. You remember, the papers made a laughing-stock of the Loch Ruin expedition, and some people involved got disgusted, and they refused to have anything more to do with Barry. But this time it did look as if he'd got hold of something. He showed us his maps, and some old records he'd turned up, and in the end half a dozen of us couldn't resist the temptation to investigate. But because of what happened to the Loch Ruin project, we made it a strict rule that we'd lie to the papers and to anybody outside the group who got curious.

"Some of us came down here during last Christmas vac. We made some inquiries. We talked to people who'd spent all their lives in this district. And we found that there was a kind of—blank area, that's what we called it, for want of anything better. There are roads which nobody seems to have bothered to use since before the last war. Some of them, in fact, don't seem to have been used since the last century. You were driving along one of them. There are fields where local people just don't go, even though they are wild now, and form a source of weed-seeds that give them trouble with their own crops. There are woods where the local children just don't go when they're out gathering mushrooms or picking blackberries. And to cap everything else, there are errors on the Ordnance Survey map of the area. A roughly circular area of about a hundred and twenty square miles is *not* as it's shown on the map."

She was breathing with a sort of agitated haste; the sound made an uneven accompaniment to his explanation.

"We only had time to make preliminary inquiries on our first expedition," he went on. "We did decide to try and follow one of the roads which we calculated entered the blank area, but the car broke down, and we were so sick by the time we'd pushed it a mile back along the road—only to find it was running perfectly again—we gave up and postponed that part."

"My engine failed," Vivien said. "In the middle of the ford. It just went dead."

"We found out why later," Miles said, nodding forgetful of the darkness. "For some reason, inside the blank area nothing seems to have changed for—well, for centuries, going by the appearance of the country and the people. During our winter trip, we worked all round the northern fringe of the area; it wasn't till a few weeks ago that we started down here. We've rented a cottage which is only a short distance from the edge of the area, and we've got a pretty elaborate set-up—we have radio communication in my car with the cottage and with our other base, which is under canvas on the north side. That's for fixing position, of course—you need two lines to fix a position.

"Directly after we came up this time, we started venturing into the blank area. We've been taking it slowly, because of what happens. Cars' engines won't run past a certain point, as you know. Cameras stop working. I had a rifle in my car, but it probably wouldn't have worked if I'd brought it with me. Hugh—that's one of my friends, Hugh Baker—went right into the area on his own about ten days ago, and met some of the people living here. He's studied Old English, fortunately, and he'd dressed himself up like—well, like a peasant—and he managed to find out a great deal in a short time. But he said he wouldn't do it again by himself. I don't know what made me decide to copy him. I must have been crazy. Because, you see, he was told about an ogre living on the other side—and we saw an ogre, and a dragon."

He heard her teeth chatter briefly, probably more from fear than from cold. She said, "But this is—it's ridiculous!"

"Ridiculous or not, it seems to be real," Miles said soberly. "It's not just that time has stood still here, as we imagined at first—though that would be hard enough to account for. It's more that some—I don't know what to call it—some other plane of existence, perhaps, crops through here into the real world. A plane where the giants and dragons of legend are somehow given substance and actuality, and where the force of progress is turned aside by an invisible barrier, just as the local people are turned aside from using those roads or walking through those woods by some unconscious reluctance to break what has the compelling effect of habit."

"I—" she began, and broke off, her hand finding his shoulder and closing on it convulsively. "Look!" she exclaimed, and moved against him.

He saw what had attracted her attention in the same moment. Through the clinks in the rough wooden wall they could see a moving yellow flame—a torch burning. And now there were sounds outside: horses' hooves, the jingling of harness, the murmur of low voices, and finally the tramping of feet.

They rose to their feet without saying anything. The door of their prison was unbarred with a scraping of wood on wood, and thrown back, revealing four brawny men with raised clubs and another man between them, wearing a cloak that showed rich red in the fitful torchlight. Miles recognised him for the young rider who had supervised the tying of Vivien to the stake.

"Come out!" he said in the harsh, antique dialect which Miles had learned to understand from Hugh's sketchy instruction. "By the rood I adjure you to come out!"

There was nothing to do but to obey.

Barry raised his head from the engine of the jeep as the others came down towards him from the cottage.

"Very funny!" he said in a shrill voice. "Very clever! I congratulate whoever thought of the joke!"

"There's no joke," Colin said. "The radio's out, too."

"No," Barry said. His eyes switched from face to face, like a trapped animal's. "No," he said again. "It's a joke. It's gone too far."

"Everything's gone too far," Colin said. "And it isn't a joke." He wiped his face with the back of his hand.

"We'll have to go after Miles anyway. On foot, since we have to," Hugh said. "Take axes with us, perhaps. And something to make fire, and some food."

"What?" Barry said. "What?"

Myra shrugged. She looked down at her feet. "He's right," she said without enthusiasm.

Barry seemed to gather himself together. His fingers curled over into his palms. He took a pace away from the useless vehicle, coming to where he could face both Hugh and Colin.

He said, "Let me get this straight. What you're saying is that somehow the blank area has got bigger."

"Exactly," Colin grunted. "We're inside it."

"And it's true about the radio?" Barry shot at Myra.

"Go try it for yourself, damn you," she snapped.

"Well, then!" Barry said. He drew a handkerchief from his pocket and started to wipe his hands clean of the grease from his fiddling with the jeep engine. "Well, then! Let's get out of it! I'm going to! We want to stay outside it—keep the base going. You must be raving, all of you, talking about going after Miles on foot. You're—"

Colin looked significantly at Hugh, whose expression was of mingled dismay and anger. Hugh shrugged and nodded, and moved towards Barry.

Doing the same, Colin said, "Let's set you right, here and now. I'm tired of the way you're behaving, Barry. We all are. You got us into this—oh, we came with our eyes open, all right, but you didn't. You seem to have been expecting this to be another Loch Ruin episode: a quiet amusing holiday with a gimmick. It's turned out to be a deadly business with real mysteries and real dangers. We bargained for that because you were so persuasive; now things have turned out this way, we're prepared to act accordingly. We're telling you to do the same, is that understood? This isn't a game with paper and words; this isn't a tricky little hobby to employ your mind when you find yourself at a loose end. This is serious, and it's got to be treated that way."

"We've got to help Miles," Myra said. "If we still can."

"Will you stop blaming me!" Barry said. He put his handkerchief away; he had to try twice before he got it all back in the pocket. "Did I order Miles to stick his neck out? Did I?"

"This isn't a game any longer," Colin said. "Stop playing with words, I tell you! Let's get back up to the cottage and put some suitable clothes on. Hugh, get out the axes, will you? Myra, make up some packets of provisions. Matches'll probably go on working in the dead area—friction is basic. We'll take plenty of those. Come on."

He started up towards the cottage. The others followed his example, including Barry, who hesitated only a moment; then the prospect of being left to himself in the midst of impossible dangers overcame his reluctance, and he hurried after them.

At what point had play-acting shaded over into reality? The question haunted Colin's mind. What they were doing still had the outward appearance of acting; until some very recent time, it hadn't been appearance only. True, they had actual physical facts to conjure with—but they had conjured, treated them like a chess-problem or like the paper "facts" in a thriller, which hold clues to a murderer who will never be hanged.

Weird, to walk into dusk across peaceful countryside, paralleling the road which Miles had driven down, and to think of dragons; to wear fancy-dress costumes of rags and tatters and try to bludgeon the mind into accepting the knowledge that Miles had spoken of a dragon as Hugh had spoken of an ogre, as a man might speak of seeing a bus and a policeman.

Dusk was gathering. It was unbelievably peaceful—if you could think of it that way. They could not. They thought of lurking menace in the twilight.

Over on his left Barry kept snicking the bolt-action of the other rifle; they had only seven rounds for this one, although they had more for the gun which had been—perhaps still was—in Miles's car. The noise was maddening and loud in the stillness. It was getting on Colin's nerves; he was grateful when Hugh's patience wore down first and he rounded on Barry.

"For pity's sake will you stop doing that?" he growled. "If we want to advertise our arrival we can hire a brass band!"

"Lord knows why he brought it," Myra said morosely. "It probably won't work. Hell of a lot of confidence he has in his own ideas, hasn't he?"

"Shut up, Myra," Colin cut in before Barry could utter his boiling retort. "And you too, Barry—and walk quietly, Hugh; your feet are like elephants'."

There was an interval of silence. The road began to decay. Colin was just thinking that Miles's car must be somewhere at hand when he caught sight of it standing on the side of the road around the next bend.

There was no sign of struggle, fortunately, or even of the car having been interfered with, but it was completely immobilised by the same strange blanketing force which had put the jeep out of action. They could do nothing about it; they just left it where it was. With some glee

Barry exchanged his gun for the one under the car's passenger seat, and filled his pockets with spare rounds of ammunition.

"Why are you going to so much trouble?" Myra said.

"Because—" Barry began, and broke off. Hugh stepped between them with a weary sigh.

"Let's settle this once and for all," he said. He took the gun from Barry's grasp and set it to his shoulder, the muzzle raised in the general direction of the rising moon. He fired.

Nothing happened, except the click of the firing-pin going forward on its spring. He ejected that round and tried a second, with the same result. He lowered the gun, emptying it with practised movements, and put it back in the car.

Then he turned sarcastically to Barry. "May we persuade you to try an axe instead?" he said.

"Don't," Myra said. "That frightens me."

"*Shut up!*" Colin yelled. "Stop riding Barry, for Christ's own sake! See if you can spot these wheel-tracks Miles reported. Do something constructive for a change!"

With a scowl at the others, Barry obeyed, and discovered them within moments a few yards further on. Standing around the tracks they held a brief conference, and came to the only possible decision: to follow them as their unique clue to Miles's path.

They went ahead again in silence for a while. Colin broke it with a low mutter. "I wish I wasn't so much of a townee," he said. "So's Miles, come to think of it."

"Why?" Hugh said, glancing round from just ahead.

"All this." He made a vague gesture. "The thought that it's getting absolutely dark—one doesn't think in terms like that without conscious effort if you've lived in towns all your life as I have. You turn on a light. But there's no light to turn on."

"There's moonlight," Hugh said. "The moon's going up."

"Maybe I can't explain it," Colin shrugged. "It's just a sort of nightmare sensation that the non-town world is uncontrollable. A town is subject to man—a place to huddle together away from natural things."

"Natural things?" Barry had overheard the last phrase and was glancing back. "Dragons and ogres—natural?"

"I'm glad you've finally been dented by what's really going on," Colin said.

"I've had enough of this!" Barry flared.

"No, I mean it," Colin said. "Stop being so sensitive, for heaven's sake. What I mean is I'm glad you've caught on to the fact that here we've got something we can't just turn the bright clear light of scepticism on for it to shrink and shrivel into dust. We're stuck with a real danger."

"You've said that before," Barry grumbled. "How about you leading the way for a change?"

"Okay." Colin lengthened his stride.

At the ford they found the baby-car stuck in the mud, and around it many footprints which it was hard to see clearly in the gloom. Out of curiosity Myra tried a match; it lit, and gave them a welcome half-minute of bright yellow flame before it burned her fingers. That was something of a relief. They exchanged wan smiles by its light.

Beyond the ford, however, they could merely follow the overgrown track, and speculate as they went on the fate of the driver of the abandoned car. In the hope of discovering some clue to Miles's fate also they began to peer through every gap in the hedge they came to, which seemed superficially sensible, yet cost them so much walking time one way and another Colin was beginning to suspect it was a means of avoiding arriving too soon in the very heart of this perilous country, when Hugh saw something lying on the ground in an adjacent field and uttered a startled oath, pointing.

"What the hell is *that*?" concurred Colin, looking past him.

"It looks too damned much like a body for my comfort," Hugh said, and started to scramble through the hedge. Their minds alive maggotwise with half-formed suspicions and terrors, they followed him.

He outpaced them across the field with his long legs, and before they had come up to him was able to turn and say, "No, thank the lord, it's not Miles. But—what is it?"

Colin stared down at the thing. Out of the corner of his eye he saw both Myra and Barry turn away, their mouths working.

"Do you suppose that's what they mean by an ogre in these parts?" he said at last, gesturing at the hideous corpse.

"I suppose so," Hugh said. "But—God, what a brute! He must have stood eight feet tall!"

Against his reflex desire to keep his distance, Colin went down on one knee and peered closely at the gash on the monster's shoulder. There was another which had split his skull, but that one was full of blood-clots and the shape of it could not be made out. He said, "I think that's an axe-blow. Do you?"

Hugh bent down also. After a moment, he said, "You're probably right. In which case Miles must have given a damned good account of himself—if it was Miles."

"Hey, you two!" Myra's voice, sharp-edged with alarm, cut across the silence. "Get away from there! It sounds as if there's people coming—a big crowd of them!"

Hugh and Colin shot to their feet like puppets whose strings had been jerked. Myra was right; distinctly to be heard was a murmur of speech and then the neigh of a horse.

"Let's get out of sight!" Hugh said. "Over there—look, under the hedge—quickly!"

They fled in the direction in which he pointed, and a moment later were sprawled together in shadow under overhanging thorn-tipped branches. Cautiously raising their heads they saw a company of people enter the field, most on foot, but with one rider at their head. This man's horse, however, perhaps scenting the odour of death on the quiet air, threw up its head and whinnied as it entered the field, and the rider was forced after some moments to dismount and go ahead like the rest on foot.

They seemed to know about the ogre's body, for none of them went near; they headed instead towards a single oak-tree standing perhaps twenty paces further away, and there drew themselves up in half a circle. Their number was about twenty, Colin estimated. They stood silent, as though waiting.

From among them their leader stood forth, facing the oak. He raised his arms. Perhaps it was an illusion, but the stillness seemed suddenly to be redoubled in intensity.

Then he began to chant, in an eldritch voice that somehow rasped the ears. Colin saw how the twenty others grouped under the tree's branches shivered and moved perceptibly closer to one another.

"Do you hear that?" Hugh said faintly from arm's length away, huddled under the hedge. "Do you hear that, for—?"

"What is it?" Barry said sharply.

"Ssssht!" Myra hissed. "They'll hear you."

"It's—" Hugh said in a barely audible voice, and broke off. He raised one hand and pointed towards the oak-tree.

The group gathered under the tree had bowed their heads, all except the man who had raised the chant. And now there was another voice answering: a bass voice, forming words at whose meaning Colin could only snatch, grasping nothing. A voice with a curious echoing quality, as though uttered from inside the tree.

v

It must be worse for Vivien than for himself, Miles thought. He could follow at least some of the coarse dialect spiked with antique French which their captors used, but even after all the tuition he had had from Hugh he was only getting the bare gist of it.

In a sense, it was both reassuring and terrifying. As he and Vivien were ordered out of their improvised prison and escorted across the moonlit farmyard outside, to walk by torchlight down a rutted lane with the four armed men in front and behind and the rider following on, there were remarks passed in a low, awe-filled tone about someone they referred to as "he"—with a little, barely perceptible pause before and after. They had hypothesised, for want of a better explanation, that the phenomenon of the blank area might be controlled by some-body, and deliberately maintained by paranormal means. If these men spoke of a mysterious "he," that pointed to their guess being correct. So much was reassuring.

On the other hand, these were frightened men. One could almost scent the terror which they were perhaps ashamed to admit openly to one another; it could be read in their eyes as they studied their cap-tives. Even the rider, his long oval face silver-pale in the thin moonglow, looked warily upon them.

It was a long walk by the light of the torch. Miles judged that almost half an hour passed, their captors making nervous jokes between themselves and sometimes speculating on the significance of the recent events. The rider spoke little, except once or twice to chide his underlings for lack of confidence in the mysterious "he."

Miles went hand in hand with Vivien, wishing that they too could talk together, but when he ventured to speak his reward was a numbing blow on the shoulder from the man walking directly behind him, and a curt order from the rider to hold his tongue. The reason could be pieced together from what was said by the escort afterwards: they were sure that Miles must be a demon, not a man, for he had laid low the ogre, and if he were permitted to speak in his unknown (to them) tongue, he might chant an incantation and so call up spirits to set him and Vivien free.

From various clues let fall during the walk, several other things began to be clear to Miles. These people, existing in a curious half-world between legend and reality, were accustomed to miracles of a sort— they endured the depredations of the dragon, they accepted the necessity of magic and once or twice mentioned charms which they wore against it, and they had known of the ogre and its savage nature all their lives. This was ordinary; they had no standard by which to question it.

Now this universe was strangely riven. The ogre was dead, but that was not all. This woman—they meant Vivien, and eyed her fearfully—had come among them dressed in outlandish garb and speaking a tongue no one could understand. They had stripped her and searched her for witch-marks, and found them; one man spoke lasciviously of the business of the inspection. Miles glossed the words automatically. What they had taken for a witch-mark must be a vaccination scar or something of the sort.

Who it was who had had the idea of pitting this witch against their ancient enemy, the dragon, Miles could not establish, but it had clearly appealed to the people. She had been rescued—by a stranger. And in this world there were no strangers. Or until lately there had been no strangers. Miles was not the first; another man, with a fair beard and speaking with a peculiar accent had been reported on the other side of the village some time ago.

Hugh Baker, obviously. He'd spoken with several of the people here. They had treated him with awkward courtesy, as he had later told the others, but were plainly in awe of him.

The attempt to feed Vivien to the dragon had failed. The ogre was dead. In this backwater world, the common people had failed to blot out the unbelievable intruders. They had consulted with some—oracle? Wise man? The word used meant "oak-tree" in their dialect, but Miles assumed it to be an ekename for someone whom they regarded with nearly as much awe as "he" himself.

And the advice given was to bring the strangers to the castle dominating the village, where presumably "he" kept his court.

Bit by bit, deliberately and artificially, Miles was bringing himself back to the state of mind in which he had foolhardily ventured into the blank area. It was the only way he could think of to armour himself against the insidious fear of what might be going to happen to them. After all, he'd been gone quite a long time now, so the others would certainly have set out to look for him, and then of course there was a chance that someone might have known that Vivien was travelling this way... but that wasn't to be relied on. No, there was only the knowledge that he had friends who would come after him to sustain him—that, and a slender hope that he might prove, if not more powerful, then quicker-witted than the mysterious lord of this weird domain.

Gradually their goal began to take form ahead, blackness against blackness: the castle. Hugh had seen it from a distance, with the village clustered around its foot. Now the washy moonlight laid a few specks of silver on its roofs and towers, hinting at its bulk but showing no details. It seemed to crouch over the tumbledown dwellings in the village like a shapeless sphinx. Almost one could imagine that at some time in the past it had reached out a clumsy or angry paw and struck at something in the village that displeased it, for the houses were twisted with age, their walls bowing outward, their roofs sagging.

It was eerie in the village. There were no lights to be seen anywhere, yet as he and Vivien were hurried along through its single unpaved street Miles had a sense of being watched, as though every blind window in those precarious walls was an eye. The last few hundred yards of their way was up a steep, potholed slope, for the castle was set on ground somewhat higher than the level of the village, and then reared up beyond that again.

A gleam of light showed on one of the battlements as the party approached; a voice was heard shouting something, and another light— a torch held high—appeared seemingly from within the vast black wall directly in front of them. Someone called curtly for them to identify themselves, and the rider spurred his horse past the others to do so.

The torch had been brought through a little postern gate in a far bigger gate, fully twenty feet high, which formed the main entrance to the castle. Glimpses of their surroundings came to Miles as the wavering torch glow picked out highlights—the heads of iron bolts passing through the wooden gate, the uneven walls which glistened, suggesting that they were coated with creeping moisture, the faces of men who came out silently to see to the rider's horse and to scrutinise the captives.

Prodded from behind, they stepped through the postern gate into the castle yard. At once the air seemed to grow colder yet, and a smell of fungus and old damp met their nostrils. The torches now picked out strands of hanging creeper on the walls, clumps of grass tilting the paving-stones, an old, almost toothless dog lifting himself on his forepaws at the end of a rusty chain and trying to growl at the intruders.

Vivien's hand closed so tightly on his that it was almost painful; he gave her a forced smile which did not change the fixed expression of terror now distorting her pretty face. She had taken her lower lip between her teeth and bitten it so hard that a trace of red showed on her chin.

Miles shivered, and tried desperately to concentrate on remaining calm.

"Come!" the rider said, and with a gesture indicated that the man who had brought the torch out to them should lead the way.

They crossed the uneven flags of the yard in silence, except for the clinking of spurs at the heels of the man ahead of them. It was possible to glimpse his face occasionally; it was very pale and drawn, and his forehead glistened with sweat.

They reached an iron-studded door on the other side of the yard. Here the man bearing the torch knocked three times with his fist. There was a pause; then bolts screeched back in unoiled runners and the door opened.

"Enter!" said the young man, and went in.

There were candles here—many of them, in sconces and candlesticks and simply planted on ledges under the windows, which were blacked out with shaped screens of canvas on wooden frameworks. By their light, almost dazzling after the night outside, they saw that they were in a raftered hall—perhaps formerly the banqueting hall of the castle. The rafters were draped in fantastic swathes of grey cobwebs that shivered in the warm updraught from the candles. A fire burned on a hearth big enough for an ox to roast there, in an iron fire-basket; a spit and turning-jack black with soot were above the hearth.

The walls were of bare stone, hung at intervals with gaudy but faded banners; some showed coats of arms, others were mere patched-up pictures of banal events, with green for grass, blue for sky, and black stick-figures imposed thereon. The floor was bare stone also, with some tattered rugs lying in front of the fire. So still that at first glance Miles took them for statues, two girl-children ten or twelve years old stood near the hearth with pale frightened faces and big eyes; they were dressed in homespun smocks and their feet were bare.

All this was the setting. What mattered was set against it like a rasping discord against a dull half-musical drone.

The young man leading them turned as he entered, bowing his head and folding his hands meekly on his chest. He said in a choking voice, "Brother! It is done and they are here."

"Push them forward," said a voice which had such a quality of wrongness that Miles clenched his fingers into his palms. He raised his eyes, and saw the lord of this impossible domain.

In the exact middle of the hall, under a candelabrum loaded with every candle it could bear, there was a table. A round table. There were chairs set up to it, some empty, their backs and legs stippled with wormholes and their seats threadbare, others containing suits of armour, polished and propped and tied into stiff parodies of natural positions. The visors on the helmets were down; the gauntlets rested limp on the edge of the table, their leather palms torn into holes.

The middle of the table was specked with drips of wax from the candles above. A few pieces of glass and china were set out, and there were some bones and crusts of bread on dishes. Opposite the door were three chairs somewhat better kept than those dedicated to the grotesque ghosts whose armour was the only token of their presence:

one held a staring-eyed woman in a gown embroidered with gold and
silver lace, now much tarnished, whose hair was knotted untidily up
on the crown of her head and surmounted by a ridiculous coronet
from which many of the brilliants were missing; one was empty, and
across the back two words were embroidered in faded gold thread like
that on the woman's gown.

And the third—the chair which faced Miles and Vivien directly
across the table—held a creature with the body of a child of twelve, a
face in which could be seen the shadow of a resemblance to the hand-
some, pale young man who had brought Miles and Vivien here, and
above that a bloated, baby-bald cranium which rose at the back into a
sort of sagging bag of tight-stretched skin traced with pulsating veins.

The eyes in that face, half-childlike, half-ancient, fixed the intruders
like steel spikes. The horrible voice, in which childish petulance was
crossed with madness, spoke again.

"Was it difficult, Brother Kay?"

The young man swallowed hard. He shook his head and muttered
something incomprehensible.

"Good, good, good!" the child-thing shrilled, and broke for a
sickening moment into a kind of neighing laughter. "I know what
you're thinking, Brother Kay, but you're wrong, you're wrong! There's
nothing they can do for you, you churl, you varlet, you scurvy knave.
Now they're here they'll have to do what I tell them, as everyone else.
Heh!" A final squirt of wet, bubbling mirth that put a streel of drool
on the narrow pointed chin.

"Tell me your names, now!" he went on after a moment. "Who
are you and where do you come from to trouble me in my private
realm of Logres?"

In the next instant, as though lightning had struck, Miles knew
exactly what had brought about this fantastic backwater of the world,

and what he himself must do to save them. He threw his head back proudly and spoke in a voice to make the rafters ring.

"The Lady Vivien of the Hill!" he cried. "And I the knight who comes fated to take the chair at your right hand!"

"What?" the child-thing said, and began to shake.

Miles let go of Vivien's hand and strode forward, not daring to betray uncertainty by look or gesture, seeing the words on the back of the empty chair grow clear enough to read.

Siege Perilous, they read. He turned, and sat down.

A phrase formed itself in Colin's mind and kept repeating over and over: *this is the weirdest thing, this is the weirdest thing…*

The sun had crept out of sight among the clouds in the west, and the night cool had followed the appearance of the stars. Wan moonlight played on the ogre's body, lying in the grass still and harmless, and the twenty people grouped facing the solitary oak. Here under the hedge no noise, except a painful and irregular moaning from Barry, so soft that although it was alarming for there to be any sound at all Colin could not in reason be frightened of anyone overhearing it out there by the tree.

Whatever was happening, it was a slow, lengthy process. The young man who had intoned the chant at the beginning of the—ritual was the word that suggested itself—ritual, then, was putting questions, most of them too faint to be understood by the four at the edge of the field; to each question came an answer in the curious hollow booming voice which seemed to emanate from the tree itself.

Not daring to speak, the listeners exchanged questions with their eyes, and in the last of the daylight Colin thought he saw that Hugh had found some sort of clue to what was happening; at any rate he was nodding, his beard white in the moonlight, as he stared across the grass towards the tree.

At last it was over, and the young man raised his chant a second time, striking curious unfinished intervals in the eldritch melody. Turning away, he spoke brusquely to a man near him, who ran to fetch the horse standing by the place where they had all come into the field. The young man mounted, and in a straggling line everyone else followed him out of sight.

"Thank heaven for that," Myra said. Cautiously they stirred from cramped positions, got to their knees, rubbed at the damp stickiness which had permeated their clothes where they lay against the moist earth.

"Let's get out of here," Barry said in a tremulous high-pitched whisper. "Let's for God's sake get out of here!"

"Shut up," Colin said coldly. "If you think you stand a better chance on your own, try it—but don't expect us to come after you, all right?"

Barry flinched under the scorn in Colin's voice and did not answer. The sound of his teeth chattering followed. Colin disregarded it. He turned to Hugh.

"You look as though you were making some sense out of that rigmarole," he said in a low voice. "What was it? Do you know?"

"I think so," Hugh said. "I *think* so. We've got to gamble anyway—agreed?"

"What else have we got to go by?" Myra said. "If our luck gives out, that's too bad."

"If I've figured this right at all," Colin said, "luck has a different meaning hereabouts from what it usually has. Go on, Hugh—what did you make of it?"

Hugh hesitated. At last he shook his head. "It sounds crazy," he said. "We'd better try it. If it doesn't work, we're no worse off. How are you with an axe, Colin?"

"I—well, I don't know. I suppose I can use one after a fashion."

"You're going to have to. We're going to go and chop down that oak."

"We're *what*?" Colin said, and in the same moment there was a despairing cry from Barry.

"No! No, you're insane! You can't just start cutting down trees—people will hear us, they'll come and capture us, and what'll become of us then?"

"Keep your voice down if you're afraid of someone hearing you, then!" Myra snapped. "Explain, Hugh—what's the point of this? Where will it get us?"

"If Barry would stop wailing and start thinking, he'd be able to tell you," Hugh said caustically. "It was his idea in the first place that there was an Arthurian tie-up in this affair. Well, that's an oak, and some people just came to talk to it. Do you see what I'm after?"

Colin retrieved his axe, nodding. He said, "It makes a perverted kind of sense, in this context anyway. Let's go."

"No you don't!" Barry shouted, and started forward to take Hugh by the arm. The big man moved reluctantly but firmly; a second later Barry was sprawling on the ground, clutching his belly, all the wind driven out of him.

"Sorry," Hugh muttered, eyeing Colin. Colin shrugged, shouldering his axe, and began to walk towards the tree.

They paused when they came close; the bole seemed very thick and formidable, and chopping through it would certainly be a slow, long job. Hugh spat on his hands and rubbed his palms up and down his axe-helve.

"One each side," he said. "You go round the tree."

He poised his axe; swung; splinters and chips of bark flew.

The tree seemed suddenly and fantastically to *writhe*, all the way up its trunk and along its branches. Colin stopped dead in mid-stride as he made to take his place opposite Hugh. He said, his voice trembling a little, "It looks as though you guessed right."

"Well, then, hurry up!" Hugh said savagely, and launched his second blow.

Colin's arms ached; his throat was raw and dry from the gulps of air he was drawing in. He was unused to such work, and when Hugh was managing to keep a steady rhythm—slower now than when he started, but still regular—he was beginning to miss his stroke, or to aim badly, and fail to widen the gash he had cut in the wood.

It was quite dark now, and the trunk was shadowed from the moon by the top of the tree; his eyes struggled with the task of distinguishing the trunk from its background. Curiously it seemed to be moving again. He paused with the head of his axe on the ground. Peering closer, he saw...

"Watch out!" Myra shrilled, and he jumped backwards, seeing that Hugh had done the same a moment earlier.

Like a man's arms flailing, the upper branches were waving without a wind. A crack had opened in the side of the bole. Splitting noises like bones breaking rent the air. And then, faintly behind the cracks at first, but growing louder, there came high moaning sounds, with a heart-stopping quality of human agony to colour them.

They stared at the tree as it rocked on the narrowed base of its trunk, where the two axes had bitten deep into it. The split ran down, and one whole side of the tree toppled with a crunching noise.

"Help him!" Myra said, starting forward.

At first Colin did not see what she meant. Then he wiped his eyes and looked again, and saw that there was emerging from the tree—*from* the tree, sliding out from the newly exposed surface of raw wood, as a ghost might slide out between the molecules of a wall—a pale, twisted, moaning figure. A man. An old, shrunken, naked man with pipestem limbs and a little wisp of white beard clinging at his chin.

*

He stepped to the ground. If Myra had not caught him, he would have fallen. But, resting on her arm, he was able to compose himself and draw himself up with a kind of pathetic dignity, nodding first to her, then to Hugh and Colin.

He said in a wheezy voice, "I thank you, gentlemen, as my rescuers. My captivity has been a long and intolerable one, and I had long relinquished hope of standing on my feet again."

Colin pulled off the ragged coat which was his outer garment and put it around the old man's shoulders. He said, "But—who are you?"

"I, sir?" The old man gave a would-be sardonic chuckle; it changed into a racking cough, from which he had to wait to recover before he could speak further. "I am, sir," he began again, "though you'd not think it from my present estate, James Richard, seventh Baron Davinside, and very grateful to you all."

"Well, I'll be—" Colin began slowly, and swung round. "Barry! Did you hear that?"

The field was empty but for the four of them clustered at the shattered tree.

"Where's he gone?" Hugh said. "Myra! Where did he go?"

"*I* don't know," Myra said. "I didn't see him go!"

"The fool!" Colin said. "The blind, stupid fool! What can have got into him? What chance does he think he stands on his own, of getting away from here?"

"We can't go looking for him," Hugh said. "We daren't."

"Of course we daren't," Colin snapped. "Ah, but—the hell with him for the moment. We've got to find out what's going *on* here." He turned to old Lord Davinside. "You, sir!" he said. "Can you explain to us why such extraordinary things happen in this area?"

The old man coughed again, clutching his chest. He said as soon as he was over the fit, "Sir, if as I surmise you come from the world beyond where things change forward with the passage of time rather than back, your ability to use so mild a word as 'extraordinary' bespeaks much knowledge, or much confidence. I can tell you what happened, but I cannot tell you why or how it happened."

He tottered on shuffling feet through a quarter-circle, groping blindly about him. "I would be seated," he wheezed. "Then let me speak."

VI

No single act in all his life had cost Miles so much effort in sheer self-control as that short walk around the table in the ghastly hall, to take his place next to the child-thing who was its lord and master. He had only that blinding flash of inspiration to guide him, and the vague hope of help from the companions who might come looking for him to sustain his resolution.

Dangerous possibilities flitted through his mind: suppose he had guessed wrong; suppose that the words embroidered on the back of that chair—Siege Perilous—were more than the symbolic expression of a child's play-acting; suppose that the terrible imagination which had been able to create a dragon and an ogre as necessary parts of this private kingdom were able to strike him down...

Yet against that he could set a little calm, reasoned knowledge. What was there to account for the failure of mechanical devices in this backwater world, except the probability that here, by some paranormal means, disbelief and ignorance could acquire tangible force? Such things had no part in this world—but this world itself had no part of the real world outside, the greater world to which he as Miles Croton belonged.

And this, here, was in effect a child.

He lowered himself into the Siege Perilous, closing his eyes for one moment; opening them again, he saw Vivien's pale face across the table, and smiled at her. Turning, he bestowed the same smile on the child-thing.

He said, "See! I have taken my place."

The chair was only a chair. Some of the gold threads on the back had broken or frayed, and they scratched his skin if he leaned against them. That was all.

But he hated to think of what might have happened if he had guessed wrong.

A look of strained puzzlement crossed the wizened, old-young face of the child-thing. He said, "Where—have you come from, then?"

"I've travelled far and had many perilous adventures," Miles said solemnly, only too conscious of the deadliness of the game he was playing. "Riding on a steed that breathed smoke, and armed with thunder and lightning."

Beyond the child-thing, the woman in the faded gown turned her vacant blue eyes on him. A flash of comprehension showed in her face for a moment, struggled and was gone. Miles felt a stir of unutterable loathing for this place and its master.

"But you are a knight," the child-thing said. "Not an enchanter." Yet a trace of greed coloured the words.

"Not many of us are so fortunate as to be both," Miles said. "But I have been—friendly with enchanters."

The child-thing's tongue showed pink for a moment between his lips. He said, "You have had strange adventures, you say? You must tell of them. Elfrida! Yvette! Bring wine! Make a place for the lady—how said you she was called?"

The two statue-still children by the hearth moved, making little wordless noises like the chattering of squirrels, one running to the hall door and vanishing, the other making shift to tug a heavy chair away from the table so that Vivien could sit down between two of the suits of armour. She did so nervously, her eyes all the time on Miles.

"The Lady Vivien of the Hill," Miles said.

At once a suspicious look crossed the child-thing's face. He said, "The Lady Vivien? The enchantress Vivien? No, that cannot be!"

He leaned forward to stare at Vivien, and the bag-like bulge on the crown of his head pulsed disgustingly. It would be apparently so easy, Miles thought, to strike now, raising one arm behind—and yet that would surely seal their fate, for all the people of the castle and the village would avenge their lunatic master.

He said as smoothly as he could, "We'll speak of the adventures which I've seen in other lands, which certainly will entertain you well."

The hostility in the child-thing's eyes died bit by bit. He sat back, nodding. "Speak, then," he said. "In truth, it grows dull here in Logres, and you must be a great hero to have slain the ogre. Of course, ogres have been slain before, and they spawn anew like the phoenix of the fable, but that you well know, certainly."

Miles hesitated. The girl who had run from the hall came back before he could speak, and brought with her a china jug—an ordinary china ewer from an old-fashioned bedroom washstand. It was very full and extremely heavy for her spindly limbs. Miles stared at it, fascinated. It was another piece of the pattern, and his suspicions were rapidly being confirmed.

The other girl set a cracked glass in front of Vivien; the girl with the jug poured something thick and black into it. Then she did the same for Miles. Reluctantly he lifted the glass up, seeing bits of dirt and specks of dust floating on the syrupy-viscous surface of the liquid.

"My wine is good," the child-thing said slyly. "Taste it, and you'll see!"

Cautiously Miles obeyed. It was a preparation of fruit of some kind—blackberries, perhaps—and it was almost nauseatingly sweet. But he made as though much impressed, and smacked his lips.

The child-thing chuckled, changeable as the sea in his moods. He said, "We are famous for hospitality, you see! We see few strangers, but those who do come by, we treat them well."

Vivien said suddenly, "But not all your people know how to treat strangers."

Miles stared at her in alarm. The child-thing said, "What said you? Of my people?"

"Is it courtesy to have me stripped, to feed me to the dragon as would have happened but that—but that Sir Miles came to my rescue?"

With a blast of amazement so strong that it almost made him dizzy-faint, Miles realised that she must have worked out for herself the key to what was happening. But that was wonderful! It meant that he was not after all alone in his deadly word-fencing.

He said sternly, "Indeed that was a keen discourtesy!"

"An ill-chance!" the child-thing said. "For know you, the dragon has sore ravaged the land these many years, and the people in fear and trembling seek to placate it that they may keep safe their flocks and herds, but it is written—yes, it is written—" A faraway look was coming to his eyes, and he rolled his head from side to side on his scrawny neck.

Suddenly his gaze fell on the young man he had addressed as Brother Kay, standing still by the door, perhaps hoping not to be noticed again. He threw up his arm and pointed, a look of diabolical cunning coming to his face, a note of screeching delight entering his voice.

"A noble champion shall come!" he declaimed. "To rescue a fair maiden! To slay the ogre who eats the people's children! Yes! Yes! And a false kinsman of the king shall seek to foil this plan and—you, traitor brother, you, it's you!"

Kay swayed where he stood. He said in a moaning voice, "No, brother! No, I swear, it isn't so! Why should I plot against my brother?"

"You *always* plotted against me," the child-thing said with venom. "You won't do as I tell you! You tell bad things about me, you tell lies and pretend they're true, you always have done. You tried to make—"

He broke off with a sidelong glance at the vacant-eyed woman in the next chair, and gave a stifled sob. A silly tear crawled down his sunken cheek. He seemed to compose himself by force.

"You try to steal the queen's love from me," he cried. "Criminal traitor, caitiff knave! False Brother Kay, I'll have no more of it. Gird yourself—here's come a champion to do battle in the name of the queen! Clear the floor, and there shall be such combat done as men will speak of it from now on and forever till your black blood gushes at your throat."

The voice had taken on a chanting rhythm. Giving a sidelong glance, Miles saw with horror that drool was trickling over the child-thing's chin. Kay stood rock-still now. Only his eyes and lips moved.

He said, "As God's my witness, brother, it's a lie. I never did such things!"

"Elfrida!" the child-thing cried. "Take armour to him! Get armour likewise for my champion!"

The girl scuttled to obey, running to the nearest chair on which armour was placed and struggling to untie the strings that held it in a quasi-living pose. Kay still did not move.

"Get you to it!" the child-thing shrieked. "Or must I call men to set it on you by force, and roast you in it till it's *red-hot*?"

★

Savagely he leaned forward, almost falling with the great weight of his abominable head, his thin, claw-like hands clutching the sides of his chair.

He would do that, too, Miles thought. He looked at Vivien and saw that she did indeed understand what had happened here, and knew as he did that the threat was no empty one.

Something had to be done, and at once. Miles snatched up his glass from the table and banged it down. He said, "I did not come here to spill a stranger's blood! I came to—to slay the dragon that threatens the village!"

"Aye!" Vivien chimed in. Miles marvelled at the lack of nervous tremor in her voice. "And then there'll be battle to gladden the eye and heroism to be told in story—"

Aware that all was not well, she broke off. She licked her lips and shrank back in her chair.

"Oh-ho!" the child-thing said. "Oh-ho! So there we see truth, like a star in darkness. Liar. Deceiver." His voice was hideously soft, almost caressing. "Not for nothing, now I see, is your name called Vivien, sweet-tongued flatterer and cheat."

She put her hand to her mouth.

"And you, deceiving knight unworthy of the name!" the child-thing said, turning to face Miles. He put out his hand to the table, feeling for Miles's glass, and hooked his fingers around it. "To kill the dragon—you have come to kill the dragon. Fool!"

With appalling suddenness he snatched up the glass from the table and hurled its contents into Miles's face. He fell back spluttering, wiped at his eyes, and scrambled to his feet as he recovered.

"To kill a dragon!" the child-thing screamed at him. "Why, fool, knave, simpleton—that dragon is my toy, the thing I made, mine, mine, *mine*! Yvette, call to me my trusty men, and bid them treat these evil-thinkers as they well deserve."

*

The girl dashed out, shouting shrilly, and Vivien got up from her chair, her face white. Unexpectedly, the woman in the faded gown, who had been staring without comprehension at the spectacle of Miles's face stained purple with the blackberry wine, burst into wave after wave of high, mindless laughter, which started insane echoes among the rafters and brought dust sifting down from the cobwebs above to play in the light of the candles.

The child-thing bestowed a loving leer on her. He said, "Well may you laugh, but there'll be better cause for mirth soon, my heart. What shall we have done with them, hey—these evil folk who come to cheat us of our rights? Shall we spit them over the fire on yonder hearth, or tie them in a treetop for the crows to pick? Shall we bury them to their necks in dung—how say you justice shall be done to them?"

The woman stopped laughing as abruptly as she had begun, and after a moment shook her head meaninglessly. She saw a puddle of the blackberry wine on the table, put her finger in it and then applied it to her mouth.

The child-thing looked away, and once again a tear ran on his cheek.

"Well, one way or another," he said. He began to lever himself down from his chair; his legs did not reach the ground. For the first time Miles saw that he was dressed in a velvet suit, of a rich brown colour, and a lace collar spread over his shoulders. One shoulder was higher than the other. When he walked, he swayed in an irregular rhythm, limping on one leg and jerking forward as though the weight of his head was liable at any moment to outrun the support of his body.

Miles backed away from him around the table. It seemed ridiculous to have to give ground before this creature who reached—now he stood on a level—no higher than his elbows, and yet there were two good reasons why he was compelled to. For one thing, he did not know if there were any limit to the child-thing's powers; for another, there were men being called to the hall.

Vivien darted to his side; when she laid her hand on his arm, he could feel a shaking that must rack her whole body.

"Ye-esss!" the child-thing said. "You're afraid of me, aren't you? That's sensible! I'm *glad* you're afraid of me. I want everyone to be afraid of me. Everyone in Logres has to be afraid of me, and you're in Logres, and you're afraid. Oh, swee-eet! Swee-eet!"

Crooning, he rocked his head from side to side again. Once more Miles and Vivien gave ground, circling the table, and he limped after them like a sort of monstrous spider, some trick of the light creating a twelve-foot shadow behind him on the wall.

"Where are the men I called?" he cried suddenly with passion. "Elfrida! Go after Yvette, bring them here, and say I'll give them twenty lashes in the morning that made their pace so slow!"

The girl obeyed, and her voice faded in the night outside, like a banshee's wail. Once more the idiot circling of the table renewed, past the limp suits of armour in their awful poses, past the woman in the faded gown who was trying to lick the last drops from the glass whose contents the child-thing had hurled at Miles.

"What can we *do*?" Vivien said under her breath. "Oh, he looks so fragile and so—pitiful!"

Miles hesitated. From the corner of his eye he could see that the suit of armour propped in the chair he would pass next had a sword in its scabbard girded by its side. It was a desperate chance to take, to try and snatch it—who could say it had not rusted fast? But this was a time of desperation.

"Move aside!" he said harshly to Vivien, and leapt to seize the sword.

*

In the next several seconds astonishing things occurred. The hilt of the sword resisted him for a moment, then gave way; he raised it, looked at it, and saw he held not a blade, but a stump of a blade. Rust had eaten the metal through. He stared stupidly at it for what seemed an age. Vivien screamed, and the child-thing gave his high neighing laugh.

Something was going to happen. It could be felt in the air, like the oppressive prelude to a thunderstorm.

And then—a dark thing rose in the air behind the swollen head. A staff, perhaps. A stick, or a club. Poised for an instant. Swept down with all the force that more than a century of hatred could put into the blow so that it sank into the sagging bag-like excrescence where perhaps the ruler of this pseudo-Logres kept the source of his mysterious, unholy powers, bringing a flow of blood, a cry like that of a child in torment, and release.

The child-thing fell, and there behind him in a shadow, his face white with the beginning of knowledge as to what he had done, was the forgotten brother Kay. He looked at his hands, he looked at the body on the floor before him, and he began to laugh, laugh, laugh with the dreadful hysterical note of mad delirium.

"Oh, God!" Vivien said. "Oh God, look at it!" She turned and buried her face in Miles's shoulder, while a clatter of feet sounded in the yard outside. Thinking belatedly of those who would come in answer to the child-thing's call, Miles scanned the hall wildly for some weapon which would serve, saw a carving-knife on the table and snatched it up.

Yet, when the hall door was flung back and men came pouring in to find their master dead with Kay and Miles and Vivien standing by, they did not move to arrest them. They fell back against the walls and spoke in hushed voices, while still more people followed them into the hall.

*

Incredulous, Miles could not trust his eyes. He thought he saw Hugh—Colin—even Myra, there in the doorway. He made to speak. They saw him, recognised him, smiled awful tired smiles of relief to see him yet alive, but motioned that he and Vivien should remain where they were.

There was an old man hobbling between them, wearing an old cloak and with sandals too big for his narrow feet. Despite his age and his rags, he carried himself with some dignity.

Leaning on the arms of Hugh and Colin, he surveyed the scene. He saw the body of the child-thing sprawled on the floor; he saw Kay, whose laughter had given place now to frenzied weeping and who had turned where he stood and was beating at the stone walls with his fists, and the monstrous parody of an Arthurian banquet at which the child-thing had so long presided.

Trembling, he let go of Hugh's and Colin's arms and walked an unsteady pace or two forward, to the side of the body. He lowered himself bit by bit, helping to support himself by holding the back of a nearby chair, until he was on his knees. He said, "So, so, so! It was to come to this—well, let it be. Now the devil can take back his spawn. Let the father of lies bring this lie to an end—God knows, God knows, it's lasted far too long!"

He bowed his chin, with its wisp of beard, to his chest. The woman in the faded gown was staring at him, and a frown had come to her face, as though she was struggling to recapture a faint, faint memory of seeing this old man before.

There was a moment of utter silence in the hall; even Kay ceasing to weep. The old man seemed to become limp; he bent, and toppled forward, and lay still—forever still—across the body of what had been his son.

*

The people of the castle did not trouble the strangers. Someone had dredged up from somewhere the almost forgotten ritual which had to be followed when the lord of this place died, and two lords were dead, and there was much to be done in the great hall where now the only candles burning were at the head and foot of the two corpses.

It was ghastly—yet no more weird than anything that had gone before—for them to be standing before the fire with corpses for company, and empty suits of armour, while they spoke in low tones and tried to explain to each other what had happened.

"The key was Arthur, of course," Vivien said.

Miles looked at her, remembering with respect how she had found that out herself in spite of her terror. He said, "It was indeed. Colin, who was the old man?"

Briefly Colin explained how they had come to bring him here, and continued, "He said he wanted to tell us everything, to lighten the burden on his soul. In his own eyes, he was the guilty one. I think he was a little mad himself long before his son imprisoned him in the oak-tree."

All those listening shivered, as though they felt the brush of supernatural beings passing.

"He was Baron Davinside. He was an eccentric, that's certain, and perhaps even a monomaniac—he was crazy about the Arthurian legends, had sunk himself in them, had tried to recreate a medieval atmosphere on his estates. Perhaps his undoing began there. He was married once to a girl he said he loved very much—Kay's mother, who died in childbirth. That too probably helped to unstable him. For he conceived a monstrous plan to salvage the family fortunes.

"There was a woman—an heiress, the only daughter of a rich family in the next county. Her father was dead, and had settled all his fortune upon her to pass to her eldest son when she married. The reason why she was single was simple. She was completely mad."

"Then—" Vivien said faintly.

"We've seen her," Miles supplied. "The woman sitting next to— *him*." He gestured at the body on the table between the candles.

Colin nodded. His voice took on a haunted note.

"He married her, yes, and what's more fathered a child on her. *That* child. The hope of riches for Lord Davinside, if he could bring him up till he was of age to inherit the entailed fortune. Do you understand?"

"God, it's disgusting," Myra said hotly. "I think he deserved what happened to him."

"So did he, at the end," Colin reminded her. "Of course, in such a condition he hoped his son would never be able to claim and enjoy his inheritance; meantime, it was his to administer.

"But this proved to be no ordinary child. Crippled, he yet had a phenomenal intelligence, and something more—something of which the secret perhaps lay in that horrible outgrowth of brain on the crown of his head. Bit by bit, helped by his father's obsession with the days of Arthurian legend, he began to create for himself a world in which he could rule.

"His father he hated, feared and respected all at the same time. Hated, because he knew there was no real love between them; feared, because he was powerful in the family; respected because he was the source of the wisdom which he took for his own."

"That fits," Hugh muttered. "Very exactly."

Colin nodded.

"He wanted his mother to love him, too. But she didn't. She was barely aware of his—or anyone else's—existence, with her mind fogged by insanity. But it seemed to him that her love had been stolen, by his elder half-brother Kay, who had obviously no mother of his own, and who doubtless often angered him by refusing to take part in his elaborate games of Arthurian make-believe.

"At what stage the make-believe turned to that horrible reality, we'll perhaps never be sure. It was when he was some ten or twelve years old, and Kay five years older. Maybe his power, till then dormant, matured. And then, all at once, the world turned to nightmare for everyone around him. The land of legend escaped from his mind and pervaded the real world."

He glanced at Hugh, requesting with his eyes that he take up the tale.

"His father, you see," Hugh said sombrely, "had called him Arthur. As a joke, perhaps. And it occurred to him that this man who claimed to be his father wasn't, after all—but the wizard Merlin, who was entombed in an oak-tree. This suited his emotional feelings about his father. That was the first direct and terrible thing he did. His father couldn't tell us how he did it, and now he himself is dead we'll never know—but it was done. He knew an isolated oak-tree on the estate, and he imprisoned his father there, leaving him only the power to speak when properly conjured."

"I get the impression," Miles said after a pause, "that in this—this Logres of his, there was a strange mingling of childish make-believe and reality."

"Oh, yes. No doubt about that," Hugh agreed. "For instance—well, the child was fantastically intelligent in his way. He would read Malory in the original, and perhaps even the older stories which his father showed to him. He knew the proper dialects supposed to have been spoken in Arthurian days, and consequently, by some unimaginable force he possessed, he brought it about that the people who served him spoke that language and no other."

"But he himself spoke to us in the English of his own day," Miles said. "And he had the little girls bring wine to us, and they brought it in an ordinary china ewer, off a washstand. And it was a sickly blackberry syrup, not wine at all."

"Logical," Colin said. "Probably, like most children, he liked very sweet things. That was his idea of a delicious drink, and wine was delicious, so that was wine in his mind."

"But the dragon!" Vivien said. "And the ogre!"

"You can explain—or rather make guesses—about them too," Hugh said. "He knew that any proper Arthurian kingdom must have its quota of strange beasts and giants. So when the estate became his Logres, there was a dragon, and an ogre. And quite possibly there are other strange things as well. We know he had a wizard imprisoned in a tree. To him, some part of the area might have been a Vale of Avalon, and there might be a Grail somewhere."

"I suspect not," Colin put in. "The result of the apparition of the Grail was the dispersal of the company of knights; he'd have let that one go by."

"Yet he had a Siege Perilous," Miles frowned. "But of course he didn't seem to take it seriously." An idea struck him. "I see!" he went on. "When I said I'd come to kill the dragon, that was when he grew suspicious and angry. I must have seemed like one of the interfering adults he hated so much, come to take his toy away."

"He called it his toy," Vivien said. "Don't you remember?"

"So he did. So he had his kingdom, and his mother to play the part of his queen, and his fantastic power to impose his will on the country roundabout. Thank God his power was limited! Only a little of the world was shut in by him—it might have been the whole of England!"

And suddenly he realised.

"Hey-y-y!" he said. "Where's Barry? Why isn't he with you?"

The others exchanged glances. Colin spoke up and explained briefly how Barry's endurance had failed him and he had vanished while they were cutting down the tree.

"What do you suppose happened to him?" Myra said after a pause.

"God knows," Hugh answered bitterly. "But if he had the wits to keep out of harm's way till now, he'll probably still be all right in the morning, and we'll find him then."

"What are we going to do about everybody here?" Myra went on. "After all, they're our responsibility in a sense—we snatched them out of their familiar little world, and tomorrow they're going to be exposed for the first time to the twentieth century. It's going to be horrible for them!"

"Are they going to go on letting us alone as they've done?" Vivien said nervously. "I mean—we have been responsible for killing their lord and master, and perhaps some of them might hold us guilty of the old man's death as well."

"No chance of that, luckily," Colin said. "When we came to the castle Lord Davinside spoke with some of the retainers—I can't make head or tail of the relative times these people have experienced; some of them, like Arthur himself, haven't grown older in more than a century, while others have grown old and died in the ordinary way—anyway, that can be sorted out later. I was saying: he spoke with some of the retainers who recognised him, and he ordered them to accept us as his friends. We're spoken for."

"That's a relief—" Miles was starting to say, when there was a sudden commotion outside. Loud noises, coupled with shouting in high shrill voices, and the sound of running feet, came to them.

They looked at each other, and all together headed for the door.

★

Outside, across the castle yard, there were bright lights. People were milling around the entrance to the yard, and the gate was grinding back on its hinges. Familiar noises sorted themselves out of the hubbub: cars' engines revving, authoritative voices calling out in twentieth-century accents.

"Well, I'll be damned!" Hugh said explosively. "I'll bet you anything you like the swine *made* it! I'd never have thought he had the sense or the guts!"

He hesitated a second, then started at a run across the yard.

"Who? Who's he talking about?" Vivien said.

"Barry he must mean," Miles said. "Lord above, what kind of a story can he have spun to get all these people here? It sounds like a small army that's arrived!"

"I don't care who they are," Vivien said with sudden overwhelming weariness. "I just want to know if they can get me out of here, back to a nice safe comfortable world where you don't have anything worse to worry about than H-bombs—no ogres, no dragons, no wizards... God, Miles! Did you ever think before what a horrible world children actually live in?"

"Children are cruel creatures," Miles said. "They have to learn to be human, slowly and painfully. And far too many people never do learn, even when they're adults. A child born of an idiot mother, jealous of his half-brother, unloved by his father who saw him only as a source of future wealth—what else could one have expected? Oh, come on! Let's get away from it. Our part in this is over."

She smiled at him. After a moment she nodded and put her arm through his, and together they walked across the castle yard to watch the arrival of Logres in the real world.

THE ANALYSTS

I

J OEL SACKSTONE BROUGHT HIS SMALL RED CAR INTO THE GROUND-
level bay of the parking block and braked within the space outlined
in white on the waiting pallet. On the left, the wheels were sixteen and
a quarter inches from the line, both front and rear; on the right, they
were sixteen and five-eighths inches from the line. That was one of
the things Joel could do.

When he had switched off the engine, he looked up into the
artificially-lit recesses of the building. Like cells in a gigantic beehive,
the girder-framed compartments stretched twenty storeys high. Nine
out of ten of the compartments already held their cars.

For the few seconds when he was staring upwards Joel seemed
to be in a state of absolutely total repose—his expression, which was
almost always a sleepy one, slack to the point of being comatose, his
gangling limbs relaxed like a rag-doll's. That was another of the things
he could do.

Simply by looking at him, it was not possible to place him. His
large face, fresh-complexioned, with its sandy eyebrows and the thick
sandy hair cropped short above his wide forehead, suggested he might
be a countryman; so did his big-knuckled hands, except that where
one looked for the skin to be calloused it turned out to be quite white
and soft. There was more sandy hair on the backs of those hands, and
also there were freckles.

His clothes, on the contrary, indicated that he was a city-dweller
and city worker. His face and build would have brought overalls to

mind, or thornproof country tweed. Nonetheless he wore a narrow suit of conservative cut, dark, with a dark bow tie and gleaming brown shoes.

Consequently people made extraordinary wild guesses when they were asked to categorise him; someone had once said he was probably an agricultural correspondent for a television company, someone else had said—at random—he was probably a publisher. He wasn't. He was a unique specialist.

His moment of repose past, he got out of the car and handed his parking fee to the attendant in the little hutch beside the entrance. The man made change and turned to his control board, which glittered with little red lights showing empty compartments. As his hand fell on a switch, Joel spoke gently.

"No—if you do that you'll have to move seven cars. If you start with G9 you only need move four. See?"

The attendant hesitated, studying the board. A light dawned on him. He nodded and said thanks.

That was another of the things Joel could do.

It took only a couple of minutes for his loose-limbed stride to eat up the distance from the parking block to his destination—a tall bronze and glass office building that had acquired a certain air of traditional solidity alongside its newer neighbours in jade-green, magenta and raw umber. Either side of the entrance were plaques of anodised aluminium indicating the names of the firms trading there.

Although he was a regular visitor, he glanced at the plaque which read *Hamilden Partners, Architectural Consultants*, and a faint frown came to his face. It lasted all the time he was crossing the lobby, all the time he was in the lift, and right up to the moment when without having to wait he was shown into Eric Hamilden's office.

Eric Hamilden had been a bright young revolutionary in his business ten years ago. Now, past forty and getting fat, he had grown a solemn dark-brown moustache as a concession to his new status as senior partner of his own company, but to Joel—who had known him a long time—there was always something of the diffident, excitable youth about him. Today it was more marked than usual.

He started on the conventional how-nice-to-see-you's, but Joel cut him short as he dropped into an armchair facing Eric's desk.

"You've got troubles," he suggested.

Disconcerted, Eric blinked and brushed self-consciously at the bristles on his lip. "How did you guess?" he parried.

Joel waved one hand. "Guessed is all. Let me know the worst. Planning Commission? County Council?"

"Neither. A client problem."

"They're always the worst," sighed Joel. "But you never met one you couldn't handle, did you?"

"There's always a first time," said Eric, so soberly that Joel sat up and took notice.

"Go on!" he urged.

"Did you ever hear of some organisation called—ah—the Foundation for Study of Social Trends?"

"Not that I remember. Are they the clients?"

"They are indeed. In fact, you're going to meet a couple of their people this morning, and you're going to tell them where they get off."

A trace of bewilderment drawing together his sandy eyebrows, Joel objected. "I can't do that, Eric—not without knowing what's going on. *Why* are they being troublesome?"

Eric picked a cigar from his desk, leaned back, and began to peel off the cellophane and the band. He said, "Well, they first came to us about—five weeks ago, it was. They have a site, apparently, about forty or fifty miles from London, on the outskirts of a village, and they want to put a new headquarters there. I imagine, though I'm not sure, that it's not just going to be an administrative headquarters; it'll be something of a research clinic, to judge by the fitments and furnishings they require."

Joel gave a slow, satisfied nod. "*I* see. Amateur dictators again."

"Yes—but not *just* amateurs. I mean, whether it's the archaic log-cabin instinct or whatever, everybody thinks he knows how to build a house; usually all you have to do is to point out that he's forgotten to put the stairs into his plan, or explain that he wouldn't want visitors having to go through his wife's bedroom every time they washed their hands. And once you catch him on an elementary point of this sort, he's so embarrassed he leaves it to you and you get on with it.

"Well—these people aren't plain amateurs. In actual fact they're very good indeed. Instead of turning up with plans, they brought a scale model twelve feet by nine, as professional a job as I could get done here in the firm. And thanks to working with you so often, we're specialists in model-work."

"You started it," Joel corrected mildly. "But—go on. I can tell you're coming to a point."

"Well, yes. Of course, this model impressed me; in fact I thought at first glance it *was* a professional job and that they might have disagreed with some other firm and come to me with it to get a lower tender. Only it wasn't professional after all. On looking at it closely it turned out there were some flaws—minor ones, but definite flaws, which would make the job of construction unnecessarily difficult as well as blowing up the cost."

"Such as what?"

"The differences in level are the most significant; there are no less than seven different levels of floor. I thought, till I actually went out to the site to see, that whoever had prepared the model had accommodated himself to the lie of the land—which would have been right and proper and if there was a lot of muck to be shifted might even have kept costs down. Preparing the ground for the foundations averages eight to eleven per cent of the labour-budget on jobs like this, you know."

"Only the land doesn't lie that way?"

"It does not! Fitting their model on the space available, it's going to take twenty-foot piling at one place to hoist the floor up where they want it. That's another thing, by the way; they want the building aligned to within one degree, major axis running due east-west and no mistake. Anybody would think they were Japanese and went to bed by the compass."

"What's wrong with that?"

"Means the wrong elevation gets the sun. Yet there's no reason I can see for not shifting the whole thing fifteen degrees or so—which would fit the site better anyway—and levelling off the floor. Mark you, there are other things too. There's a lot of space wasted on the east wing, and there's a false shell-roof over it which is going to be the devil's own job to scaffold while building. Oh, it could be done, no denying. But it'll cost them an extra three thousand at least."

Joel grunted. "If you can say all this yourself, why bother me?"

"They're absolutely immovable. They say flatly—either build it our way, or let us go somewhere else." Eric looked unhappy. "You know how I feel about turning in a job that's not as good as I can possibly make it—maybe it's not good business-sense, but it's the way I work."

Joel hauled himself to his feet. "Where's this model?" he demanded. "Let me see for myself."

"In the boardroom. We've got a couple of minutes before the clients get here, and I'd really like your views."

The model was superb, right down to the colour-scheme of the walls and furnishings. The roof lifted off first, then the upper floor from half of its roughly cross-shaped layout. Joel nodded his experienced approval of its quality.

"If you could knock up models like this for me to work on, Eric," he said banteringly, "my job would be half as difficult. Damn it, they've even got a couple of pictures on the walls no bigger than postage-stamps."

"I noticed those," Eric agreed. "But here's the site-plan, do you see? Notice how the rise of the ground at present goes directly contrary to the layout of the east wing."

Joel's acute power of visualisation converted the stark contour lines on the map Eric was displaying into information so real it was like actual experience. A rising bank there; a ridge there; two deep gulleys there...

"You're absolutely right," he said. He rubbed his chin with the back of his knuckles in a puzzled fashion. "Hang on—I'll just see if there *is* a purpose behind it all."

He bent to the model, narrowing his eyes, while Eric remained quite still and silent. This was the thing Joel did best of all and better than anyone else, the thing which had made him a unique specialist. He could work from plans if he had to, but a scale model like this saved him asking a hundred supplementary questions.

What he could do was get inside the model. Reach for a door-handle and find it an inch too high for comfort. Open a window and discover that it caused a draught where people would likely sit. Turn on a light and find that he shadowed what he wanted to read. Wash up at a sink and find that his elbow knocked a dish off the draining-board, or switch on a washing-machine and realise that the power-point was sited a yard too far along the wall. Count his steps between door and door and note that he had to change hands to open the second one—awkward if he were carrying anything heavy, irritating at all times.

These were the things he could put right. This was how he made his living.

II

He was inside this model now. Consciously, deliberately, he was erecting the finished building about himself. He began at the entrance because that was where experience of a building would in any case begin. Recognition of the exterior. Roughcast walls and that peculiar shell-roof on the east wing. The extraordinary lack of co-ordination between the building and the ground on which it was set, introducing a jarring note at once.

The main door... He hesitated for a second, debating whether to be let in or to go in. He glanced at Eric.

"Give me some idea of the work that will go on here," he suggested.

"Ah—I know very little about it," Eric confessed. "But I believe they analyse news-stories, deduce things from the ways they're handled, then test their theories on volunteers. Sort of social-psychological research, I gather."

Joel felt blank for a moment. Then he shrugged. All right. He could experience this as one of the volunteer subjects, and let the details go hang.

Open the door. Someone—a secretary—taking his name, asking him to wait in the curiously-shaped main hall, which was mainly light woods and textured plastic. Windows with a view of trees.

In imagination, he walked about the hall. Good. Original. Craftsmanlike. Only...

He had been there a little longer now; he knew his way about. Perhaps he was a member of the staff. Twenty newspapers making a huge bundle under his arm, he went up the flight of opentread steps at the far side of the hall and turned naturally the way they seemed to indicate.

Towards a blank wall.

Startled, he tried again. This was a thing he could experience vividly—the logical thinking behind a structure. A staircase, he felt, should imply its destination; a passage likewise, or an entrance-hall.

Yes, no doubt about it. That flight of steps logically led to a blank wall. A point worth correcting. He made a mental note of it and went on walking. Turning right at random, he went up a step and into one of the big-windowed rooms around the exterior of the upper floor. Change of level.

There were several of these rooms, interconnected. Their shape had a definite implication of direction. By that, he meant that they suggested to someone who wasn't thinking about where he was going that he should go a particular way. The reasons for this sensation were complex; partly, they were to be found in lines created by the furniture and walls, which narrowed perspective-wise towards a distant point.

Arbitrarily he made the time midday in summer, and looked at the shadows.

They also pointed in the same direction.

Eastwards.

With sudden rising dismay, he returned to the puzzling stairs which had seemed to him to lead to the wall and nowhere else. That too was eastwards—east of the stairhead.

Accident, he thought at first. Then: *No. This is too consistent to be an accident!*

What was beyond that wall, then? He figured it out. One of the upper rooms; you could get to it through *that* door, and there was this other change of level and the logical way to turn when you had passed through was—eastwards again...

In a room with very ordinary furniture, decorated conventionally enough but with a strange subtle compulsion in it which no one would see unless he were deliberately hunting for the petty irritations and bothers which spring from minute inconvenience, Joel Sackstone figured that he was supposed (supposed? By whom?) to turn left, go up that little step, turn, go a pace forward...

His mind suddenly shrieked silently. That was the way! But that was not a way at all!

"Joel! What the—?"

Abruptly he was back in the boardroom, with Eric Hamilden clutching at his arm; he had come close to falling on his face across the model on the long table. He was sweating, and he thought his teeth were going to start chattering.

"Joel!" Eric said again.

"I'm all right," Joel said with an effort. He straightened up, and his head seemed so far from the floor he was dizzy. "I don't know—what happened. Bit faint for a moment, I suppose."

Anxious-faced, Eric urged him towards one of the chairs arranged at the end of the table. "Sit down for a moment," he said. "Have you been ill at all? You looked ghastly."

Joel was going to say something more; at that moment, though, the door opened and a pretty brown-faced girl looked in.

"Oh, you're here already, Mr. Hamilden," she said with relief. "Mr. Angelus and Miss Bailbrook just arrived. Shall I show them in?"

Eric hesitated, glancing at Joel.

"Oh, I'm all right now," Joel insisted—and he was, except that the astonishing thing the model had done to him was still making his mind reel like a dying top. Eric gave him a lingering uncertain glance before making his mind up.

"Yes, Tracy," he said to the girl. "Bring your pad and join us. And get Mr. Low as soon as he's free."

The girl nodded and disappeared.

"These are the clients?" Joel suggested, knowing the answer. Eric nodded, and he put on a grim expression.

"I look forward to meeting them," he said. "Because—make no mistake, Eric—this job they've done is for a reason. All for a reason. I don't know what the reason is, but I'm burning to find out!"

Eric was so taken aback that he still had not formulated the question on his lips before Tracy returned with the clients.

Mr. Angelus was a dark, saturnine man of forty or so, rather slim, who moved with a grace suggesting he might have been of Indian descent. He wore a light grey suit and a mauve tie, and carried a large portfolio.

Miss Bailbrook, in contrast, was extremely fair. Long hair pale as corn-silk was coiled on her nape and held by fashionable magnetic clasps of rich blue cobalt steel. Her narrow face was dominated by large eyes and a wide but thin-lipped mouth; it could not have been called pretty, but certainly it was a very interesting face because of its vivid mobility. Her expression never seemed to stay the same for more than a second or two; as she entered the room, a smile of thanks to Tracy for guiding her and her companion, a smile of greeting to Eric, a look of inquiry in respect of Joel, a look of recognition of the model on the table, a look of expectancy at Mr. Angelus.

Joel studied the two new arrivals thoughtfully as Eric saw them seated, as Tracy took a chair in the background with her notebook open, as

Christopher Low—Eric's costing expert, whom Joel had often worked with—came from his office to join the discussion, bringing a package of papers.

"We're fortunate to have Mr. Sackstone with us today," Eric was saying, and Miss Bailbrook's eyes met Joel's as he spoke. Those eyes matched the cobalt clips in her hair, exactly; they were the darkest blue Joel had ever seen.

Almost, it seemed he could hear a clash as he met her gaze, like two swords struck together. For a second there was an expression on her eternally mobile face which said to him as clear as speech, "I think you know too much. I think your sleepy appearance is camouflage. I think you understand more than you are going to admit. Don't meddle with me."

But the look vanished, and Miss Bailbrook was complacently smoothing down the black and white sheath dress she wore as if she had taken Joel's gaze simply as an admiring tribute to her very shapely figure, and Eric was continuing, "Mr. Sackstone, I may say—though he'll certainly deny it from modesty—is without equal in the world as a visualiser."

Keep 'em off balance. Deliberately Joel relaxed back into his chair. In his laziest tone of voice, he said, "I wouldn't deny it, Eric—not at all. It's merely true."

Taken aback, Eric shot a bewildered glance at him. Into the hiatus Mr. Angelus put a measured question. His voice was deep and purring, catlike.

"What is a visualiser, exactly? I'm sorry, Mr. Sackstone, but I'm not well up on architects' jargon."

"A visualiser is—" Eric began. Joel cut him short.

"You want to find out what's wrong with a projected building—or what's right with it? You send for me. You give me a model, or just the plans, but if I only have plans I want to know the colour-scheme, the furniture, the purpose, the mean temperature, the environment and all the rest. I will tell you whether the building is going to be ideal for its purpose, and if it's not, why not. You follow me?"

He addressed Mr. Angelus, but obeying some whim of his subconscious he looked directly at Miss Bailbrook.

Something was definitely amiss with Eric's plan for this discussion. He hurried on, "Yes, that's it. Mr. Sackstone can as it were visualise the actual building about him, and discover inconvenient points about its layout which can then be corrected before it's put up. I asked him to sit in on our talk today in the hope of making clear beyond doubt the things which need to—uh—which might at considerable saving be put right in the model you've prepared of your proposed building."

He glanced at Low. "You have the costings, Chris?" he suggested.

Low fanned the papers from his hand to the table. He began to talk persuasively. Joel caught occasional phrases: "This will run to twenty-seven thousand approximately, if you do such-and-such only twenty-four... strongly recommend this owing to the economy it will effect in labour charges..."

But Joel wasn't listening with attention. He left that to Mr. Angelus, who sat patiently and wearily nodding at what Low had to say, his entire air that of a man whose mind is made up and who refuses to be muddled by facts. Joel's eyes were on Miss Bailbrook. And that shifting face was speaking to him with closed lips.

You really can do this, can't you?

Joel smiled, saw that Tracy, pencil poised, saw him smile, and knew she took it for granted that he had been badly smitten at first sight; knew also that with the inevitable automatic judgment of the brown, Tracy felt a stab of envy for all who were pale and fair.

That was bad.

How much more than what you admit have you done?

He wasn't going to respond. He folded his hands on his lap and twiddled his thumbs; then he realised that was a response in itself.

Go on—say it. You're proud of what you've found out because no one else could have done it.

All right, that was true enough. But he was also frightened by his discovery; it was astonishing how badly frightened. That direction in which he had been guided—*wasn't* a direction at all! It was between directions, and this was ridiculous.

Low had finished. Mr. Angelus was shaping his reply, flat denial of all he had heard, and Joel broke in.

"It's no good, Eric, you know," he said. "If there's one thing that building is not, it's a collection of amateur's mistakes."

Eric—and Christopher Low as well—looked as startled as gaffed fish. Eric recovered first. He said, "But, Joel—! The changes of level! The site! The—hell, everything!"

Sleepy-eyed, Joel shook his head. "Everything in that building is there for a purpose. *Everything.* That's a unified design job in a class by itself, ahead of anything I ever saw—"

"Joel!" Low snapped. "Have you gone crazy?"

"I'm telling you, Chris!" Joel sat up in his chair and was abruptly wide awake, sharp-voiced, taut. "There's an air of purpose about that building. It's right from ground to roof. I can't tell you what the purpose is. But it *breathes* purpose like a good machine. If they're willing to pay for it, Eric, you go ahead and build it. Whatever it's actually for, it'll be worth putting up just to find out."

Mr. Angelus beamed on Joel. "A man of superb perception!" he applauded. "I trust you no longer think we are silly amateurs, Mr. Hamilden."

Eric said something which Joel didn't hear. He was staring at Miss Bailbrook, and somewhere deep inside he was chuckling. Because he had startled her out of showing any expression except pure amazement for five whole seconds together.

III

Joel was not normally the sort of person who got pleasure from behaving in an unpredictable manner, and his buoyant sense of certainty evaporated bit by bit under the impact of the looks of hurt puzzlement which Eric gave him from time to time during the negotiations that followed. Nonetheless he preserved his air of assurance, and by lunchtime—when Eric had to break off the discussion and go to lunch with another client—he was fairly certain his friend was resigned to deferring to the expert's judgment.

Of course, Eric had never really been able to more than tolerate Joel's criticisms of his work, though he was so sure of their value that he had not undertaken a major scheme for years without consulting Joel first. And it had to be Joel, of course; this wasn't a talent in which you could train a person, but a natural gift. Moreover, Eric was well aware of the head start Joel had given him over some of his rivals, who had only recently got around to retaining him. So…

Nonetheless, Joel was not as happy as he had been when he emerged into the fine outdoors again, in company with Mr. Angelus and Miss Bailbrook.

Mr. Angelus was purely delighted with what had happened, and turned to Joel now with a broad smile, extending his hand.

"Your services have been invaluable!" he exclaimed. "The reputation of Mr. Hamilden's firm stands very high, and we were eager that he should handle our job rather than one of his competitors. But until today he was so adamant in his own view that we were beginning to despair."

"He must place great faith 'in your judgment," Miss Bailbrook murmured. "Tell me—in all honesty, Mr. Sackstone—was he right to say you were the best visualiser in the world? That you're unique?"

Joel felt uncomfortable now before her blue-steel gaze. He shrugged. "I won't claim to be unique," he said. "But I do believe I have a most unusual talent."

"I can imagine." Miss Bailbrook glanced at her companion. "Marco, should we not ask Mr. Sackstone to join us at lunch? After all, I don't think I've ever before met a unique individual."

Mr. Angelus pursed his lips. "A very good idea," he agreed. "Though before extending the invitation, Mr. Sackstone, I ought to warn you that if Letta speaks that way, you'll likely be—grilled, I think the word is. Our own line of work is a somewhat unusual one, though not as remarkable as yours."

There was nothing Joel wanted more at the moment than to learn something about these extraordinary people. For the sake of appearances he hesitated, and knew that Letta Bailbrook was not in the least deceived.

"I'd be very interested," he said at last.

He was prepared for his companions to question him first, once they had taken their places at table and made their orders. He was equally prepared to hold off until they had told him something about themselves. Accordingly, he parried patiently for some minutes, until Letta Bailbrook gave a sigh and smiled at Angelus.

"I suppose he's entitled to ask first," she agreed. "Well, Mr. Sackstone, we're with a somewhat peculiar organisation. I presume you know its name—the Foundation for Study of Social Trends. It's privately endowed; I can't tell you who by, but I can say it's a famous charitable industrialist. At present we're engaged in trying to reduce the vast mass of what is known—and half-known—about human society to a workable form. We take in individual psychology, mass psychology, politics, economics, religion, culture of all kinds from cheap popular to the most rarefied intellectualism—but we're not just compilers of scrapbooks, which we like to think is what distinguishes us from similar organisations. We're sufficiently wealthy actually to test out our theories. Or we think we are. That's why we're building our new headquarters."

"At present," Angelus chimed in, "we're operating from a suite of offices here in London, but we're forced to rely on friends in various hospitals for experimental facilities, and this is inadequate."

"Experimental facilities?" Joel raised his sandy brows.

"Oh yes." Angelus broke off as the waiter delivered their first course to them; all three were having *cannelloni*, and it came in bright-polished chrome dishes, thickly sprinkled with half-melted Parmesan. Joel was very hungry.

That was perhaps why he missed the significance—at the time—of the glance that Angelus exchanged with Letta.

Picking up his fork, he said, "Please go on."

"Ah—yes!" Angelus seemed momentarily at a loss, but soon caught the thread of his thoughts again. "We have developed—I say 'we,' but we have a staff of almost a dozen experts: psychologists, statisticians, students of political science, and so on—we have some rule-of-thumb theories which we are now testing out. A great objection to previous work like ours had been lack of control experiments, we found."

"But how can you experiment with—what do you call it?—a social trend?"

★

Letta answered with a smile. "Why, one takes a person who is as close as possible to an average, and if he is willing to forego a weekend or a week—well paid, mark you—to help us, we then expose him in miniature to various social situations. We weight everything, the circumstances, the things that are said, the various stimuli—and sometimes the results are helpful, sometimes not."

"Such as—?" Joel went on addressing her rather than Angelus. He was sure she was the dominant partner.

"One on which we are working here, now," Letta answered, "is one you yourself have been exposed to this morning."

Suddenly her face was stern. The change was shocking, for the stern look endured where most of her expressions did not. Joel searched his mind, and hazarded, "Ah—to do with Eric?"

"No... The secretary who was taking notes of our conversation."

The brief look of envy that had passed over the face of the girl Tracy came back in memory to Joel. He nodded.

"In this part of the world today," Letta pursued, "you have just passed the beginning of a phenomenon which exists elsewhere in full force. About three-quarters of one per cent of the population of Britain is coloured—not enough to make a major problem, but enough for the problem to exist. It has had—what? Fifteen to twenty years to become established, to allow attitudes to harden. But it will be another fifteen before it is truly serious. Meantime, we compared the situation here with the same one elsewhere, where it is more developed, and we draw conclusions."

"With a view to what?" Joel put down his fork and sat back with a satisfied feeling; the food was delicious. He put it down to too much talking when he saw that Letta had barely touched hers.

"With a view—" Angelus spoke, then hesitated, then resumed. "With a view to curing the sickness of human society, Mr. Sackstone."

It didn't fit. Unless... He said slowly, "Tell me, Mr. Angelus: that building of yours. Is it a kind of—of maze, like the ones they put rats in to test their intelligence? Is it all one big psychological experiment?"

Angelus looked curiously relieved for a moment—not for long, but Joel had spent the morning watching the far more mobile expressions that came and went on Letta's face, and he caught it before it vanished. "No," Angelus said. "Not exactly. But we do think it will serve to put people off balance a little. To disturb their habitual ways of thinking and make them more receptive to information."

It could work. Joel had to concede that. A building of this sort could serve as a stimulant, simply because if you didn't know it extremely well it would always be taking you by surprise. But there would have been a hundred simpler ways to achieve such an effect, and a twenty-seven thousand pound building was overdoing it, in Joel's view.

The fact remained: that design was not the work of a bumbling amateur!

Neither Letta nor Angelus had eaten more than a mouthful of their food. The waiter, disappointment plain in his face, took the chrome dishes away and brought the next course. Joel saw with surprise that whatever had kept his companion from enjoying the *cannelloni*. it hadn't been lack of appetite, for they ate their second course with relish.

He said hesitantly, "Curing the sickness of human society is a tall order, isn't it?"

"Very tall. And we have little time," Letta agreed. "We scarcely knew where to start at first. Indeed, we were afraid we would be wasting our time."

There was a movement under the table. Joel was almost sure that Angelus had kicked Letta on the ankle. And that was perhaps more puzzling than anything so far.

"We hope eventually," Angelus said with buttery smoothness, "that we shall establish such a reputation that governments will consult us on the best way to handle their problems. We are in fact compiling information specifically for use at governmental level."

"What else do you tackle?" Joel demanded.

"All forms of intolerance, anything which leads to war and destruction. At present we are concentrating on—as Letta has said—the colour question, and on the Christian paradox."

"The what?"

"The paradox that adherence to a religion can cause on the one hand the most selfless dedication to the cause of human welfare, and on the other the most ruthless savagery against one's fellow creatures."

Joel gave him a steady look. He said, "To be quite candid—well, I can't figure you out. But I like your ideas."

Letta leaned forward, cobalt-blue eyes glowing. She said, "Mr. Sackstone, it's because some people do like our ideas that we think it's worthwhile going on with them."

Joel grinned at her, sipping his wine. He said, "In a way we're in the same trade, you and I. It's rather rarely that I get a chance to tackle something as big as your new building—most of the things I do are quite simple, like studying a new design for a kitchen and saying that the housewife will have to walk fifty per cent more paces from stove to refrigerator than she has to. Oh, sometimes I get factory plans thrust at me, and I have to spend a month studying how to run a lathe, for example, or a hydraulic press, before I can think myself into the position of an employee and say whether the factory is going to produce contented working conditions. In theory, I can run just about every machine that we've ever thought up—"

He stopped short.

"Go on," Letta encouraged. "This is very interesting. We have very few chances to speak to a unique individual like you, because we deal generally in averages."

Joel said slowly, "Why did I say, 'We've ever thought' and not 'That's been thought up'?"

There was a total silence between the three of them for a long moment. Joel was conscious that they were waiting for him to go on—that they were themselves afraid to say a word in case it was the wrong word.

Wrong? Equals *dangerous*? To whom?

He said, "What direction does your building lead in?"

The silence congealed and became completely frozen. In the heart of it Angelus got unsteadily to his feet, his face pasty.

With difficulty he said, "It was—I'm sorry! The cheese with the first course. I'm allergic to it—"

Joel made to rise also. He said determinedly, "You're not going to weasel out of it that easily! I asked a question and I want an answer—"

"But it's true!" snapped Letta beside him.

And in definite proof that it was true, Angelus went more pale than ever, arched suddenly and with a look of impossible embarrassment over his plate, threw up.

IV

"Joel Sackstone," he said to himself under his breath, "you may be hell on wheels as a visualiser, but when it comes to people you're no damned good."

In pursuance of this opinion he sipped the brandy in front of him.

It was going to take him days to get over the shock he had felt. He had been so certain that he was on to something—he wasn't the kind of person who worried about the Freudian slips he might make in conversation, and it was entirely out of character for him to have placed so much emphasis on a chance choice of words—"we've thought up." *We* as distinct from whom else? No one! Who else was there?

And—well, maybe it sprang from his professional ability to put himself in someone else's place, but the terrible embarrassment Angelus had felt on vomiting in public that way had hurt Joel as acutely as though it had happened to himself. Worse, perhaps, because he'd inflicted it on someone else unthinkingly. Had it not been for his own, Joel's, insistence poor Angelus would have made his way to the decent seclusion of the toilet.

Oh, well—set it against the service they had had from him this morning.

What service?

Well, they'd said they preferred to have their work carried out by Eric Hamilden's company, rather than by any one of umpteen other firms who would have accepted their brief without question.

Why? What special distinction? Joel knew of several firms—none of whom retained him, purely as a point of interest—who would have been delighted to follow clients' instructions exactly, and who would have charged the clients handsomely for the privilege. Yet cost obviously wasn't at stake in this matter; Eric had been eager enough to reduce the expense for them.

Principle, then? What principle? What distinguished Eric Hamilden's firm from the competition? Basic honesty, perhaps; Eric was regarded as very reliable. But then, so were other firms beside his. For every company Joel could think of who might have chiselled Angelus and

Letta, he could call to mind another who would have been equally determined to stop them wasting their money.

Was it a distinction to have employed Joel's own services before anyone else—ten year ago, when Joel was still a student? It would have been flattering to think so. Nonetheless Joel was sure Letta hadn't feigned her lack of knowledge about his work. Angelus? Perhaps. But not very likely.

Which brought it down to…

The idea was bred, probably, from what Letta and Angelus had said regarding their work, plus the look of envy he had surprised on Tracy's face when she thought that he had been staring at Letta because he had fallen for her. But it was a valid point, however you looked at it. If Letta and Angelus, and their peculiar Foundation, regarded this as one of the symptoms of mankind's sickness, it might well be important to them. The more so as Angelus looked like a person of Indian descent, despite his Italianate name.

So they might have gone to Eric Hamilden as one of the few people in his field who made it a matter of virtually religious principle to employ on a basis of merit and not prejudice. Who probably leaned over the other way to avoid being suspected of prejudice. Whose personal secretary was Tracy—Tracy what? He didn't know. But he had a valid point.

He moved his glass around on the table in front of him. He'd said to Letta and Angelus that he liked their ideas. He remembered the warmth with which Letta had replied. Liking an idea, theoretically, was a long way from putting it into practice.

And Tracy what's-her-name was indisputably a pretty girl.

Joel Sackstone, age thirty, would have been an architect only he found he had his gift for putting himself in other people's places. He was retained by Eric Hamilden, mainly; he'd gone to Eric when Eric was just branching out on his own, and badly needed, in an overcrowded field, something to give him a lead over his rivals. Joel Sackstone was a lead. Joel ensured that a Hamilden development was *that* much more satisfactory as a living unit than another development—that petty awkwardness never intruded to spoil the pleasure of living. At first he hadn't been perfect; he had a long reach and a man's way of looking at things. So Eric had said to him one day, quite candidly and directly, "Joel, you're remarkable, and you're worth gold to us. But you're not perfect."

There had been a layout which was unsuitable in some rather important respect for mothers bringing up small children. It called to Joel's mind the cartoon of the harassed mother at the Ideal Home Exhibition saying to a salesman, "I want one that a child *can't* work!"

So Eric had said, "Get yourself a girl, Joel!"

Fair enough.

Well, it was Sadie, and about the most important thing he learned from Sadie was that women have a habit men can seldom stand—a determination to make the best of things. She left him after a year because of his perfectionism.

There was May. There was Janet. There was Peggy, and she was much better. Nonetheless, it didn't last. Well, it was probably intolerable living with someone whose business was figuring out better ways of doing things; even if, during the time spent figuring out the better way, you could have done it twice over.

He shrugged. He had drunk rather a lot of wine with his lunch, because neither Letta nor Angelus had more than sipped at their glasses. And now he had had a double brandy to settle his nerves after the dismay of what he had done to Angelus...

But damn it! That building of theirs—whatever specious excuse Angelus might trot out, it wasn't simply meant as a way to unsettle

people. It would have that effect, but that was incidental. The purpose
behind it was...

He moved his glass through the well-remembered series of motions
he had followed when he was imagining himself inside that building.
To him, the directions were as clear as signposts. But he could not
complete the series. At the last instant his mind rebelled. Because this
direction—the way implied by everything around him—was not a
direction at all.

Well, yes—it was. *And* it wasn't. It shared this of the characteristics
of an ordinary direction: it meant that if you went that way you'd get
somewhere. But it lacked this characteristic of a normal direction: that
you would know where you were going.

How was that *possible*?

He tried to make it clear to himself as he would have done to a stranger.
There are always clues to direction in any environment: names on the
walls of houses at street-corners, moss on the north side of trees in
a wood, the fact that the parallels of a railway line converge towards
the distance. Something very important in his line was to make sure
that a new environment was not confusing; that the new occupant of
a house was never disturbed by its layout unnecessarily, that the new
employee in a factory was able to go from entry to machine to canteen
to toilet to machine to exit as smoothly as might be.

Hence: provide clues to direction. Build in lines that suggest a way
to follow. Focus the attention on the best course.

This had sprung from time-and-motion study originally. Now it
was part of design in every field—ergonomics, human engineering.
He called himself a visualiser, because he worked in collaboration
with architects. But he was a human engineer. His job essentially was
putting himself in other people's places.

What place was that which the indicated direction (he could not think more clearly of it) led to?

He closed his eyes. Once more, with maximum concentration, he thought the movements through. And snapped his eyes open again, shaking all over.

"I want to meet the guy who designed that layout," he said to himself under his breath. "Because his mind doesn't work the way mine does!"

It was simple enough, naturally. That was a way you could follow by walking—not a difficult way, requiring artificial aids. Provided you had the right clues to go by, you might chance across it at any time. Neither forward nor back, neither up nor down, neither left nor right. Just another direction leading to…?

If somebody were to wander about that building when it was completed, in an absent-minded state, heeding the random advice of his subconscious, he would very probably walk all the way.

And vanish?

Joel stopped there. He could not imagine where the new direction led to, and wasn't going to kid himself he could. But he did know that the architect of that extraordinary building was aware of what he was doing. That must be why Angelus and Letta refused categorically to allow a detail to be altered. That was the purpose he had sensed from the model.

Like a trap? Like a baited trap?

Confused, he got up from his stool and paid for his drink. "Is there a phone I can use?" he demanded of the bartender.

There was. He waited for the called number to answer, and when it did said, "Mr. Hamilden's secretary, please."

Click. A soft voice. Joel said, "Tracy?"

"Yes—who is that?"

"Joel Sackstone here."

"Just a second, Mr. Sackstone. Mr. Hamilden is engaged with a client at the moment, I'm afraid—"

"Tracy what?" Joel broke in, scarcely hearing.

There was an interval of puzzled silence. Then—"I'm sorry, Mr. Sackstone? I didn't catch what you said."

"I said Tracy *what*? You've been working for Eric how long?"

"Uh—well, two years." Still puzzled.

"Two years. And I don't know your last name."

She was beginning to catch on. There was a giggle. It was quite a nice giggle.

"Tracy Duchin, Mr. Sackstone. Shall I spell it?"

"No thanks—I'm in no state to write letters right now. Duchin. All right, Tracy Duchin, what are you doing this evening?" As an afterthought, he added, "And my first name, which apparently you don't know, is Joel."

My job is putting myself in other people's places.

All right: here was a place to put himself in. A place as next-door in quality as the place this impossible new direction led to. A place coexisting with the world he knew well, and different from it at every turn. A place in which Tracy Duchin lived—as distinct from worked—which was so close to him that he could reach out and take her hand, and yet which was so distant he had never before noticed it.

It was a very strange evening to spend. There was the beginning, when she was uncertain why he had paid her attention at all, when she was wondering so loudly he could hear her think whether he had simply been turned down by Letta Bailbrook and thought of her on the rebound.

There was the middle, when she came to recognise that he was temporarily adrift, and decided she liked him well enough not to mind taking advantage of his drifting. During that period they went to a dance.

There was the end, when he delivered her to her home in a street which seemed to have taken a strange direction all of its own and found its way to somewhere in the Caribbean. As he got out of the car, people looked at him questioningly; they saw Tracy with him, and either their faces lit with smiles or they darkened with displeasure. This was a street new to him—new to Britain as such things commonly went. A street in the new ghetto.

A little unhappily, he opened the passenger door for Tracy and was about to say the conventional things about hoping she had enjoyed the evening, when he saw—recognised—completely failed to understand.

A tall young woman there on the pavement, walking past, who suddenly quickened her step and averted her face: milk-chocolate skin, hair like midnight, but the manner, and the movements, and the reactions, of…

Forgetful of everything, he took a giant stride sideways, blocked her path, stared disbelievingly and saw in the fraction of a second before she recovered her composure that he was right.

He said in a shaking voice, "Letta!"

V

He *knew* he was right. But she had fully adjusted now, had begun to pretend the start of recognition had never happened. She spoke to him with a sudden lazy smile, and her voice was the same, but her accent was perfect and breathed Trinidad sunshine into the night-lit London street.

"The name's wrong, big boy—but the rest is right. Mm-hm!" A trilling hum of approval, that, delivered with all the brazenness she could manage as she swept Joel's tall frame with her eyes. Two or three men idling nearby exchanged grins and moved closer to see what developed.

Suddenly helpless, Joel spun on his heel and appealed to Tracy, who stood irresolute beside the car a few paces from him. He said, "Tracy, don't you know her? In spite of the wig and—and the paint?"

Tracy's small brown face set like supercooled water into which an ice-crumb falls. She shook her head.

The woman he was *sure* was Letta gave a chuckle in which a note of triumph was almost—not quite—buried. She said. "My wig don't flip, big boy. Want I prove it?" Eyes laughing, she put her hands to her hair.

There was a long moment of silence. Ending it, Tracy said in a cold voice, "Thanks for everything, Joel." And turned, and walked with a quick clicking of high heels along the pavement towards her door.

Joel felt as though the entire world had followed the impossible direction now. He shook his head, which was spinning giddily, and did the only practical thing which occurred to him—got back into his car. Letta-who-wasn't spread her hands in an exaggerated gesture of not understanding, and the men who had moved up to watch burst out laughing. She joined in.

Joel slept very badly that night. He kept dreaming he was back in the weird model building, following the subtle implied directions and coming again and again to the point at which he woke up shaking, damp with sweat and very frightened.

Between whiles, he kept encountering Letta turned brown with black hair, Angelus turned albino, himself turned dark.

In the morning he went back to Eric's office. Eric was on the phone to a client when he arrived; he had to wait in the outer room with Tracy for a few minutes, and at first walked about uncertainly while she, apparently quite composed, attended to the sorting of Eric's mail. There had been two minutes of uneasy tension before he halted his pacing abruptly and planted his big hands on the edge of the desk before her.

"Tracy!" he said. "Do you think I went crazy or something last night?"

Dark, quizzical eyes met his. She shrugged.

"Well, I didn't!" Joel asserted hotly. "That girl we ran into—that was Letta Bailbrook, I swear it! Voice, manner, expression—everything except her colour."

"It doesn't sound possible to me," Tracy said shortly.

"Didn't you see the likeness at all?" Joel persisted.

"A likeness, yes," Tracy conceded. "But darn it, Joel—there are just so many ways you can put a person together, and you always run into people who look like other people, don't you?"

It sounded very reasonable, put like that, and for a moment Joel's certainty wavered. Before he could go on, there was a click from the intercom on Tracy's desk, and Eric was heard asking for his mail.

"Mr. Sackstone would like a word with you," Tracy murmured.

"Oh, send him in!" Eric exclaimed grimly. "I want a word with him, too."

Joel had never seen him looking quite so stern as he was this morning, though his voice was neutral as he said good morning and waved at a chair. Accordingly Joel decided he had better make his point first.

Leaning forward, he fixed Eric with his eyes. "Eric, you may not have realised this yet—but there's something peculiar about this Foundation set-up."

"Not realised!" snapped Eric. "To me the whole affair's crazy."

"You feel badly about my taking their side against you yesterday. Fair enough. But listen to this."

And he recounted his sensations as he studied the model, and his encounter with Letta Bailbrook last night.

The second part of his story had no effect on Eric at all; he only shrugged.

"It wouldn't surprise me," he said. "When I inquired about the nature of their work, they mentioned that the colour problem was part of it, and that sometimes they set up identical situations in which that was the only difference. And they said that sometimes they disguise a person and compare the reactions they get—"

"Well, I'll be damned," said Joel softly. "Now why didn't I think of that? That *would* account for it. A kind of field trial of people's attitudes. All right, forget that side of it. But their building, Eric! How about that?"

Eric was having some trouble controlling himself. In an edgy voice, he said, "Joel, I recognise your gift. Nobody appreciates it more than I do. But don't you think that because of your talents you may look for more than is actually there?"

Patiently, Joel shook his head. "Eric, I've worked with you closely enough for you to understand me better than that. Put yourself in mind of all the dwelling units we've redesigned in order to make them imply their layout better, just as an example. You're a master hand yourself at focussing the lines of a room or a hall, aren't you—bringing the occupant's attention where it ought to be?"

Eric gave a reluctant nod.

"Well, this building of Angelus's isn't any ordinary building. There are virtually no distractions anywhere. The entire layout is made to—to converge on a particular direction. But it isn't a direction you can follow!"

Sceptically, Eric brushed at his moustache, and Joel knew he had failed to convince him.

"Joel, I don't get you. There are just *so* many possible directions. Who do you think the designer was—Einstein?"

"No!"

"Then he must be a lunatic, and the whole bunch are probably lunatics. A nonexistent direction, an impossible dimension—rubbish! Joel, I warn you, if you go on about this you're going to shake my confidence in you and I'll cancel the agreement I made with Angelus yesterday. I don't like it today any better than I did then."

Joel got to his feet with a disgusted expression. He said, "All right. Wait till the damned thing's actually built, and—and I'll take you through it and *show* you."

"By then you'll have got over your excitement," Eric muttered, and bent his head to look at something on his desk.

Fuming, Joel went back to Tracy's office and paused in front of her desk. "Tracy, have you the address of this Foundation for—?"

"Study of Social Trends? Sure, just a second." She turned up a pad beside her phone, copied the address on to a scrap of paper, and handed it to him. "Are you going to go and see them?"

"This very minute," Joel confirmed.

Seeming not quite sure how to phrase her next sentence, Tracy hesitated. At length she said, "Joel, if maybe they are doing what they seem to be—"

"Yes?"

"Well—I sort of like the idea. I mean, I've got reasons to like it. Follow me? Would you let me know what you find out about them?"

Joel shrugged. "By all means," he said. "But I don't know what there's going to be to find out, more than what I've already been told."

That proved to be a pretty accurate judgment. The Foundation for Study of Social Trends occupied a block of offices on the ground floor of what had formerly been a wealthy family's home in Belgravia. Joel subconsciously expected there to be something extraordinary about the premises, in line with the building they proposed to have erected. Instead, he was faced with a rather dull-looking middle-aged female secretary, who informed him that neither Mr. Angelus nor Miss Bailbrook was available, but if he wished he could speak to Mr. Harty.

Joel did wish. An hour later, he felt he would have done better not to. For Mr. Harty—an elderly stick of a man with a rasping voice—had nothing extraordinary about him either, except a remarkable capacity for repeating himself. He was simply an administrator, probably a very good one, but at heart a book-keeper cum office manager.

Despite his pride in the way he handled his work, Joel got the distinct impression that Mr. Harty was in some way puzzled by the Foundation's activities. But he could not pin the idea down, and when he eventually left he was more confused than on arrival.

Point: the Foundation existed and operated exactly as Angelus and Letta had claimed.

Point: the organisation was a wealthy one, and plainly it was highly regarded by many distinguished people. Among the research projects of which Mr. Harty had given him details he had noticed some being conducted by famous psychologists and sociologists.

Point: their aims were admirable. To cure the sickness of society, whether manifested as intolerance, or violence, or fanaticism.

Point: other people had set out to tackle these same problems and got precisely nowhere—perhaps because they paid too little attention to the real way in which people's minds work, and too much to their own preconceptions. The Foundation was apparently determined not to make this mistake. The emphasis they placed on control experiments convinced Joel of this.

Had it not been for the far deeper conviction his experience in studying their model building had impressed on him, he would have been content to admire and wish the Foundation well. As it was...

In accordance with his promise, he called Tracy when he was through at the Foundation's office, and when she finished work he took her to dinner and told her as much as he could. As an afterthought, he included the strange affair of the impossible direction, wondering whether she would disbelieve him as completely as Eric had done earlier.

Well, she was tempted to, he could see. But she tried not to show it. Frowning, staring down at the table, she made a gallant effort to see some sense in his words.

"I understand what you mean about the layout of a place suggesting directions," she said hesitantly. "You made that very clear. But... well, if a staircase naturally leads towards a blank wall, isn't that simple carelessness?"

"If it happened once in the building, it would be. But it goes on and on happening, and always points the same way."

"Even so... I don't *see* how there could be a direction between directions, that isn't the same ordinary normal kind of direction as any other."

"Nor did I!" Joel agreed helplessly—and an idea hit him. He dropped his big hands to the table beside his plate.

"Tracy! Will you act as a witness for me?"

"Ah—and do what?"

"Look, I remember as clearly as though I were still in the middle of it exactly how that layout works. I'm beginning to sound crazy to myself. So—in spite of the fact that the idea gives me the screaming meemies—I want to see if I can rig up a kind of analogue of the original, and follow it all the way through."

"What happens then?" Tracy said sceptically. "You saw me in half, maybe?"

Joel closed his eyes, re-visualising the model building. This time he almost managed to figure out what would happen; it was as though he was getting used to the possibility. He spread his hands.

"Probably nothing will happen," he said sourly. "Probably I've just slipped a gear somewhere."

"This Foundation sounds like it's thinking in all gears," Tracy said with unexpected decision. "Okay, Joel, I'll buy it."

VI

It didn't have to be exact—only close enough to prompt his memory and jar him into reacting from subconscious impulse rather than conscious intention. So it could be done with the miscellaneous objects available in his largest room. He liked plenty of space, especially free floor area, because that increased the number of direct routes he could take from one point to another.

Tracy sat in a big sling-back armchair shoved back against the wall, her expression mildly puzzled as she watched him arrange odds and ends—sofa cushions, stacks of old newspapers, cans from the kitchen—to represent changes of floor level. He kept walking back to the door and following the kind of maze-like path he had created, shaking his head and making a scarcely noticeable alteration. As he worked, he talked.

"I'm coming to see one way in which it could be done," he said. "Look at it like this. Normally we move in three dimensions—six directions—and exist in a fourth as well."

"I read about it once," Tracy said. "Time."

"Correct. Only if you come to think of it more closely, primitive man—we'll neglect time for the moment—primitive man like a good many other animals really only exists in two dimensions: forward-back, left-right. He extends in the third, up-down, but to move in it he has to have some kind of assistance to be successful. He can jump up, but he can't stay up owing to gravity. He has to climb a tree, or a mountain, to move successfully in the third dimension. Follow me?"

"I think so."

"Okay. But man is a special case. I mean he can look at a tree and think, 'If I climb that tree I shall be high up.' How about some much simpler creature—a snail, for example? A snail can crawl across the ground, or up a wall, or up a tree. But as far as the snail's concerned, the essential difference is that it's hard going straight up. Being higher or lower doesn't signify."

"Ah—yes, all right. Are you coming to the point?"

"Any moment now." Joel made a final adjustment in one of his piles of cans, placed a foot on top and found that it would comfortably take his weight. "Suppose there's a direction we don't know about for the same reason the snail doesn't know about up and down—that we haven't got organs of perception adequate to let us select a path along it. But a genuine physical direction nonetheless. By mere chance, like a snail climbing a wall, we may stumble across it without knowing."

"You're beginning to confuse me," Tracy objected.

"I'm talking to keep my spirits up," confessed Joel. "Not really to explain. Because I'm honestly afraid I may be right."

Nervously Tracy sat forward on her chair. "What exactly is going to happen?" she asked.

"*I* don't know." Joel cast a final glance at his handiwork, nodded approval of the weird arrangement he had created, and dusted his hands together loudly. "As far as I can see, if I begin at the door I shall end up by walking straight into that wall." He pointed to his left. "I planned it this way to drive the lesson home if I'm mistaken; I'll bang my head hard enough to knock sense into it. Well, I might as well start now, I suppose. Watch carefully."

He went to the door, turned around, and revealed to Tracy that in turning he had closed his eyes. Yet he did not come hesitantly forward again; he walked as though he were actually seeing what he was presenting to himself in imagination—the interior of the Foundation building, which was so far only a model, but was already an enigma.

He moved with absolute precision. When he took a step up or down, there was something to give his feet purchase. He had planned to a fraction of an inch. He did not hesitate at all during the time—about half a minute—it took him to navigate along the imaginary path and reach its end.

Watching him, Tracy firmly repressed the desire to cry out and warn him he was about to walk into a wall. He knew; he had said he knew. And he gave the impression of utter competence in this his specialist task.

Not checking his pace, Joel reached the wall, took a long final stride, and went through.

Tracy did cry out then, though not very loudly. Partly that was because she was half-prepared for something of the sort; partly because she could not rid herself of the sneaking suspicion some kind of trickery was involved. She couldn't think of a reason for Joel tricking anyone, but it wasn't impossible.

She got to her feet and walked to where he had vanished. It was not until she had crossed the room that she found she had the knuckles of the first two fingers of her right hand clenched between her teeth to stop herself crying out again; when she looked, she found the teeth had left deep indentations in the flesh.

Beginning to shake a little, she went to the telephone at the far side of the room and picked up the receiver. She made two mistakes when she tried to dial, which was silly because she had called this number enough times in the past couple of months—for Eric—to know it perfectly. She was dreadfully afraid that no one would answer. The relief when a reply did come was so overwhelming she took twice as long as necessary to make clear the one essential point.

"I've *got* to get hold of Mr. Angelus or Miss Bailbrook—right now, this very moment!"

One pace past the point at which he was prepared to bang his head against the wall, Joel stopped walking so abruptly he rocked on his feet. His eyes snapped open like camera shutters, and impossibility made real blasted into his awareness.

Blue sky—a good, plain, ordinary summer sky, with an ordinary yellow sun in it. Good. Grass, the correct green, and in the distance some trees which looked like ordinary trees. Good.

But underfoot! Some firm elastic pinkish material extending like a pathway ahead of him, towards buildings of golden colour and unpredictable shape—cycloidal domes, pyramids, cylinders offset on one another. Beyond the buildings, towering twice their height towards the blue sky, were objects like tremendous eggs so black the eye could barely endure to look at them because they seemed to suck the light from the world.

As he stared in that first incredulous moment, one of the eggs vanished with a clap like thunder; its place remained vacant for perhaps seconds, and was filled again.

There was movement. There were people in front of the strange buildings—perhaps a hundred yards from where he stood—who caught sight of him and begun to hurry in his direction, calling out to him. At first Joel could not distinguish any details of their appearance; then he saw that there were both men and women among them, and that they wore something more like harness than clothing. What at first glance he took for close-fitting tan garments proved to be their own skins.

He glanced about him, not yet thinking coherently, his mind full of visions of flight. But there was nowhere to flee to; behind him, the pinkish pathway led to another cluster of buildings, another group of night-black eggs in cradles of white girders, and another group of people—fewer, but also hurrying towards him.

It was not until they had come very close indeed to where he stood rooted by terror to one spot that he saw among them a—a creature.

This was a being nearly as tall as a man, but having nothing in common otherwise: running on short limbs from which a pale grey trunk tilted forward as a skier tilts his body when running fast down hill, swinging a group of more limbs—five or six—that sprouted from that trunk as counterweights to save itself from toppling over when it came to a halt.

It was mainly because he was so fascinated at the sight of this unprecedented creature that he did not yield to his instinct and flee blindly. One moment after he found himself surrounded by the harnessed, brown-skinned strangers he was again in the grip of mindless fear.

Only slowly did he manage to convince himself there was nothing aggressive in their manner, or in the tone of voice with which they put startled questions to him. He could make nothing of what was said to begin with, though he fancied he caught a hint of meaning here and there. At last he licked his lips and heard his own trembling voice say, "I don't understand you."

Instantly a man in the front rank of the group slapped his forehead. "Ancient English!" he said clearly. "You're speaking Ancient English. Why didn't I guess from your clothes? How did you get here? What happened?"

"*Ancient* English?" echoed Joel. The sun was warm and welcoming, but he felt a wave of icy horror sweep across his mind. "Ancient—English?"

With a strange pitying expression the man nodded. "You are probably from the twentieth century of the Christian era, aren't you? Well, by that reckoning, you're now—four and a half centuries ahead of your own time."

The pale grey trunk on legs turned to the man speaking, and addressed a question to him. With incredulous amazement, Joel felt a pattern drop into place in his mind. He said, "You—this—"

There was instantly a tension in the air. The group about him seemed to stiffen, prepared for some unseen disaster. The pattern Joel had worked out fitted that, too. He swallowed with a tremendous effort, and said clearly, "Would you—uh—introduce me to the—uh—gentleman from—uh—another planet? I never had the opportunity of…"

He broke off. They were laughing all round him. For a moment he thought that his guesswork was all wrong, and that they were amused at his absurd mistake. Then he realised it was the laughter of relief, and was suddenly weak and unsteady on his legs.

"Hey!" the spokesman said warningly, and put out his arm, supporting Joel. "Well, friend, I don't know how you got into this act, but—you seem to know a surprising amount about it. How come? I mean, I wouldn't even be surprised if you said you knew you were going to turn up in your future this way."

Painfully, but immensely proud of the fact that he wasn't hysterical from shock, or worse, Joel forced a grin. He said, "Well as a matter of fact I rather think I did."

The spokesman's face revealed him deciding not to waste more time on being puzzled. He shrugged. "Obviously, we've got some explanations to attend to. Ah—you asked to be introduced to our friend… Well, that's not so easy, because he's not exactly a gentleman or anything else; he's a colony of mutually interdependent cells somewhat like a jellyfish but very highly evolved, and he hasn't a name, and there are certain human-based concepts he can't understand of which personal singular identity is one. So if you don't mind I'll leave it at that…?"

"Well—uh—of course," said Joel, and was still unable to take his eyes from the greyish trunk of the creature. With a further shock he saw that what he had taken for its tegument was actually protective clothing of some sort, and there were artifacts—filters, perhaps—dotted up the front of the trunk like buttons.

"I don't quite know what we're going to do about you," the spokesman was saying thoughtfully. "But, at any rate, let's get over to the control building and talk in comfort. I must say that for a—forgive me, but you are, you know!—a virtual primitive, you're taking this extremely well."

Joel was going to say something about his actual state of mind, behind his automatic sleepy calm. But he was interrupted.

From behind him—from a mere yard or two distant—three voices suddenly cried out. Two of them said, "Sackstone!" The third said, "Joel!"

He whirled, and all the harnessed men and women with him. There on the pinkish path a few paces distant, starting forward, were Angelus, and Letta Bailbrook, and Tracy.

VII

"My friend Chamberel here," said Angelus in his suave manner, "tells me that you seem to have worked out for yourself an astonishingly accurate idea of what's happened to you." He waved in the direction of the man who had been spokesman for the group that met Joel on arrival. "So perhaps you'd like to tell us what you think...?"

Joel cupped between his big hands the cool container he had been given a few moments before, which held a sparkling reddish liquid, tart like fresh red-currant juice but with a strong rich scent like wine. A lot of things hadn't changed; the cup was essentially a cup; this chair he sat in was recognisably evolved from a chair of the mid-twentieth century, and the room had walls and a door and windows and tables.

He said, "Is there something in this drink you gave us?"

Angelus nodded. "What you would call a tranquillising drug. Although you support your experience very well, there is necessarily a psychical traumatic effect which it's best to counteract at once. You don't object?"

"No, of course not. I just thought I was overdue for some delayed shock-reaction, and I couldn't feel any." Joel glanced at Tracy, and found she was staring at him with narrowed eyes as though preferring to fix her attention on something familiar. Her knuckles were pale around her own cup of drink.

Speaking in as reassuring a tone as he could manage, for Tracy's benefit, Joel said, "The way I figure it is this. We human beings exist in four dimensions and we have knowledge of direction in six of the eight possible ways. Or seven, if you like. Because we travel all the time forward into time. The big difference is simply that we're able to reverse our journeys in the ordinary dimensions; we can go and come back, we can jump up and drop down again. Having gone left, we can then go right, and so on.

"I was working it out for Tracy in terms of a snail, which is three-dimensional all right, as much as a man is, but which can really only perceive and work in terms of the directions proper to two dimensions. A snail, going up a wall, is just going along as usual, not consciously going *up*.

"Maybe—I thought—there's a way of using the directions proper to a fourth dimension, which people sometimes stumble across. Which they can be impelled, or urged, towards. The way the layout of your weird building will impel people." He looked direct at Angelus.

But it was Letta who commented. "Marco!" she said. "Did I not say we ought to pay attention to this unique individual?"

"Unique hell!" said Joel. "*I* think a lot of people have disappeared by accidentally walking in—in a temporal direction. Absent-mindedly, perhaps."

"That is very probably correct," Angelus nodded. "Though we have no definite record of any such case. You see—oh, I would have to demonstrate this either mathematically or in the language of my own time which has evolved to cope with the concepts; English never did, I'm afraid. Human has supplanted most other languages gradually over the past hundred and fifty years, you see.

"But very broadly, you're right in your surmise. Only the direction you yourself have now followed is not identical with the time-dimension;

if it were, in going to the past I would become my original component atoms, of course, not preserve continuity as a thinking individual. It is perhaps closer to compare it to—well, say that a savage who cannot swim comes to a deep, wide river. He has to go around its headwaters to reach the other side. But with his own unaided muscles, and some grasp of the concept involved, he could swim across. I can't bring it any nearer to you, I'm afraid."

"But Mr. Sackstone has an excellent grasp of the principle," Letta put in. "The—what was your expressive phrase?—the jury-rigged arrangement in his room, which we ourselves used to come after him, was an amazing first attempt."

Joel felt ridiculously proud of himself, and a bit embarrassed.

He said, "Uh—but all the paradoxes they talk about…?"

"Such as causing a building to be erected in our own past? Such as interfering with the lives of our ancestors?" Angelus smiled. "I'm afraid you'll have to take it for granted that there are no paradoxes. Remember what I said—the direction involved is not identical with the time-dimension. It simply intersects with it."

"I give up," Joel said after a moment's struggle.

"I'm afraid so. Actually, though we've known of this direction for a century or two, only very exceptional persons like yourself, with astonishing powers of spatial visualisation, can follow it without complex artificial aids like the ones built into our proposed headquarters in your own century. I imagine you might after training do it unaided; if you care to find out, we'll be overjoyed to give you facilities, because that's one of our chief problems at the moment."

Tracy broke in unexpectedly. Leaning forward, she said, "I want to know—Joel, ask them what it's all for, please!"

Composedly, Letta crossed her legs. "I believe Joel will make a successful guess at that, too. Go ahead, Joel."

Joel closed his eyes, re-visualising the vast black eggs in their girder-cradles outside, re-visualising the strange pale grey trunk of the creature from some other world. He said, "Ah—all right. Is it a kind of psycho-analysis?"

Angelus's normal composure broke to pieces with a strangled grunt of surprise. He said something in his own tongue to Letta, who burst out laughing, before addressing Joel again.

"This is more than I bargained for, Mr. Sackstone! Because you're so *exactly* right I just accused Letta of speaking too freely to you! I haven't any idea what we're going to do with you, but we're not going to let you slip lightly, so if you want to listen I'll tell you just how right you are."

"Please go ahead!" said Joel, alarming excitement rising inside him.

"In strictly psychological terms, then, we're trying to get rid of a guilt-complex," Angelus began.

This planet Earth was not the only one to bear intelligent life. It had turned out so far, though, to be the one where the dominant species had taken the most violent and bloody path towards eventual civilisation.

Those men who first ventured into space came from a society sick with fear and suspicion—fear of annihilation in an ultimate war, suspicion that the motives of others were as selfish at bottom as their own.

The first manned probes to distant planets drew the attention of other races who had long ago entered the starways, who came cautiously but with welcoming intent to greet the toddling infant Man as he moved into the adult universe.

And Man—fearful, suspicious—feared, suspected, and attacked.

It had taken the better part of two hundred years for those fears and suspicions to die down, and even now the consequences of what had been done hastily, from panic, had not been atoned for.

"That's a long time for a conscience to take to evolve," Angelus said greyly. "But it came. It came, in the end. And you can guess the result. One of the saving graces of our sometimes repulsive race is that we are capable of feeling ashamed.

"Only shame is just as much a handicap to a rational person as fear, hatred and suspicion. So what was to be done? Only one thing. We had to fetch up into the light of day the unpleasant impulses which now made us ashamed. We had to lay bare for analysis and eventual understanding the forces which prevented us from believing in other races' good intentions. We had to carry out—as you almost said—a socio-analysis of human history. We had to come to understand, through personal contact with people in every epoch of history, the forces at work in their minds."

"And by experiencing them for yourselves?" Joel suggested.

Angelus caught his meaning instantly. He inclined his head with a faint smile. "Yes… Letta told me she was not sure she had convinced you you were mistaken when you ran into her in her—ah—alternate guise. I may say that by recognising her you upset a good many of our preconceptions about the role of pigmentation in twentieth-century society. And add incidentally that you might also occasionally have encountered myself looking more blonde than usual."

"Wasn't that pretty risky?" Tracy said.

Angelus shrugged. "The risks in that are fairly predictable. Others aren't. We went to a restaurant yesterday; we're not intimately acquainted with twentieth-century cuisine, and as it happens some minor genetic shift has left me, and a good many people of my generation, unable to endure the enzymes which turn milk to cheese. Consequently I ordered something by mistake which turned out to be dressed with cheese, and the result was calamitous."

Joel made to apologise, but Angelus shook his head, smiling.

"I said to you the other day," put in Letta quietly, "that we were afraid we might be wasting our time. You see, when we first looked into the particular aspect of the situation which has been assigned to us—your own period—we had a horrible sense that disaster was ultimately unstoppable. On every side we found people of goodwill, with high, civilised ideals—and yet a pattern of nastiness which had occurred a thousand times over elsewhere was steadily evolving as though no one raised any objection to it.

"But that was just a momentary aberration, of course. It springs from the sense of shame Marco was referring to. We so much want to emerge into the community of civilised races, but we fully understand that the prerequisite is to know our own worst shortcomings and to guard against them so efficiently that they will never again cause calamity."

Joel gave a thoughtful nod. It all made sense, barring one thing. He said, "But the—the creature I met on my arrival: how about him? What's he doing here if we aren't open to contact with these other races?"

Angelus and Letta exchanged glances. Letta said after a while, "Well… That's a brave person, you see, Joel. He's exactly as brave as a missionary in your own time who chose to live among a tribe of headhunters."

"What in heaven's name did we *do*, then?" Joel demanded.

"I'm not going to tell you!" said Angelus violently. "If you make up your mind that you would rather disappear from your own period and allow us to work on your—talents, you'll be told sooner or later. But I'm not going to burden you with details of the things we're ashamed of."

Joel was silent for a long time. After a while, he grew aware that Tracy was still looking at him. He thought about some corollaries of that.

And finally he said, "Well, it scares me stiff. But as I told you before, I like your ideas. Having got in your way like this I wouldn't feel right about doing anything else."

It was a hell of a big decision to take on such short notice. But he knew it would last.

"I like your ideas too," said Tracy determinedly. "Do I get a chance to come in on this?"

Angelus glanced at her, and was going to shape a doubtful answer, when Letta put her hand on his arm.

"Everybody's in on this," she said crisply. "Whether they like it or not, from—from Adam and Eve through to us here. And nobody can set us straight but ourselves."

She turned to Tracy and Joel. "Don't delude yourselves it's easy. It isn't in the least. You'll certainly be tempted to change your minds, and you won't be able to. Think it over for a while, and give us an answer then."

"I know already," said Joel, and with mild astonishment realised that Tracy had spoken at the same instant in the same Words.

BRITISH LIBRARY
SCIENCE FICTION CLASSICS

SHORT STORY ANTHOLOGIES
EDITED BY MIKE ASHLEY

Nature's Warnings
Classic Stories of Eco-Science Fiction

Lost Mars
The Golden Age of the Red Planet

Moonrise
The Golden Age of Lunar Adventures

Menace of the Machine
The Rise of AI in Classic Science Fiction

The End of the World
and Other Catastrophes

Menace of the Monster
Classic Tales of Creatures from Beyond

Beyond Time
Classic Tales of Time Unwound

Born of the Sun
Adventures in Our Solar System

CLASSIC SCIENCE FICTION NOVELS

By William F. Temple

Shoot at the Moon

Four-Sided Triangle

By Charles Eric Maine

The Tide Went Out

The Darkest of Nights

By Ian Macpherson

Wild Harbour

By Muriel Jaeger

The Question Mark

The Man with Six Senses

We welcome any suggestions, corrections or feedback you may have,
and will aim to respond to all items addressed to the following:

The Editor (Science Fiction Classics)
British Library Publishing
The British Library
96 Euston Road
London, NW1 2DB

We also welcome enquiries through our Twitter account,
@BL_Publishing